PARADISE
AND
PINK PLASTIC SHOES

PAT HOLDEN

Matador
Unit E2 Airfield Business Park,
Harrison Road, Market Harborough,
Leicestershire. LE16 7UL
Tel: 0116 2792299
Email: books@troubador.co.uk
Web: www.troubador.co.uk/matador

ISBN 978 1805140 474

British Library Cataloguing in Publication Data.
A catalogue record for this book is available from the British Library.

Printed and bound in Great Britain by 4edge Limited
Typeset in 11pt Minion Pro by Troubador Publishing Ltd, Leicester, UK

Matador is an imprint of Troubador Publishing Ltd

For my mother Amy
who taught me to read and love books

UGANDA 1972

ONE

Freya's navy seersucker dress was glued to her skin with sweat, and her nylon stockings were hot and itchy. She had never flown before, and she had stayed wide awake throughout the eight-hour flight to Entebbe, staring straight ahead, afraid to look through the window, her stomach lurching with fear every time the plane hit turbulence.

After a long wait in the arrivals queue, she handed her passport to the officer at the desk.

'Mm, twenty-three. Too young to be alone. Where's the husband?' he said.

Before she could answer, he laughed, stamped the passport and turned to the next passenger.

The customs officer opened her case, picked up a sanitary towel and inspected it. Roger had said that she should bring enough to last for a few months. It had been difficult to squash all the packets down the sides of the case, so she had opened them and scattered the towels across the top of the clothes. For a moment, she was afraid

3

that she had done something wrong, but then the man slammed the case shut and waved her on.

Outside the terminal crowds of people, pressed behind a barrier, waved and shouted. Car horns blared. There was a smell of burning wood and sweet rotting fruit. The weather at Gatwick had been foggy, dark and cold. It was as if she was in a movie that had changed halfway through from black and white into technicolour.

She squinted in the bright sunlight and looked around for Roger, afraid she would never find him. The plane had been five hours late. Perhaps he had given up waiting and gone home? Then she spotted his red curly hair. A porter grabbed her case before she could stop him and they pushed their way through the jostling crowds until they reached her husband. She hadn't expected to see him dressed all in white, in shorts and long socks. His pale skin was tanned and freckled, his red hair bleached with blond streaks. His broad shoulders were wider than she remembered.

They had been apart for three months and she was shy at the thought of touching him. He was always careful, even nervous about kissing her in a public place. But when she reached him, he pulled her closely towards him and hugged her so that she was almost suffocated against his sweat-stained shirt. There was a faint smell of gin.

'At last! I thought you would never get here,' he said.

They pushed their way through the crowds, found the car and drove out of the airport onto the road that would take them to the project.

*

'Damned *watu*!' Roger shouted as he jammed on the brakes. 'If they would only keep off the *waragi*.'

'I don't understand,' Freya said.

'*Waragi* is the local booze. And *watu* means people. It's Swahili. You'll soon learn a few words. I was beginning to think that you'd never get here. They kept changing the arrival time until I almost gave up. I spent quite a lot of time in the bar while I was waiting.'

'Is it okay to be driving if you've been drinking?' she said.

'They don't bother about that kind of thing here. In fact, I think it keeps me more alert. We'll soon be there. It usually takes about an hour. We're up and down this road a lot, taking and fetching people from the airport. Some of the government offices are still in Entebbe. It's the old capital. And the botanical gardens are there. It's a good place to have picnics on a Sunday.'

The road to the project was long. It was suddenly dark and the car headlights caught the jagged edges of the tarmac where it met the dirt path. Tilley lamps inside the doorways of small houses and open-fronted shops threw shadows on the people who were walking or running, sometimes barefoot, along the sides of the road, narrowly avoiding the traffic. Women were dressed in long, brightly coloured dresses, pinched at the waist and with large padded shoulders, or in long wraps and shirts. Others wore smart office clothes. Schoolchildren in cotton uniforms straggled along the roadside.

Freya's eyes closed from sheer exhaustion. She forced them open and saw her face in the car window. It was sallow, with dark rings around her eyes. Her almost black hair, carefully bouffanted at the hairdresser's two days before, was flattened and wet with sweat.

She turned to look at Roger and felt a glimmer of excitement when she saw the place where his shirtsleeve tightened on his muscular arm. Everything would start to get better now that she was here. She could begin to forget the months of fear and anxiety. She wanted to say something to him, to let him know that she was ready to make a go of things, as her mother might say. Instead, she gently placed her hand on his thigh and felt his soft, bare skin.

'No, please, I have to concentrate,' he said as he pushed her hand away. 'These people have no idea how dangerous it is to walk so close to the road.'

There was an old, familiar jolt of fear that she had done something without thinking through the consequences. Her mother always said she was a dreamer who never thought things through properly.

Rows and rows of short green trees, forming a thick wall, lined the road. She tried to stay awake but her eyes closed once more and the trees moved towards her, like a waving green army. The car braked suddenly and she opened her eyes. She was afraid but she didn't know why. What was behind those trees?

Roger's blue airmail letters had arrived in bundles every few days. They were mostly about what she should bring with her: a jar of Marmite, sanitary towels, serviette rings. He had mentioned the names of Don, the project manager, and his wife, Mavis, and talked a bit about his job as the project engineer responsible for keeping all the tractors and heavy vehicles going properly. But the letters had said nothing about what she would do to fill her time.

'What are those trees?' she said.

'Green bananas. The *watu* eat them steamed in their leaves in big pots. They call it *matooke*. They use the leaves for other things too: umbrellas, house covering, ropes, plates.'

There were so many new things to learn about. She could hear impatience in his voice. Was this really the same quiet, shy young man she had waved off at the railway station?

The car turned suddenly off the main road, leaving the tarmac behind. Red dust clouded around them and filled the car as they sped over the bumpy track. She coughed and covered her eyes.

'A lot of the roads are made of this stuff; it's called *murram*,' Roger said. Along the sides of the dirt road, people sat outside their houses eating and chatting. Occasionally someone would look up and wave at the car, as if they were royalty.

After about a mile, the car stopped in front of a gate. Through the dust, Freya saw a sign that read: BUGELERE AGRICULTURAL DEVELOPMENT PROJECT.

Roger pressed the horn.

'Asleep as usual, I suppose,' he said.

Two African men dressed in khaki uniforms and red fez hats ran forward, opened the gate and saluted.

They drove through the gate and onto a smooth tarmac road. In the darkness she saw identical bungalows set back from the road and lit by veranda lights. They passed two houses and then turned into a driveway.

'This is it. What do you think?' Roger said.

The spacious, white-walled bungalow had a red tiled roof. The light on the veranda shone on a hedge of trailing orange flowers. There was a large garden with neat flowerbeds and brightly coloured shrubs, surrounded by tall trees. Freya caught a sweet, sickly scent that suddenly reminded her of her father's funeral.

'What is that smell?' she said.

'It's the tree with white flowers, a frangipani,' Roger said.

She wasn't sure what she had been expecting. The house and the garden were like the bungalows in the posh outskirts of the Midlands town she had just left.

'It's much bigger than I thought it would be,' she said.

Warm air came in through the car window. Everything felt quiet and calm. What had happened was all in the past now. People would soon forget. There was nothing to be afraid of now. She could start to be a real wife. The word still sounded strange. No one taught you what to do to be a good wife. That was all that she wanted, to make a go of things.

A golden Labrador ran towards them, barking. She tried to push it away as it nuzzled its nose under her sweat-drenched dress. She had been afraid of dogs since a growling Alsatian had knocked her over when she was a small child.

'Come here, boy,' Roger said, pushing his face into the dog's yellow fur. 'This is Jock. I inherited him from the Scots chap who used to live here. You need a good guard dog, especially when you're on your own at night. They can tell the difference between the *msungus* and the *watu*. It's something to do with the smell.'

'*Msungus?*'

'White people, Europeans,' Roger said.

The veranda door opened and a tall woman wearing a faded pink cotton dress and headscarf came out of the house onto the driveway. She made a movement like a quick curtsy and said, 'Welcome, Memsahib.' No one had ever bowed to her before.

The woman laughed as she said something to Roger in what Freya guessed must be Swahili.

'This is Keziah. She has left us some cold food in case you're hungry,' Roger said, 'and I was explaining about the late plane.' The woman helped Roger unpack the car and then went back inside.

'She does everything around the house. You won't need to do a thing.'

He carried her case through the veranda door. It opened directly into a large living room. A ceiling fan gently moved the hot, musty air. The parquet floor was bare except for a small, red-patterned oriental mat. There was a settee with wooden arms and two matching chairs with bright blue and yellow seat cushions. A coffee table, desk and bookcase were the only other pieces of furniture. A black, shiny wooden carving of what looked like a man with a large head stood by the door, and at the furthest end of the living room there was a dining table covered with a white cloth and a plate of sandwiches made with thick slices of white bread.

'The room is a bit bare,' Roger said. 'I thought you might like to get a few things. You know, give it a woman's touch.'

The room looked nice as it was. It reminded her of an

old film she had seen about Africa. She thought about her mother's living room with the faded settee and the mantel shelf covered in dusty ornaments. They hardly ever moved things around.

Roger pulled her towards him.

'At last you're here. It's been a long time,' he said.

During the long journey, Freya had tried to distract herself from her fear of flying by replaying in her mind the few times when the sex had been good. They had usually done it clumsily in the cramped front seat of Roger's Mini, or hastily in her bedroom on the evenings when her mother was out at the Women's Institute. Occasionally there were strange, pleasurable sensations.

After the hasty marriage, she had been afraid to have sex in case it hurt the baby. And then, after it had happened, after the miscarriage, the sex had stopped altogether. The doctor had said it was better to leave it for a while. Besides, it would have been difficult not to make a noise in the cramped back room of her mother's council house.

When they had heard that Roger had been offered the job in Uganda, there had been little point in trying to move out and find their own place. His salary would be almost double what he was earning at the tractor company and so they would be able to save up enough for a deposit on a house.

Freya heard the kitchen door slam shut. The curtains were open and she felt as if they were being watched. Through the back window she could see a dimly lit, small concrete building that reminded her of the public toilets in the local park.

'What's that?' she said.

'The servants' quarters. It's where Keziah stays. But she's not always there.'

Freya thought that it didn't look big enough for anyone to live in.

Roger pulled her towards him and kissed her. She opened her eyes and, over his shoulder, watched Keziah walk from the back of the house to the quarters, stop and turn round. Freya was sure she was staring at them.

Roger led her into the bedroom. 'Leave that,' he said, as she started to unpack her case. A gently moving mosquito net was hung round the large bed. She was nervous about making love after such a long time but Roger was gentle and said things she had never heard him say before. He shouted and shuddered as he finished. It was as if she was watching it from afar, trying to enjoy it and yet secretly hoping it might end soon.

TWO

The breakfast table was laid with the grey checked tablecloth, the silver cutlery and the blue earthenware pottery that Freya and her mother had carefully chosen together from the big department store, some months before. Her mother had worked in service when she was a young woman and she had known what to choose to suit Freya's privileged new life. White serviettes lay folded by the plates.

Through the window, Freya saw a small girl sitting outside the servants' quarters washing pots in a tin bowl.

'Who is that child?' she said.

'Oh, I don't know. One of Keziah's relatives, I suppose. Let's have some breakfast,' Roger said. He tried to kiss her but she moved away from him.

'Come here, what's the matter?' he said.

'Please, she'll see us,' Freya said.

Roger pulled her more tightly towards him. 'I'm sure Keziah is used to seeing this sort of thing. Pretend that she's invisible.'

Over his shoulder, she saw something darting across the wall and jumped in fear.

'It's only a gecko, a small lizard. They're harmless,' he said.

She had heard stories of bats that flew in through bedroom windows and became tangled in women's hair. She shivered at the thought that a lizard might drop on her head while she was asleep.

'Let's eat,' he said.

A threadbare white cotton doily covered a plate of boiled eggs. Freshly cut pineapple slices were carefully arranged alongside wedges of a green-skinned, pinkish orange fruit that she had never seen before.

'Pawpaw,' Roger said. 'It's delicious.'

Freya sat down at the table. It was all so different from the plastic kitchen tablecloth and stained knives and forks of home.

Roger picked up a small container from the middle of the table and opened the lid.

'It's Paludrine. Take one. You'll have to remember to do this every morning if you don't want to get malaria.'

He stood behind her to kiss the top of her head and his hand reached down to touch her breast. The door opened suddenly and Keziah came in carrying a jug of water.

'It's all right,' Roger whispered. 'She doesn't care. It's not her business.'

Keziah was wearing a faded yellow cotton uniform dress. The buttonholes down the front were stretched tightly across her chest as if the dress had shrunk from too many washes. She wore pink plastic sandals and her toenails were painted red. Across her forehead there were two neat rows of small raised bumps. Freya wanted to ask Roger what they were but was afraid that she might say the wrong thing. Instead, she whispered, 'How old is she?'

'Oh, I don't know, probably eighteen or so,' Roger said. 'You can never tell with these people. Does it matter?'

Freya felt a rush of homesickness for her usual breakfast of cornflakes and toast, hurriedly eaten at the plastic-topped kitchen table.

'Can't we just eat at the little table on the veranda?' she said.

'This is how I've told her to do it. We don't want to upset her routine.'

The pawpaw tasted sweet and sickly. Freya took one of the little white pills out of the box and played with it in her hand. She tried to swallow it but it stuck in her throat and she coughed, afraid that she might be sick.

The room was already hot and there was an acrid smell of rubbish from the kitchen bin every time Keziah opened the kitchen door.

'Have some toast and eggs. You've hardly eaten anything,' Roger said.

'I'm sorry. I just can't,' she said. A familiar flush of warmth pushed up through her body. After the miscarriage, the nurse had said that it was probably her hormones. She had thought that it was only old women, like her mother, who suffered from hormones.

She needed to get up from the table to go back to the bedroom and lie down. As she reached out for her serviette, wanting to fold it neatly before she got up from the table, her hand trembled and she knocked over her glass of water.

'What are you doing?' Roger said and called for Keziah,

who burst through the door. She made '*chichi*' noises as she mopped the water and then turned to Roger and said something in Swahili.

'What is she saying?' Freya said.

'She says, can you be more careful?'

The woman who had bowed to her the night before was now telling her off. She was a naughty child being scolded for something that she didn't realise she had done wrong.

'I'm sorry. I feel a bit unwell,' Freya said.

'I expect you're still tired after the long journey. And everything is so new for you.' Roger tried to put his arm around her. She breathed deeply. She was trapped. She couldn't leave the table now.

'Does she know any English?' Freya said.

'Yes, a bit, but it's not very good. We all have to learn a bit of Swahili. Maybe you could teach her some English.'

Freya had no idea how to teach anyone anything.

She hadn't thought about what it would be like to live all the time with a stranger in the house. A stranger who spoke a language she couldn't understand.

There was a film of dust on the coffee table. Her mother cleaned the house every day from top to bottom and did the washing every week in the twin-tub washing machine.

'Do we really need a house girl? It's just you and me. And I won't have much else to do all day,' she said.

Roger folded his arms and clutched them tightly.

'Don't be silly,' he said. 'It gets very hot by about ten o'clock. The clothes have to be washed in the bathtub every day. The dust is back after five minutes and we don't have a hoover. Then there's the ironing to do.'

Her friends at work and her family had said how lucky she would be, looked after hand and foot by the servants.

'And you'll want to have coffee mornings, or do things at the club. Oh, and I've been entertained by all of them while you've not been here. A bachelor is always useful to have around for dinner parties,' Roger said.

A bachelor was what they called her Uncle Cecil, a fusty old man who was always sorting his stamp collection.

'You know what I mean,' Roger said. 'I was on my own. So we'll have to do a bit of entertaining to pay them all back.'

Freya had never been to a proper dinner party, let alone given one. There were evenings out at the pub with her work friends. And when the rare visitors, family or friends from work, came on a Sunday afternoon, her mother would serve tinned salmon and cucumber sandwiches, and homemade fruitcake on a trolley that was otherwise never used. Apart from Christmas, no one ever came to the house for a sit-down meal.

'Don't look so worried. Relax. Keziah knows the ropes. She can do all the cooking and the shopping. You won't even have to make a list,' Roger said.

Keziah opened the kitchen door and said something to Roger, who smiled and nodded. Then she walked across the room to the bookshelf, switched on the radio and stood listening to it, shaking her head occasionally and making noises of what sounded like astonishment.

'She likes to listen to the eight o'clock news. She doesn't have a radio. They are all getting worried,' Roger said.

'What about?'

'Idi Amin and what he's up to.'

Freya had heard things on the news about Idi Amin, but she had taken little notice. She had been too busy getting ready to leave. Her mother's tantrums had been difficult to cope with when it had dawned on her that she would be left all on her own.

Roger spoke carefully to her as if she was a child.

'When Amin took over after the coup last year, everyone, including the Brits, thought it was a good thing. Milton Obote, the old president, was doing some awful things and he was very unpopular with a lot of people.'

A child coughed and retched outside. Keziah went to the window, shouted something to the child, and then went back to listening to the radio. It was difficult to concentrate on what Roger was saying.

'Amin was in the King's African Rifles after the war. He seemed to like the Brits. The people who live round here – that's the Baganda tribe – were very happy to see Obote go, and even happier when Amin brought the body of their king, the Kabaka, back from Britain. But right from the start there were rumours. Things started happening.'

'What sort of things?' Freya watched as Keziah got closer to the radio so that she was almost kneeling. 'You didn't say anything in your letters.'

'It's not always safe. You never know who might open them. A lot of them go missing in the post.'

Freya's father had been a postman. He would have known about missing letters.

'And Amin's got it in for the Asians. Most of them were born here, so it's their home now. But he says they've been stealing businesses from the Africans. He's threatening to kick them all out. But he won't do it. He needs them. They keep the economy going. You'll find nearly all the shops here are owned by Asians.'

The bright, early morning sunlight streamed through the room so that Freya had to shade her eyes as she caught a glimpse of the strained expression on his face.

'And there is a bit of a worry that he might be turning against the British as well. He's been making friends with Gaddafi in Libya. And he's kicked out the Israelis who have been helping him. And a couple of *msungus*, Americans, disappeared last year.'

'Disappeared?' Freya asked.

'Well, it could be anything, attacked by wild animals? Who knows?'

Freya could smell his sweat, mixed with aftershave and cigarette smoke. Why hadn't he tried to warn her about all this before?

'Don't look so worried,' he said. 'They won't do anything to us.' The newsreader began to speak in English, reading out the names of people asking for a record to be played. It was a Jim Reeves song, and it sounded very sad. Keziah switched off the radio and went back into the kitchen.

'She's from the North. Different tribe from the people around here. Life might start to get difficult for her,' Roger said. 'It's okay. We are safe here on the compound. No one is interested in us.'

Freya saw the flashing lights and felt the nausea that meant one of her headaches was coming on.

'What is it?' Roger said.

'Just a migraine. Perhaps I should lie down.'

'I hope I haven't upset you. Honestly, it's okay. We just

have to keep out of the politics. We're here to do a job. We can't get involved. They are independent now. It's their problem.'

'Everything seems strange. I'll get used to it, I'm sure.' Freya glanced towards the door, expecting it to open suddenly. She had to ask him something.

'I don't quite understand,' she said. 'It's just that I thought people usually had houseboys. That's what it said in that Blue Book they sent us.'

Roger spoke quietly, as if afraid someone might hear him.

'Well, I did take on a boy when I first came, but it didn't really work out. Actually, he was stealing things. Just little things: salt, sugar, rice and, oh … a few spoons went missing. I put marks on the jars and checked a few times. It's no good if you don't trust people.'

Was this the same shy young man she had met in the coffee bar on the high street hardly a year before? The gleaming white shorts, long socks and his tanned skin had turned him into someone she hardly recognised, someone confident and in charge. And she had never noticed the strong smell of cigarettes before.

'And then I thought that maybe you'd feel happier with a woman around the house.'

He looked away from her and lit a cigarette.

'And a house girl can always …' he hesitated, 'be an *ayah*.'

'*Ayah*?' Freya said.

'Sorry, someone who looks after the children.'

Freya's heart was beating fast and she practised the breathing exercises the nurse at the clinic had taught her.

'I'm sorry,' he said. 'I shouldn't have mentioned it so soon.'

They had hardly talked about the miscarriage or even thought about the child as a person that would one day need looking after.

Her head throbbed. She was afraid that if she went to lie down he would want to follow her and make love again.

Through the window she saw a man with a towel around his neck, sitting under a tree in the garden. Another man stood behind him, cutting his hair with a large razor.

'Who is that?' she said, distracted for a moment from the panic fluttering inside her.

'Oh, that's Keziah's brother or something. These people call everyone brother, aunt or whatever,' Roger said, sounding relieved to be changing the subject.

'Does he live here, too?' Freya said.

'I don't know. There are project rules about who can live in the servants' quarters, but no one bothers these days. Even Mavis has given up complaining.'

'Oh yes, Mavis. You mentioned her in your letters,' Freya said. 'And Don, he's the project manager, isn't he?'

'Be a bit careful with Mavis. Try not to upset her. They've been here for years. She likes to help settle the new wives in. So you'll be hearing from her soon.'

Freya didn't think that she had ever really wanted to upset anyone. She had watched her mother do it too many times.

A pair of pink plastic shoes had been left by the kitchen door. Keziah walked around barefoot in the house.

'I was just wondering,' she said, 'where did Keziah come from? I mean, where was she working before?'

He sighed. Was he becoming bored with all her questions?

'She used to work on the project as an *ayah*. The people she worked for sacked her. The kid said that she stole one of his toys. A bit of a brat, I hear. Anyway, she came to the door looking for work and all her other references were okay, so I took her on.'

The door opened and Keziah came into the room. She said something to Roger.

'*Ndio*,' he said, followed her into the kitchen and shut the door. Freya could hear them talking. It sounded like an argument but then you could never tell when people spoke another language. Freya got up from the table and left her serviette crumpled on the table. Her head was pounding.

A water glass on the table was full. She felt faint and held on to the table to steady herself. If she tugged at the corner of the tablecloth, gently at first and then harder, the glass would fall off the table and smash to the ground.

THREE

Freya was sitting on the veranda as she did every day to escape from the house while Keziah swept the stone floors and then polished them, skating around in large goatskin slippers.

She was reading a book with a tattered orange cover called *Things Fall Apart*. It was a story about what happened in a Nigerian village a long time ago. It had all seemed harsh and violent at first, but she was beginning to get drawn into the strange stories. She wondered if Uganda had been as brutal in the past. The neatly cut lawn and the carefully planted flower beds made it difficult for her to imagine a world of killing and sacrifices.

They had brought only a few books in their luggage. Roger read very little except for newspapers and magazines. Freya liked novels and she had found a handful of old books that had been left by visitors to the project rest house.

'Memsahib,' Keziah called from the kitchen. Freya still couldn't get used to being called Memsahib, and Madam felt even worse. 'Memsahib,' she called again.

Freya could hear the impatience in her voice. She pulled herself up from the sticky plastic seat and went into the kitchen.

'What is it?' she asked.

'She got something for you,' Keziah said.

The small girl Freya sometimes saw sitting outside the quarters stood at the kitchen door. Her torn, faded pink dress hung over her protruding stomach. Freya guessed that the child had been told to always go to the back door.

'Memsahib Mavis ask me to give you this,' she said, as she pushed a blue envelope into Freya's hand.

It said:

Dear Freya

Welcome to the project. I'm so sorry I haven't invited you round before now. We like to get to know the new wives and help them settle in as soon as possible. But Don and I have been up-country and only got back last night. If you are free, do come over for coffee, around 10.30.

Mavis

It was already ten o'clock and Freya began to search for something suitable to wear. The fashionable miniskirts and short dresses that barely covered her bottom already felt as if they were a mistake. Roger thought they were sexy, but the day before, when he had run his hand over the top of her thighs, he had whispered that she needed to be a bit careful as some of the local people were offended by short skirts. By people he must have meant men and old people, as almost all the young women she had seen in Kampala wore short skirts when they weren't in some kind of traditional dress.

She found a green and white, leaf-patterned cotton shift dress that came to rest just above her knee. Then she pulled her straight long black hair into a ponytail.

She walked down the project road until she came to the bungalow where Don and Mavis lived. It was larger than the other expatriate houses on the compound. A white woman, wearing a long blue cotton skirt and large straw hat, was cutting flowers in the garden, while a man dressed in ragged, stained shorts and shirt stood close by, as if waiting for his instructions.

A large Alsatian growled at her.

'Milton, you bloody idiot, come here!' the woman shouted. 'Hello, you must be Freya? Do come in. I'm Mavis, so pleased to meet you at last.'

Mavis' face was smooth and free of wrinkles, and strangely pale for someone who had probably lived for many years in Africa. Her eyes were startlingly childlike and her hair was blond and looked newly permed. It was difficult to tell how old she might be. There was a slight curve to her back. She could be about forty, Freya thought.

'Excuse the garden clothes,' Mavis said.

Freya followed Mavis into the house through the kitchen door. The cook, a tall man dressed in a long blue gown, was peeling potatoes. There was a sweet smell of oil or perfume. She could feel his strength and his handsomeness and wondered if she should feel ashamed or embarrassed to be looking at a house servant in that way.

'This is Simon,' Mavis said. He briefly looked at Freya without meeting her eyes, and then returned to his careful peeling.

Mavis led the way into the large living room. There was just one small shelf of books. The name Wilbur Smith was printed on several of them. Faded framed photographs of lions, buffalo and deer covered the walls alongside various-sized masks. The room was crowded with carved wooden figures of people and animals. A large drum stood in the corner. Brightly coloured oriental carpets covered the shiny polished floor. Red, green and yellow leather pouffes were scattered around the floor. The room was so crammed, so full, that accidentally knocking one thing over might bring it all tumbling down like a stack of cards.

As if she had read Freya's mind, Mavis sighed and said, 'This is what happens when you've lived here for so long. You just collect all this stuff and you can't bear to give it away.'

Freya had glimpsed small groups of oddly dressed tourists, wearing identical khaki safari clothes, searching for souvenirs in the clean, quiet Kampala Craft Shop. They wandered around examining different-sized drums, statues of animals, ivory ornaments, stone carvings and other things that they would buy to remind them of Africa as they wanted to remember it.

She thought about her mother's house and the seaside souvenirs and ornaments that crowded the windowsills and the old dresser.

Simon brought in the coffee pot and two small porcelain cups on a silver tray. He carefully placed them on the low table and the two women sat facing each other in large leather armchairs. Roger had explained that the identical furniture in the project houses was PWD, on loan from the Public Works Department. Freya could see that Mavis and Don had their own furniture, which she guessed they had taken from posting to posting.

'How are you finding things? I know it's not always easy at first,' Mavis said.

Freya nodded. She wasn't sure what to say.

'I was in my twenties when I first came to Uganda. I was young, like you, and I wanted to go back years ago,' Mavis said. 'But Don has always loved it here. We thought we might go at independence. A lot of our friends did. But we've stuck it out. Difficult to know where we'd fit in now. I don't know if we could put up with the UK, with all the strikes and everything. You newcomers are different with your short-term contracts. We have our roots here.'

Freya wasn't used to talking about politics or even having a fixed opinion on anything. Arguments at home were usually about what to have for tea or what to watch on TV, now that there were three channels.

'When we go back home on leave, I hardly recognise the place,' Mavis said. 'It's quiet at our cottage in the village, but go into town and you can't move for foreigners. And that mad dog Amin is threatening to throw out the Asians. I mean, they work hard and we know a lot of them, but if he goes ahead with it the place will be overrun.'

Freya's mother would often say that the country couldn't cope with more foreigners. But she usually said it quietly, aware that people might think she was colour prejudiced. There had been a young Indian called Prabhat in the office where Freya worked. She liked him and they had got on well but one day he had asked her out. She had felt confused because she hadn't thought of him in that way. He had seemed hurt when she had made a feeble excuse, mumbling that she had to visit her elderly aunt that evening. She blushed as she thought about it, and felt ashamed that she might have rejected him because of what her mother would say.

Outside the window, Freya heard the loud buzzing of hornets and bees. A gecko darted about on the wall above the window, chasing mosquitos. There was a faint sound of drumming in the distance and the voices of children shouting in a strange language. She had no idea how she would ever fit into this muddle of a place. Everything was so different. She felt tears in her eyes. Mavis stopped talking, got up, came towards her, and put her cold, dry hand on Freya's arm.

'What is it, dear?'

'I'm sorry. I don't know,' Freya said.

'Homesickness, I expect. We all get it at first. It can be difficult until you learn how to settle, to fit in. You just need to keep busy; play tennis, bridge or something. The servants keep me occupied. You just never know what they're up to. And I expect there will be children, sometime.'

Freya's heart beat faster. She wanted to leave before she said something that might peel away her armour. There was a moment of awkward silence.

'I should go,' she said.

'No, stay for a little while, until you feel better,' Mavis said.

Simon seemed to know the exact moment when to come in and clear away the coffee things. He moved silently and unobtrusively. Mavis said something to him in Swahili and he laughed. Freya was surprised at how easily she spoke to him. Perhaps this happened when you had been here for a long time.

Mavis broke the silence.

'I hope you don't mind me asking you something.'

When someone said that, it was usually a sign that you had to prepare yourself for a question that might turn your world upside down. The doctor had said that before he had asked her if she was married, when she had gone to see him because her period was late.

'How are you getting on with your house girl?' Mavis said.

There was a painting on the wall of an African. He was carrying a large corn cob on his head. His face looked still and without expression. Would anyone ever know what he was thinking?

'I don't know. I'm not sure.' Freya hesitated. She felt nervous about confiding in a woman she hardly knew. 'It's just that I'm not used to anyone strange being in the house all the time.'

'Well, we have all been wondering,' Mavis said.

It was like a punch in the stomach. Had Mavis and the other project wives been talking about her? She imagined them at the bar in the clubhouse, drinking *waragi* and tonic and laughing at her.

'Perhaps I should leave,' Freya said. 'I really don't feel well.'

'No, dear, please, I didn't mean to upset you. I just meant we were concerned.'

Freya felt her face flushing. She hesitated and then

said, 'I expect I'll get used to her. I've never had servants before.'

'Well, take it from me, dear, house girls don't usually work out. A houseboy is much better. House girls can be difficult. A bit of competition over the *bwana*, maybe? You can't have two women in the kitchen.'

Freya heard the sudden sound of heavy rain beating down on the roof. The two gardeners were running to escape the storm and were shielding themselves with large banana leaves which they used as umbrellas.

Mavis shouted above the noise. 'You see, it's rather like a dog with its master. Roger has been her master and she is used to pleasing him, and now she is probably just confused. You really will have to show her who the boss is.'

The storm had stopped as suddenly as it started. Through the window, she could see the houseboy and the gardener chatting and smoking, and looking around to see if anyone was watching them.

'Don't worry, dear,' Mavis said. 'We're not surprised you don't get on with her. She has been around this project for years. She is the daughter of one of the old houseboys who died last year. One or two people took her on out of sympathy, I suppose. She's good at what she does but she's sulky.'

Freya didn't want to hear any more. She tried to think of an excuse to leave.

'And we were a bit surprised,' Mavis went on, 'that Roger took her on as she's got a bit of a reputation.'

What did Mavis mean? The storm had stopped and the air suddenly became stifling and humid so that Freya struggled to breathe.

'Reputation?' Freya said. 'For what?'

Simon opened the door. 'Madam, it's the gardener, he wants you,' he said.

Mavis stood up. 'I'm sorry. I'm not trying to get rid of you, but I do need to check on what's happening.'

Freya walked towards the door, relieved to have a reason to escape, but Mavis hadn't finished.

'Look, if you want my advice, I'd get rid of her if I were you. There are plenty of good houseboys around.'

The word reputation echoed in Freya's head. She knew what her mother would have meant by it. An image of Roger and Keziah laughing together flashed through her mind.

She tried to focus on something else. Roger had said that she had to make an effort. She would have to learn to live with all this. There wasn't any other choice. She took a deep breath, smiled at Mavis, and said, 'Thank you for the coffee. We were wondering, would you and Don be free for dinner sometime soon?'

'That would be lovely, dear,' Mavis said.

As she walked down the drive, she could hear Mavis shouting in Swahili and trying to make herself heard above the barking of the dog.

When Freya got back to the house, she looked anxiously for the book that she had been reading. It would help her to stop thinking about what Mavis had said. But the book had disappeared. She heard Keziah talking to someone in the kitchen. She opened the door and saw that the small girl who had brought the note from Mavis was sitting at the kitchen table reading the book she had left on the veranda. Her finger was pointing to the words. When she saw Freya, the girl got up hurriedly from the chair and knelt on the floor.

'Please, no,' Freya said. 'Please tell her not to do that.'

Keziah spoke sharply to the girl, who stood up and then held out the book as if to give it to Freya.

'She took it. She give it back. She my little sister, Comfort,' Keziah said.

'It doesn't matter,' Freya said, as she took the book from her. 'How old is she?'

'Not sure. Seven, I think.'

'Does she go to school?'

'She likes to. But we haven't got the money for the fees.'

'Oh,' Freya said, 'that's not good.' She suddenly felt ashamed that she had taken notice of what Mavis had said about Keziah's reputation. She was just a young woman trying to make a living, with a small sister whom she had to support.

She would ask Roger what he thought about trying to help with paying the school fees. She could hear what Mavis might say, that it was no good trying to help people as you would never know where it might end. Then Freya decided that she didn't need to ask anyone's permission.

'I can give you money for the fees,' she said.

'We don't need. *Bwana* said he will give us,' she said and walked away.

Why hadn't Roger said anything about the fees? There was no real reason why he should but it felt like a punch to her stomach.

Freya looked out into the garden and saw the pants they had worn the day before hanging on the washing line. She shivered with embarrassment. From now onwards, every day except Sunday, Keziah would scrub away the stains. Had she heard someone say that houseboys wouldn't wash women's pants?

Was it the heat or just the strangeness of the place that was giving her these confused, muddled thoughts? She needed something else to think about.

Two aprons were hanging on the kitchen wall. She recognised the striped one. Roger had bought it when he had done a metalwork course at the local night school. A pair of kitchen scissors lay on the sideboard. She imagined taking the apron from its peg and cutting it into pieces.

FOUR

The day before the dinner party for Don and Mavis, Roger had decided what they would eat and made a list of things for Keziah to buy from the market. He said he would help Keziah with the cooking. Freya was surprised. She had never seen him in the kitchen at home. At least that explained why his apron was hanging on the kitchen door.

On the day of the dinner party, the preparations began as soon as Roger came back from work. Freya turned on the radio to drown out the sounds of Roger and Keziah talking and laughing behind the kitchen door. She tried not to think about how they would have to squeeze past each other in the cramped kitchen.

'You don't need to do anything,' Roger had said. 'But you can be in charge of tidying the living room, putting out the ashtrays and those little bowls of nuts.'

Freya opened the kitchen door nervously and went in to collect the bowls. An old, tattered copy of the *Settlers Cookery Book*, which a previous occupant had left behind, was open on the table and sprinkled with flour. Roger was beating a whole fillet steak with a rolling pin and Keziah was concentrating on making pastry, delicately crumbling the margarine into the flour.

After she had carefully arranged things for the tables, Freya went into the garden and watched the young boy called Jimmy who came every day to water the flowers and the vegetables. His skin looked dry, his trousers were torn and his shirt was ragged. He looked as if he didn't get enough to eat. She would ask Roger how much they paid him.

The sky turned rapidly from purple and red to pitch darkness. It all felt so peaceful that it was difficult to imagine that there might be things to be afraid of beyond the project gates. The *askari* who patrolled around the house every night had taken up his position outside the veranda and was lighting a cigarette. Roger complained that he was always asleep, and would check at intervals during the evening to make sure he was awake. The *askari* stood to attention and saluted Freya. As usual, she didn't know how to respond but just nodded at him and looked away. She thought she saw him smile briefly and wondered what he thought of the *msungus* whom he guarded night and day. She wanted to ask him his name but familiarity with the *watu* was discouraged. *Give them an inch and they'll take a yard*, Roger had said.

The mosquitos began to bite and she went indoors. The table was laid with a white cloth and the best cutlery and glassware. Lighted candles made the hard wooden PWD furniture look more elegant and appealing. There were butterflies in her stomach. If this all went well, it would show Roger that she was making an effort and settling in.

Don and Mavis arrived promptly at seven-thirty. Don was tall and upright and looked quite a bit older than Mavis. He could be about fifty, Freya thought. He was wearing a dinner jacket. His skin was tanned and leathery, and his black hair, which was still thick and wavy, was greasy with Brylcreem. His moustache was neatly trimmed.

'Good to meet you at last,' he said as he shook Freya's hand. 'I hope you are settling in? Can take a while.' He turned away to greet Roger before she could answer.

Mavis was wearing a tightly fitted black and white polka dot dress. Her face was heavily powdered and she wore bright red lipstick. She reminded Freya of her Aunty Eileen, who still wore the fashionable clothes of the 1950s. Mavis smiled at Freya as if they were already in some kind of women's conspiracy.

Don looked at his watch. Freya knew that he had asked Roger if they could bring along two young men.

'They should be here shortly,' he said. 'Sorry, I should have explained. They are the godsons of Fred Brearley, one of the tea plantation managers. He's retired now, of course, but he got in touch and asked if I'd keep an eye on them. They are here to do Voluntary Service Overseas, VSO.'

Don looked at his watch again. 'I'm not sure what good that VSO stuff does. And the way they dress rather lets the side down. Doesn't help in trying to get the *watu* to smarten up and turn up on time. And I've heard that some of them are mixing with the locals all the time. Of course, they don't get much money so I suppose some of them have to live on *matooke* and rice and beans.'

A few minutes later, two young men appeared at the door and Roger ushered them into the living room.

'Meet Sam and Mike,' Don said.

Sam had red hair. He was wearing light-coloured cotton trousers and a loose, brightly patterned *kitenge* shirt. Mike, who had John Lennon wire-rim glasses, wore dark trousers and a white shirt, as if he hadn't quite got used to life in the tropics. The two young men looked awkward, seeming unsure whether to sit down or stand.

Freya guessed that they might be about twenty-one, only a couple of years younger than her. She accidentally met Mike's eyes and wanted to say, *I know how you feel, I can't get used to all this either. I'd rather have dinner on my lap in front of the TV.*

After drinks, they all sat down to dinner. Roger looked anxious and smiled at Keziah as she brought in the small plates of egg mayonnaise for starters. This was followed by leek tart, and then fillet steak, which had been marinated in herbs and wine and then cooked slowly in the oven. Chocolate mousse completed the meal.

'Great stuff; well done, my dear,' Don said to Freya.

Freya blushed. 'Actually, Roger did most of the cooking with Keziah's help,' she said.

There was a moment of silence.

'Yes, of course, we heard she was a good cook. Worth hanging on to. And yes, all the best chefs are men, eh, Roger?' Don said.

'I see they've opened a new supermarket. Has anyone tried it yet?' Mavis said hurriedly as if she was trying to change the subject.

Roger stood up and signalled that people should move

from the table. He offered liqueurs, and everyone began chatting and laughing. Roger smiled at Freya. Things were going well for their first dinner party. He would be happy that she was learning how to do these things.

Don asked the young men what they were planning to do.

'I'll be working at Mulago Hospital, helping with the admin. You know, registration of patients, bills, that sort of thing,' Mike said.

'Wouldn't be in your shoes,' Don said. 'That place was wonderful when they opened it. 1962, I think? State of the art. A lot of expat doctors working there then. Now it's just gone downhill. The *watu* don't know how to look after anything. Fact is, a lot of them prefer their own medicine men.'

Sam said that he would be working with a small charity. Freya had seen TV programmes about African charities. White people with concerned faces gave medicines to grateful mothers of starving children. One of her old school friends had become a nun and gone to work with a charity somewhere in Africa. Freya had thought briefly about doing the same, after she had a crush on a tall, good-looking vicar at her local church.

'Oh, one of those church mission things?' Don said. 'They're doing a great job. Can't be easy.'

'No,' Sam said. 'Actually it's run by an Asian guy called Satish Kumar.'

'Didn't realise the Asians were involved in these things,' Don said, 'though I suppose a lot of the rich ones are giving big handouts now to keep in with Amin.'

'I don't think it's like that, sir,' Sam said. 'This is just a small charity that tries to do things where it can. They are helping to pay my salary so that I can teach in a primary school about twenty miles from here.'

'Well, do be careful,' Don said. 'There are some terrible stories going around.'

Mavis looked at him as if signalling him to be quiet.

'Yes, we've been warned. But we're not really expecting any trouble out there. The politics is going on in the towns,' Sam said.

'I wouldn't be so sure of that,' Don said.

Mike looked at Sam, and Freya thought she saw him move his eyes as if to signal, *Here we go again, this old bloke is such a bore.* Then Mike said, 'If you don't mind me asking, sir, what is it that this project is doing?'

Don stroked his moustache. 'Oh, mostly developing new crops for export, building a few roads and dams, fish ponds, that sort of thing. We're trying to get these people into the twentieth century and away from their *pangas* and hoes and into using tractors and modern equipment.'

He looked towards Roger. 'That's his field, of course. Can't say any of it's easy.'

'Wasn't there a groundnut scheme in Tanzania after the war that went horribly wrong?' Sam asked.

'Yes. Actually, I was there briefly, before I came here. Place just wasn't suitable for growing groundnuts, not enough rainfall, that sort of thing,' Don said.

'Shouldn't they have thought of that before they began?' Sam said.

Don's face went red. 'Sometimes you just have to get on with things. These people never want change.'

Before Sam could say anything else, Don turned towards Roger and said, 'By the way, I heard today that Bobby will be coming over next month.'

'Who is Bobby?' Freya said quietly, hoping that she hadn't asked a stupid question.

'He's the project supervisor from London,' Don said. 'He visits two or three times a year to check that everything is going okay. We all have to put in a bit of extra effort when he comes.'

Don was sitting next to Freya and he lightly rested his damp hand on her back.

'Even you girls.' He laughed as he said it. 'Bobby likes to think everyone's happy, settled in and keeping occupied.'

Freya's eyes were sore from the cigarette smoke, and the smell of Don's cigar nauseated her. Keziah moved slowly and coughed loudly as she cleared the table and took things into the kitchen.

'More drinks, anyone?' Roger said.

Freya saw Mike smile at Sam and she hoped they weren't going to start another argument with Don. Then there was a sudden coughing and retching sound from the kitchen.

'Has your girl been at the drink?' Don said and laughed.

Roger stubbed out his cigarette. 'I'd better go and see what's happening.'

'I can go,' Freya said.

'No, it's okay. She doesn't always understand what you're saying.'

Roger went into the kitchen, shutting the door behind him. Freya wanted to get up and follow him but Don was looking straight at her, meeting her eyes relentlessly as he talked about the old days, how the *watu* had been so much easier to deal with, how they'd always been grateful for what the *msungus* did for them. How things had gone downhill since independence; first the overthrow of the Kabaka, the old king, by Obote, and now Amin and his cronies.

'It's all down to tribalism,' he said.

Mike looked agitated, as if he was plucking up courage to speak. 'But don't you think, sir, that a lot of these tribal things are the result of colonialism, with the British and other countries just carving up the country and favouring one tribe over the others?'

Don became red in the face again but before he could speak, Mavis interrupted.

'Come on, Don, it's half past ten, time we were on our way.'

Sam stood up and tilted his head towards Mike.

'Yes, if you don't mind, I think we ought to be going as well,' Mike said. 'We have to walk down to the main road and get a taxi.'

'Good heavens. Don't they give you transport?' Don said.

'We'll have a scooter. But they haven't arrived yet,' Mike said.

'You can't possibly go home on your own like that. Your godfather would never forgive me if anything happened to you.'

'It's okay, thanks,' Sam said.

'Nonsense, someone will give you a lift. But we are all a bit worse for wear,' Don said as he finished his second liqueur.

Freya was relieved that they were all leaving. She and Roger could finally relax and chat about how things had gone.

'Oh, actually, I'm okay to drive,' Roger said as he came back from the kitchen. 'I can take them. Keziah's not feeling too good. She wants a lift down the road as well.'

The guests got ready to leave and gradually went outside onto the veranda, chatting loudly.

'What's the matter with Keziah? You were in the kitchen for a long time,' Freya said.

'I don't really know. I suppose she's tired or got malaria or something. These people get it all the time.'

'It's late for her to be going out,' Freya said.

'She's probably meeting her friends, or getting some local medicine of some kind. Look, don't wait up for me if I'm not back in an hour or so.'

Keziah had changed out of her work clothes. She was dressed in a shiny red satin dress and high heels. Instead of her scarf, she wore a black wavy wig.

Freya heard them all laughing as the car moved off down the drive. She poured herself another gin and tonic. She wondered if the evening had been a success. There had been a few arguments, but perhaps that was expected at dinner parties. Don seemed happy as long as he could have the last word.

Had she imagined that Roger had seemed distracted, too eager to rush into the kitchen when he heard Keziah making that strange choking noise? Perhaps it was her own fault? She would have to start learning to cook.

Freya switched on the record player and took her

Carole King LP from its sleeve. The songs were sad and romantic and it had been played so often that it crackled.

She poured herself another gin and tonic. It might help her sleep. The room spun a little but she felt happy and she stood up and began swaying and dancing to the music. Something crunched under her foot and she jumped away and tried to stifle a scream. A large cockroach ran across the floor, stopped and then looked at her defiantly. She picked up a book and hit it, but it refused to die. She picked up the spanner that Roger had left by the door in a box. She hit the cockroach harder and more violently until at last it lay squashed and wriggling.

The spanner had made a small crack in the concrete floor and she hastily covered it with a mat. She sat down trembling, surprised at how violent she had felt towards the cockroach.

There was a knock on the door and she jumped. The *askari* who kept guard outside the house every night was standing in the doorway. There was fear and concern in his eyes. He had a handsome face. She hadn't really looked at him before. What would it be like to run her finger down his cheek? Would he respond? Or think it was just part of his job?

'*Memsahib mzuri*?' he said.

She thought she saw disgust in his eyes. She knew she was drunk and she looked away and mumbled, '*Mzuri, santa sana*'.

She sat down and tried to calm herself with another gin and tonic, then fell asleep. She woke suddenly, unsure for a moment where she was, or whether it was day or night. The noisy ticking clock on the wall stared at her. It was two-thirty. Where was Roger? Had he taken his key? She wasn't sure if she should lock the door. Her mother had done that when her father was late back from the Post Office Club and he had had to sleep in his car. She despised her mother for doing it. It had seemed so childish.

She felt dizzy as she stood up. As she undressed for bed, she thought about the young men. Their life was just beginning. They had views and ideas and didn't care about saying what they thought. They were excited about what they were going to do.

Freya shivered with fear. Other people had already decided what her life would be like and what she was supposed to think.

FIVE

Freya woke with a pounding headache. When she lifted her head, the room spun around her. She knew it must be a hangover although she couldn't remember ever having one before. Roger's side of the bed was empty. She struggled to remember if he had come back during the night. Had she woken and heard the front door open in the brief early morning silence when the crickets stopped chirping? The sun was coming through the curtains and already the air in the room felt warm. Freya pushed the bedclothes away, looked at the clock and saw that it was nine o'clock. What had happened? Keziah always brought the tea in at six-thirty, apart from Sundays when it was her day off.

She put on her dark blue silk dressing gown. In the mirror, she saw her black, sweaty, tangled hair and her tired, crumpled face. She looked in the spare room. The bed was untouched.

In the living room, Keziah was polishing the floor. Freya watched as her body swayed from side to side and her breasts shook. After a few minutes, she plucked up the courage to speak to her. The brother of one of the project mechanics was giving Freya Swahili lessons every week. But when she tried to say anything it still sounded strange, as if she was speaking like a character in a *Woman's Weekly* story about Africa.

Freya cleared her throat and said, 'Please stop.' Keziah ignored her. She shouted 'Stop' again, louder. Keziah stood still, mopped her brow and stared at Freya.

'The *bwana*, have you seen him?' Freya said. Keziah pointed towards the kitchen door. Roger appeared in the doorway dressed only in his cotton shorts.

'What happened? When did you come back?' Freya said, trying not to sound angry.

'Oh, I don't remember, half past two or so, maybe.' That was the time she had finally gone to bed. Perhaps her watch had been wrong. She couldn't remember very clearly.

'I didn't want to wake you. So I slept in the spare room.'

'But the bed hasn't been slept in.'

'I can make a bed. I'm not completely useless around the house.'

'I wouldn't have minded being woken,' Freya said.

'Oh, don't be grumpy.' He put his arms around her and pulled her towards him. Through the silk pyjamas she felt his erection. She tried to meet his eyes but he was looking at Keziah.

'Breakfast, *Bwana*?' Keziah said to Roger and he nodded.

'Why aren't you at work?' Freya asked.

'I took some leave they owed me.' Roger held her more tightly. 'We could go back to bed,' he said.

'But she's getting breakfast,' Freya said.

'She won't mind. She'll just leave it on the table for later.'

He smelled strange, as if he had been eating something unfamiliar. She pulled away from him, and looked through the side window into the garden. Jimmy was watering the plants before he went to school.

'How much do we pay him?'

'No idea,' Roger said. 'I leave it to Keziah. She knows him. I give her the money to pay him. Is it important?'

'She seems to be in charge of a lot of things,' Freya said.

Roger tried to hold her hand.

'What's the matter? I'm sorry I was so late coming back. I didn't want to wake you when I came in.'

'So what happened?' Freya tried to pull away from him again but his grip was tight and she felt as if she couldn't breathe properly.

'I dropped the boys off at the nightclub, the one at the top of the Bata building.'

'And Keziah?' Freya said.

Roger looked towards the closed kitchen door and whispered, 'I left her at the bottom of the road, near her sister's house.'

'She looked quite dressed up, as if she was going somewhere,' Freya said.

'How should I know? It's not any of our business anyway.' He tried to kiss her. Freya escaped his grip and walked to the other side of the room.

'Oh come on,' Roger said, 'I don't know what's wrong with you.'

'So where were you all night?'

'I'm trying to tell you. I was on the way back when I had a puncture. The spare tyre was missing. Someone must have taken it. So I had to flag someone down to help me. It took me ages and then when this bloke, an Asian guy, did stop, we had to find a *duka* that was still open. I was quite scared actually. Anyway, we found a tyre eventually. By the time I got back it was late. So I just crashed in the spare room.'

It was strange because he was always saying that it was important to be properly prepared for the road. If there was an accident or the car broke down and you had to stop and get out of your car you might be set upon, robbed or even beaten up.

Freya stood by the bookshelf. A small porcelain figure of a shepherdess had been carefully placed on one of the shelves. It was tiny, just a few inches tall. Roger's mother had given it to her after she had said that she liked it. His mother was a widow who was always dressed neatly in tweed skirts and cardigans, her grey hair pulled back in a bun. Roger was her only child and she had tried to stop them getting married. She had said they should wait until after the baby was born and not rush into anything. Freya could tell she wasn't happy that her only son had been trapped into marriage with a girl from the council estate. When she had given the little porcelain figure to Freya, it had been like the sign of a truce, something to show that she might eventually get used to her being married to her beloved son.

Freya picked up the figurine and felt the rough edges of the chipped pottery. The porcelain girl wore a white dress flecked with gold stars. One hand was on her forehead, as if she was searching for her sheep. The other hand had been broken off. The girl was attached to a hollowed-out tree trunk. Freya felt a shiver of fear at the sight of this slight, delicate woman, always stuck to the heavy tree trunk, never able to break free. There were tiny white flowers in the trunk. Keziah must have put them there.

There was a sudden loud bang outside and Freya jumped with fear. The tiny figurine slipped from her grasp, fell and shattered on the floor, the water spilling on the broken china.

'It's just a car backfiring,' Roger said as he picked up the broken pieces. His face reddened. 'What have you done? We've had that since my grandmother died.'

Keziah came in with the broom, shook her head and began sweeping up the broken pieces.

Was it the sound of the car backfiring that had made it slip through her fingers, or had she dropped it on purpose? Why would she do such a thing? It must be the heat. The Blue Book had said that it sometimes made people behave strangely.

'I'm sorry,' she said.

'Oh well, it's just an ornament. My mother will never know. And you need to get dressed.'

Then he pulled her towards him and led her to the bedroom.

SIX

Freya walked along the project road. It was mid-morning. The project people drove everywhere and only walked when it was cool in the late afternoon. Walking was another sign of failure, a sign that she couldn't drive.

A high wire fence surrounded the project compound. The bungalows, the office buildings, the rest house, the club, the swimming pool and the tennis courts had been set down like a neat model village in the middle of the Ugandan countryside.

Some days it felt like a prison. *There is no real need to leave the compound. Everything you need is here*, they all said. *When you want to go to town for shopping, Oketch, the project driver, can always take you.*

Through the fence, Freya watched people hoeing and planting crops in the land between the banana trees. If she wanted to breathe properly, she knew she would have to go through the project gate and out onto the road.

As she walked towards the gate, the *askari* said something to her in rapid Swahili. He looked scared and she was afraid to go any further. A car drew up behind her and she heard Mavis' voice.

'Are you okay, dear? I know it's tempting, but you really shouldn't go walking outside the gate. I was looking for you to ask if you'd like to come along to the tennis this afternoon. One of the regulars is sick.'

'Oh, I'm not sure. I can't really play,' Freya said.

'Don't worry, we are used to newcomers. You'll soon pick it up. Meet us at the courts at four, when it's a bit cooler.'

*

'How was the tennis?' Roger asked.

Freya's short, white tennis dress was stained with sweat marks and flecked with the red dust from the courts.

'You look nice,' he said as he tried to brush the dust marks from the front of her skirt.

'It was awful. They all pretended to be patient with me, but I could tell they were annoyed that I kept missing the ball. And I couldn't bear the way they shouted at the ball boys all the time.'

Roger looked disappointed.

'You could have some lessons. Those kids don't mind being yelled at. It's money for them.'

'And I didn't know what to talk about.'

'I know some of them are a bit of a pain. But don't give up straight away.' He pulled her close to him, kissed her, and added, 'For me?'

'I just can't. I'll make some excuse to Mavis,' Freya said.

There was a long silence as Roger sat down and lit a cigarette.

'Well, you will have to find something to do soon. I don't really understand what it is with you. The other wives all seem to be perfectly happy, running the house, supervising things.'

There was the sound of rattling pots and pans in the kitchen as Keziah got things ready for dinner. She was talking loudly to someone.

'I've got nothing to do. She does everything. She doesn't like it if I try to do anything,' Freya said.

There was silence. Roger avoided looking directly at her.

'Perhaps it's time that we thought about ... you know ... trying?'

Freya was caught off guard. Her heart pounded. She pressed her eyelid to hide a tear. An image of her blue broderie anglaise wedding dress flashed through her mind. *It can't be white, of course,* they said. Freya and her mother had bought it from the posh dress shop with money from their holiday fund. Weddings were supposed to give you something to remember, to hold onto. She just wanted to forget the shame, the embarrassment. She heard her Aunty Eileen whispering to her, 'I'd get rid of it if I were you.'

There were so many things she hadn't been able to ask him. Would you still have wanted to marry me if I hadn't got pregnant? Do you really know how it feels to have something like that happen to you? But she didn't know how to ask him. And she was still scared of what the answers might be. Whatever she said, he would think that she was accusing him of something, or it would show him once again that she was a failure.

He lit a cigarette and stared straight ahead.

'I just think it might be a solution. You know, something to keep you occupied. You'd have something to talk about to the other wives.'

Was that how he saw it? She should have left the conversation there and given him some excuse as to why it was too soon to think about having a baby.

'You didn't really want me to keep it, did you?' she said quietly.

After a moment's silence he said, 'It wasn't easy for me, either.'

It was the first time that they had talked about it other than as a problem that needed to be solved.

'I could just see it was all going to be difficult, with not much money coming in and nowhere proper to live. How do you think I felt, living in your mother's house?'

Then he sighed, turned and looked directly at her.

'It's true. I did feel a bit … trapped. And when you lost it, it was a sort of relief.'

She could feel tears coming.

'I'm sorry. I know it must have been awful for you,' he went on. 'Now we're here and I've got this job, everything's different. We have a future. We can save money for a deposit on a house.' He tried to put his arms round her but she moved away from him.

'I just don't understand what you want,' he said.

At the time, no one had asked her what she wanted. When she had finally blurted out, 'I'm pregnant, I'm sorry,' her mother had slapped her face and then shouted and screamed for days about the sacrifices they had made so that she could go to the grammar school.

All she could do was struggle with the morning sickness, with the awful tiredness and with thinking about how she could hide the growing bump.

Her mother had gradually calmed down and said she would give up her job at the shop to look after the baby so that Freya could carry on working as a clerk at the furniture factory. It was taken for granted that they would get married. There was no discussion about it.

Everyone had been relieved when Roger was offered the job in Uganda. Peoples' memories were short. There would be nothing strange about a young woman with a baby joining her husband overseas.

It had happened three days before Roger was due to leave, just when she was beginning to feel a growing tightness at her waist and the first gentle kicks. The pain was sudden and violent. She had gone to the hospital on the bus, on her own. She waited in the cubicle for the midwife to come but by then blood was everywhere. She had screamed as something dropped heavily from between her legs. It had reminded her of a small bloodied frog. The nurse took it away and told her to forget it all.

'Good riddance,' her Aunty Eileen had said.

Roger had tried to comfort her, but she knew he was embarrassed. The blood of periods, of dead babies, was something he couldn't cope with, something that had nothing to do with men. Besides, he was busy getting ready to leave for Uganda.

'I don't think I could go through all that again,' Freya said.

'But it's been a few months since it happened. It will be different this time. You can take it easy.'

Freya knew that she should have 'got over it' by now. If you didn't pull yourself together, you only had yourself to blame. But nothing could stop the strange dreams or the sinking feeling she had in her stomach when she woke up in the morning.

Roger put his arms around her.

'I'm sorry if you're upset. I do love you,' he said. She was surprised. He only ever said that when they were making love, as if the words just went with his need to finish and had nothing to do with her personally. She felt angry. She wanted to hear him say he loved her but not just as a way of making him feel bad if she wouldn't agree to try for a baby.

'Look, why don't we give it a try? You could just stop taking the pill,' he said. He pulled her towards him. The idea seemed to excite him.

'Promise me that you will,' he whispered.

She didn't say anything and just nodded. That seemed easier than saying I can't, not yet. She wanted the conversation to end.

'I need a shower,' she said.

'I'll come with you.' He had never suggested that before. She pretended not to have understood what he meant.

After they had made love, he said, 'Oh I forgot to tell you that Amin is visiting the project on Monday.' It seemed like some sort of strange joke and she laughed nervously.

'No, it's true. The High Commission has organised it. They want to show him what British aid is doing and it seems he's very interested in farming.'

'Will I have to go?' Freya said.

'Yes, Don says we all have to go along.'

SEVEN

Freya was both scared and excited about seeing Idi Amin in the flesh. Mavis had heard a rumour that he had murdered one of his wives and thrown her to the crocodiles. Surely that couldn't be true? The newsreaders on the radio were always saying that people shouldn't listen to rumours.

Would you be able to tell from just looking at someone if he was really a monster? Newspapers and magazines from the UK arrived by airmail every few days. Sometimes there were jokes or cartoons about Amin as if he was an African Tommy Cooper or Norman Wisdom.

She would at least have something to tell her mother in her weekly letter home. It wasn't always easy to find things to say.

A large crowd stood outside the project offices, waiting for him to arrive. The sun was hot and they were fanning themselves and wiping their brows. Freya recognised the project people and the house servants. But there were other people there too. She guessed that they had come from nearby villages, or perhaps they were his supporters, ordered to attend. Bored-looking drummers and musicians stood by a microphone on a stand. The smell of *matooke* was mixed with the sweet smell of locally brewed beer.

Freya felt as if she was at a party, nervous but waiting for something exciting to happen. She spotted Keziah laughing and talking with her friends. She hardly recognised her in her long patterned dress and matching turban. Comfort stood with a group of schoolchildren dressed in green checked school uniforms, all holding or waving the black, yellow and red Ugandan flag.

The wait felt endless. Then a large Mercedes-Benz with the windows blacked out arrived. Two burly men jumped out of the back seat and opened the car door and Amin stepped out. He was a tall, large man with a belly that overhung his trouser belt. He could have been someone's friendly uncle.

Freya tried not to stare at the puffed, round face that she recognised from the newspapers. The project men lined up and Amin shook hands with them all. Freya had brought her new Polaroid camera and she took a photo as Amin shook hands with Roger. The two burly men who had arrived with Amin turned and stared at her. She was scared for a moment. Perhaps taking photographs of the President wasn't allowed. But the men quickly went back to talking and laughing with the young girls who were standing at the front of the crowd.

Everyone followed as Amin and Don inspected the fields where the experimental crops were being grown. Freya heard Amin talking to Don about farming and the work he used to do on his *shamba*. The crowd suddenly cried 'Eeeh'. A young girl had fainted. Amin turned and walked back to where she had fallen and gently picked her up.

After the walk around the fields, Amin took the microphone and began speaking. It was difficult to hear what he said because it wasn't working properly. She could hear a mixture of English and Swahili and she heard the words, 'These are good men, you people are lucky, very lucky to work with these *msungus*'.

The white people shifted around uncomfortably, as if they were hoping it would all end soon. The Africans had their eyes fixed firmly on the President. They made sure they didn't laugh until he laughed.

Then the drumming started and Amin began dancing. People gradually and nervously started to join in. The project people and the man from the British High Commission jigged around, trying not to look embarrassed. Freya had never been any good at dancing and she swayed awkwardly in time to the music. She was sure she saw Keziah laughing at her.

A group of local women wearing tee shirts with Amin's face printed on the front performed a traditional dance. The mouth on the face opened and closed as they danced. Amin laughed and clapped when they stopped. The women looked away or bowed their heads, as if nervous of looking at him directly.

Then Amin beckoned to a woman in the audience. Freya couldn't see who it was at first, then she saw that it was Keziah. They began dancing. They laughed and chatted to each other as if they were old friends.

The music stopped and Amin sat down and mopped

his brow. The two burly men waved their hands at the crowd, signalling that they should start to leave. People began to drift away, leaving Amin and his men with the project people. There was an awkward moment when it seemed as if no one knew what would happen next. Then Amin said, 'Some refreshments, I think?'

Don said, 'Of course, sir,' and he led Amin and the others to the clubhouse. Don ordered beers and soft drinks for everyone.

'He's a Muslim. I hope Don hasn't done the wrong thing,' Mavis whispered to Freya. But Amin was holding a glass of beer and smiling. He climbed the two wooden steps onto the small stage in the clubhouse. Everyone stopped talking and Amin held up his glass.

'I'm telling you sincerely to drink, for overdrunk will not make you happy,' he said.

Everyone laughed nervously, unsure of what he was saying. Then he made a toast to the 'wonderful Queen of England' and raised his glass to her picture on the wall.

They all stood waiting for the Ugandan national anthem. There was an awkward silence as Don tried to get the old record player to work, and Amin's large round cheeks began to droop. But when Don told him nervously that the record player was broken, he laughed and said, 'Next time, maybe.'

As he walked away with his party of officials, he stopped and said something to Keziah. She knelt down in front of him and then got up. He talked to her for a few more minutes while his party looked away as if they were wearily familiar with him doing this when he saw a young girl that he liked the look of.

After he had left, the project men began taking off their jackets and loosening their ties. Some of the project wives took off the hats they had found for the occasion and kicked off their uncomfortable shoes.

'Well, thanks everyone,' Don said. 'That went well. I think we'll all be fine. I can't think he's got it in for the *msungus*. I asked him about rugby, thinking he'd be interested. Remembered his time in the army. Seems he likes cricket as well. Apparently, there's some West Indian chappie in the country playing and doing a bit of coaching. He used to play for Surrey, it seems. He asked if I knew anything about him.'

Freya tried to meet Roger's eyes to signal to him that she wanted to leave. But he was sitting at the bar with his back to her. She knew that if she slipped away, no one would miss her.

As she walked back to the house, she heard footsteps behind her. She started to move quickly, afraid to turn around. She should have waited for Roger to drive her the short distance from the clubhouse to the bungalow. She wanted to run but her feet felt heavy. Then she turned and saw with relief that it was Keziah. Should she walk back to the house with her or let her overtake? It was odd to see a memsahib and her house girl walking together like two people who knew each other. She slowed down until Keziah was by her side. She tried to think of something to say to her but she only knew the words for telling her what to do in the house. They walked together in awkward silence.

A man passed them on the path. He was carrying a large canvas bag. He stopped, greeted Keziah, then took three paintings from his bag and showed them to Freya. They were pictures of an African man. In each picture, the man was carrying different things on his head. She had seen pictures like these somewhere before. It was at Mavis' house, she remembered. The man had the same sad, passive expression in all the paintings. Freya said, 'No, thank you,' and he put them back in his bag and walked away.

The wind rustled in small gusts through the fields of corn.

'You know him?' Freya asked. Making conversation felt awkward.

'My man from same tribe. They from the same village.'

Freya had never thought of her as having a man. She had a life outside the house and the servants' quarters but Freya knew nothing about it.

'Your man? Who is he?' There was silence and Freya was afraid that she had made a mistake. It felt wrong to ask such a personal question.

'In army,' Keziah said, slowly and quietly as if she was afraid to be overheard.

'You think Amin a bad person?' Freya asked.

Keziah didn't answer. Freya thought she looked tired. When they reached the bungalow, Freya went through the front door while Keziah walked round to the back of the house.

*

Roger came back from the club later that evening. He put his arms around her.

'I think Amin's all right, really. Very interested in the machinery. Seems he's just bought a whole load of tractors. Asked my advice.'

Freya smelled the gin as she showed him the Polaroid photo of him shaking Amin's hand. He pulled her more closely towards him. 'It's the time of the month, isn't it?' he said. She wanted to pretend that she didn't know what he meant. She had agreed to stop taking the pill but she couldn't do it. She was still too scared of another miscarriage. She felt guilty about the lies. But he would never know.

It was nine o'clock in the evening. That was the time when she usually took her pill. She pulled away from him and said, 'Not now, later.' She went to the bedroom and opened the underwear drawer where she hid her pills. She moved her hand around in the place where she usually kept them. The packet wasn't there. Her panic grew as she rummaged through the neatly folded pants, throwing them on the floor as she grew more frantic. Where was it? No one could have moved it. Then she remembered that Keziah sometimes tidied the cupboards and draws, even though she had asked her not to.

In the living room, Roger was sitting at the desk, doing some paperwork.

'Where is Keziah?' she said.

'In her house, I assume. It's late. Why do you want her?'

'I've lost some aspirins and I thought Keziah might know where they were.'

'Is it that important? Are you ill? Do you need them now?'

'I've suddenly got a really bad migraine,' she said. 'It's

the drink and the excitement, I expect. I need to lie down and sleep.'

He looked disappointed, but nodded. In the bedroom, she looked again for the pills, searching her memory for where she might have put them. It was the last packet before she was due for the next prescription.

When Roger got into bed, she pretended to be asleep.

*

As she woke the next morning, she heard Roger moving about, getting dressed. He suddenly cursed as he knocked his ankle against the bedpost.

'What are you doing?' she said.

'I'm trying to find my other shoe. It must have slipped under the bed.'

She pretended to go back to sleep and wished that he would hurry up and leave the bedroom. She needed to get up and start looking for the packet again. Then she felt him pulling on her shoulder, as if to wake her.

'What is it?' she said.

'Are these your aspirins?'

She sat up and saw that he was holding the contraceptive pill packet.

'So you have been taking them?' he said.

He turned away from her. His white shirt strained across his shoulders as he folded his arms tightly.

'It's just too soon,' she said. 'I'm still afraid.'

'I don't know what of, and you didn't have to lie about it.'

She could see that he was trying to control himself.

'You know, you will have to make up your mind about all this … sooner or later.'

It was no use arguing with him. It was so difficult to explain how she felt. In any case, arguments were difficult when houseboys, *ayahs*, gardeners were always around listening and then gossiping about what they had heard.

'I have to go. I'm late already. I'm not sure when I'll be back tonight, might be late,' he said.

She watched him get into the car. He revved the engine loudly and drove so fast down the drive that he almost hit Jock.

Freya was still wearing her nightclothes when Keziah came in to start her daily cleaning. She stood for a moment and then said, 'I need money. Advance. I pay you back.'

It was unexpected and Freya was caught off guard. Mavis had said, 'Be careful, houseboys and *ayahs* are always asking for loans. If you pay them properly, they have enough. They're better off than most people.'

Freya looked away into the garden. There was a noise outside of a child coughing as if choking and then crying.

'What's that?' Freya said.

'It Comfort. We think she got measles. We need money for the hospital.'

Measles, surely that wasn't serious? Freya remembered having measles when she was six. There had been awful headaches, long days in bed with fever, and little spidery creatures running up and down the closed curtains whenever she opened her eyes. And then terrible pain when they opened the curtains. But surely children got over measles without going to the hospital?

'My cousin, she died of measles.' Keziah frowned.

Freya remembered that she had read somewhere that some diseases could be more dangerous in the tropics.

'We need money for medicines. Pay doctor.'

'I thought it was free,' Freya said.

'You have to pay or wait long, long time to see doctor.' Keziah turned to go back into the kitchen.

She knew Roger would be annoyed if she gave Keziah money without asking him. She wouldn't tell him.

'How much?'

'Twenty shillings.'

That seemed a lot but Freya opened her handbag and gave a note to Keziah, who took it and put it inside her dress.

There was a knock on the veranda door. Simon, Mavis' cook, stood there holding a letter. She took it from him, afraid to open it in case she had unwittingly done something wrong again. After he had gone, she opened it and read:

Dear Mrs. Templemead

I didn't know your address so I sent this via Don. First of all, thank you very much for the lovely evening at your house. I hope you don't mind me writing but I just wanted to say that we are looking for volunteers for the Charity. Things are getting a bit difficult and the Chief Executive, Satish Kumar, has asked me if I knew anyone who might be able to help, even for a few hours a week. Do let me know if you might be interested. If so, could you let me know your qualifications and what you have done before.

Yours sincerely

Sam Miller

She remembered how uneasy he and Mike had been at the dinner party. Perhaps he had sensed that she was finding it difficult to settle down in the claustrophobic world of the project.

She crumpled the letter in her hand and dropped it on the floor.

A child outside was coughing loudly and she turned the radio on to drown out the sound. The newsreader was describing Idi Amin Dada's visit to an Asian-owned tea plantation.

Was this what her life would be like from now on? Roger nagging her to get pregnant, seeing her as a failure if she didn't? Always being afraid to say what she wanted to say at dinner parties? Always failing at tennis, golf and bridge?

The Jim Reeves song was on the radio yet again. She turned it off and shouted 'Bugger!' She turned round and saw Keziah laughing at her.

Keziah picked up the crumpled letter from the floor.

'No, don't throw it away,' Freya said. Then she opened the desk drawer, took out her blue writing paper, and wrote:

Dear Sam

Thank you for your letter. I would like to come and visit the charity office and talk to the Chief Executive. I don't think I can help but it would be nice to hear about it so that I can decide. I have 5 O levels in English, Maths, History, Chemistry and French. Since I left school, I have been working as a typist in a furniture factory.

Yours sincerely
Freya

Roger got back late that evening. She thought that there would be a difficult silence at least for a few hours, but he said, 'Look, I'm sorry about this morning.' He hesitated as if struggling to find the right words. 'If you're not ready … for a … baby, I understand. We can wait a little while.'

She knew that he wanted to have sex. And she knew that something was happening to her so that she wanted it too.

*

After they had made love, she decided that she had better not have secrets from him any more. When she told him about the letter from Sam, she could feel his body becoming tense beside her. She was afraid that he was going to be angry again but he just turned away from her.

'Well if that's what you really want to do,' he said. 'But look, I can't really help much at the moment, I'm very busy with work. Bobby will be coming from London for the inspection in a month or so. And it's important that everything goes well.'

EIGHT

Sam had written back almost immediately saying that the director of the charity would like to meet her as soon as he got back from safari.

The charity office was on the Makerere University campus and Roger dropped her off at the entrance gate.

'Be careful,' Roger said. 'You don't know who these people are. I'm sorry I haven't got time to wait for you. Oketch will pick you up and take you home.'

Freya walked up the hill, following the signposts. The bungalows on the campus were built in the same style as those at the project but the gardens were less well kept and the lawns were spattered with brown patches. Students were standing around chatting in groups. House servants stood by the side of the road, taking a break. A soldier was sharing a cigarette with a policeman. He said something and stared at her and she tried to walk more quickly.

It was eleven o'clock and the sun was hot. She had forgotten her hat, but she was happy just to be walking freely, somewhere that wasn't in the gated confines of the project.

She kept taking the wrong turns down the backs and sides of buildings until she finally saw a sign for the Makerere Demonstration School. She knew that the charity office was somewhere near there. Then she saw a line of people and realised that they must be queuing at the entrance to the charity. It was a small one-storey building attached to the side of the school. The white paint was peeling. A sign on the door said Village Aid.

Most of the people in the queue were women. Some were sitting on the floor, and most had sick-looking, crying babies on their backs. Freya hesitated, wondering if she should wait her turn, but a woman beckoned to her to go ahead of them.

She knocked on the door and a female voice called out, 'Wait'. After a few minutes, the same voice said, 'Come'.

She pushed the door open gently. Inside the room a woman sat typing at a desk covered with papers. Unopened cardboard boxes were lying all over the floor. An air conditioner rattled loudly on the wall.

'Yes?' the woman said, without looking up from the typewriter.

'Excuse me,' Freya said.

The woman looked up. 'Oh, you're here?' she said. 'Over there, that door.'

The door had CHIEF written on it. Freya knocked tentatively. An Asian man wearing a khaki safari suit opened it. He was medium height and had a neatly trimmed beard. She thought he could be about thirty. He shook her hand firmly.

'You must be Freya. Come in, please, it's good to see you. Excuse the mess. We're really busy at the moment.' He waved a hand towards the woman at the typewriter and said, 'This is Prudence, my assistant. I'm Satish.'

His office was as chaotic as the room outside. His in-tray was overflowing with papers. She thought about the typing pool in the office where she had worked at home, with everyone sitting in neat rows at carefully arranged desks.

'They call me the Chief Executive, but that's a bit grand as there are only five of us.' He laughed and rocked back in his old, torn office chair.

The phone rang and he picked it up and said something quickly in Swahili before putting it down. 'So what would you like to know?' he said.

Freya spoke slowly, unsure of what he might think of her.

'What is the work you do? I don't really know if I can help. But I'd like to know more about what you do.'

'It's good of you to come. Sam told me about … where you live. It can be quite tough for someone who is new to life here. We have quite a few…' – he didn't seem to know what word to use – '… ladies who want to do good, but find it all quite difficult. So I won't be offended if you decide it's not for you.'

Was she someone who wanted to do good? She hadn't thought of herself in that way.

'The people we try to help live outside the towns, in rural areas. There is no running water or electricity. The health posts are miles away. The schools don't have much equipment, probably no books.

'We raise money for things like wells and school

buildings. We work with VSOs to get teachers for the primary schools. Your friend Sam is doing a very good job teaching English to primary school kids. They didn't have anything in the school except a few old desks and chairs, and the roof leaks. Oh, and sometimes we work with Social Scientists at the university to do surveys for them. We haven't got much money. We get some from the local Rotary and the Kampala Sports Club, and the sugar and the textile people give us a bit now and then.'

He met her eyes and said, 'So, as I said, it might not suit you.'

Did he mean that expatriates like her were all spoilt and overprotected?

'I understand,' she said. It had been a mistake to think that she had anything to offer to something like this. Roger had said it would all be a waste of time.

'Thank you, I'm sorry, but maybe...' she said as she stood up.

Satish wiped his brow with a grey handkerchief. 'No, don't leave,' he said. 'I didn't mean to put you off. I wanted to make sure you understood that things are not always as straightforward as you think they might be. Helping people can be complicated.'

She knew that was true. People had tried to help her when she had the miscarriage. They didn't know what kind of help she needed. She had wanted to be told that getting pregnant wasn't her fault.

But she knew it was. She shouldn't have been so easily persuaded by Roger that he would make sure she wouldn't get pregnant, even though he wasn't wearing a condom. She shouldn't have tried to get rid of it.

'Are you all right?' Satish said. Freya tried to concentrate on what he was saying. She looked at him and met his eyes. They were dark brown and kind. Was he gently teasing her?

The phone rang. Prudence came into the room.

'Where are the aspirins and the chloroquine?' she said. Satish ignored the phone, took a few packets from the drawer and gave them to her.

'We're not supposed to give these things to people,' he said, 'but they know we keep some here for emergencies. That's why the women are queuing outside.'

The office really did look untidy and chaotic.

'You can see what a mess everything is. I really just need some help with filing and things. Prudence only works part-time. Maybe you could come in on Fridays, answer the phones and do a bit of paperwork? My family is in the East and I like to visit them at weekends, especially now, with things getting so difficult for us Asians.'

There were rings of sweat under the armpits of his jacket. Freya knew about Amin's threats to expel the Asians but she hadn't met anyone who might be directly affected, who might have their life torn apart and disrupted.

She had come to the charity because she wanted an escape from the project and as a way of passing the time. This all felt like something much bigger. She could hear Roger saying, 'Don't get involved with politics.'

'I don't think ...' she said.

Before she could finish, Satish interrupted and said, 'I understand. It's fine. Don't worry.'

Then she thought about Roger shaking hands with Amin, about Keziah's man in the army. Just being somewhere could make you part of politics. It was no good just running away from it all the time. It was only office work, after all. She knew how to do that.

'No… I mean yes, I can help you,' Freya said.

'Oh thanks, that would be great.' He mopped his brow with the handkerchief. 'And there is something else. The people who give us money like to have reports. Sometimes I need help with that.'

'I'm not sure I could do that,' she said.

'Well you said in your letter that you'd got English O level and that you had done clerical work.'

'Yes, but I never write anything, just type things for other people.'

'I'm sure you could do it. But it would mean occasionally going outside Kampala, off the road a bit. Mostly it's safe. But you will have heard the stories going round.'

'Even…?' She stopped, afraid that it was the wrong thing to say.

'Yes, even the *msungus* have to be careful,' he said. 'Come along next Friday, then. We'll see how you do.'

In the area outside his office, the queue of women had grown longer. Satish said something to them in what she was starting to recognise as Luganda, the language spoken by the Baganda, the tribe that came from the Kampala area. The women looked disappointed and began to mutter as they picked up their things, hoisted their babies on their backs and began to walk away. Some of them put their hands together and made a small bobbing curtsy as they left.

'It's a shame,' he said, 'but we have to close at lunchtime. By the way, you might want to learn a bit of the language.'

'I'm learning some Swahili.'

'Well, yes, that's useful but it's not really a local language. It's mostly used with houseboys and house girls. A lot of them come from Kenya. And most of the army and the police use it because they come from the North. You need Luganda for the villages.'

The job already sounded more complicated than she had imagined.

She walked back down the road to the entrance gate and out onto the busy road and watched the lorries, scooters and cars narrowly avoiding each other. The project Land Rover stopped close to her and Oketch opened the door for her.

'You should stay inside gate,' he said. 'Road dangerous.' He was like a fussy old mother hen. Mavis had said that he was very loyal. 'Not like some of the *watu*,' she'd said. 'You can always trust Oketch.'

Freya climbed into the Land Rover. As they drove along the busy road, she stared straight ahead without looking at him. She never knew what to say to him and she was scared that if she talked to him it might distract him from the dangers of the road. She wondered what he thought of these people whom he ferried endlessly up and down from the project to Kampala and back. Did he understand what they were talking about or saying, or even care? They treated him like the Invisible Man.

She hesitated and then said, 'Where are you from?'

He laughed and said, 'Uganda, where you think?'

She was ashamed that she hadn't realised that she was asking a stupid question. Did anyone ever really know where they were from, and did it matter?

73

*

When Roger came back from work, he asked her how she had got on at the charity.

'I'm going to help them. It will only be for one day a week and it's just helping in the office.'

'Well, as long as that's all it is, I suppose it's okay. I'd probably better check with Don,' Roger said.

Why did Don have to be told? Freya decided not to mention the trips to the villages. Don would most likely disapprove.

'I've been thinking,' Roger said. 'Things would be better for you if you could learn to drive. There's an old Hillman Imp for sale. I'm thinking of buying it for you.'

NINE

It was Freya's second Friday at the charity office. It was already beginning to look a bit tidier. Freya and Prudence were drinking tea. It had been brewed in an old kettle and flavoured with condensed milk.

Prudence had been standoffish at first, but after they had both tried not to laugh at the man with the strange-looking, long, dangling penis who came every Friday and stood completely naked in the queue, they had become friendlier. Prudence had gradually told her about her divorce, her young children and the elderly mother-in-law who lived with them. It sounded like a complicated story. And she was teaching Freya a few words in Luganda.

The door opened and Satish came into the office looking sweaty and dishevelled. The back of his safari suit jacket was tucked into his trousers. The two women smiled at each other.

'The student who usually comes to the village with me can't come as she is sick. It's going to be difficult. I have to have a woman with me to talk to the women there. Prudence, can you do it?' he asked.

'No, sorry. Got to pick up the children. No one else is around to do it today. And I got a lot of typing to do.'

Satish rubbed his forehead and sighed. Then he looked at Freya and said, 'What about you?'

She had told Roger that she would just be working in the office. But how would he know, unless she told him? It would be good to get out, to see the countryside, to find something else to write about in her letters to her mother.

'Yes, all right. I'll come along,' she said hesitantly, 'if you think I can help.'

On their way to the village, Satish drove fast. He turned and looked at her when he spoke and occasionally took his hands off the steering wheel to make a gesture. As if sensing her fear, he said, 'Don't worry, it's much safer to drive fast and I've done a bit of rally driving.'

'What are we going to do in the village?' Freya asked.

'Sorry, I should have said. The university hospital is doing research into a disease called bilharzia. They have asked us to do a survey in the village to find out how many people have it.'

Freya had never heard of it before.

'It's caused by a kind of worm,' Satish said. 'You get it from water, ponds, rivers, lakes, even puddles. It makes you feel ill and pee blood, and if you're poor and malnourished you can get very ill and even die.'

They turned off the main road onto a dirt track. The Land Rover struggled forward slowly, lurching over the large mounds of earth in the road. A signpost pointed to Kyasimi. The name sounded familiar to her. Was it one of the project villages where they tested the crops and the machinery?

As they got nearer to the village, men, women and children ran alongside them, shouting and banging their hands on the sides and windows of the vehicle. Freya moved away from the window.

'Don't be scared,' Satish said. 'They are just welcoming us.'

A small crowd of people gathered round as they reached the centre of the village. Satish opened the back door and gave the head man a sack of cassava and three large bunches of *matooke*.

'We can't give them money but we have to show some kind of appreciation otherwise no one would talk to us,' he said.

As she climbed out of the Land Rover, her tight-fitting sheath dress rucked up above her knees and she looked around to see if anyone was looking. But they were too busy shouting and arguing as they carried away the cassava and the *matooke* to notice her.

There was a strong smell of burning wood. People were sitting around outside their huts, eating from tin bowls and plates. Others were sleeping on the dirt floor of their compounds. People got up early to work in the fields. One morning she had woken at four o'clock and heard a thudding noise in the distance. It was the sound of women pounding maize.

Freya and Satish stood together under a tree.

'I want you to talk to the women and ask them if anyone is ill in the family at the moment. Then I can follow up with them and get more details,' he said.

A group of small girls in green checked school uniform dresses stood nearby, as if waiting for something.

'One of these girls will help you translate. Their English is quite good,' Satish said.

'Why aren't they at school?' Freya asked.

'Sometimes the school starts really early and finishes by lunchtime. Or maybe they have just been kept at home to work or look after the younger children.'

She watched Satish as he sat down on the floor with a group of men. They were waving their arms and their sticks and they sounded angry.

Freya was nervous about being left alone and she wasn't sure what she was supposed to do. It was difficult and intrusive to ask people about their lives. If she saw anyone standing in the street with a clipboard, she would always cross the road to avoid them.

She chose the tallest girl. The others made noises of disappointment and walked away. She followed the girl until she stopped by a hut where a woman was sitting outside on a stool. The woman's skin was covered in dust and she looked tired and lethargic.

'She is sad because the baby came soon and died this morning,' the girl said.

Freya felt sick in her stomach. She couldn't ask any more questions. Her hand trembled as she wrote her note.

They moved quickly to another hut where a man sat on the floor, smoking. Part of his leg beneath his knee was missing and his rusty prosthetic leg was lying by his side. He spoke quickly and coughed as if he was out of breath.

'He says his new leg is broken and he wants to know if you can get him another one. Everyone in the house is sick. It's the time for malaria,' the girl said.

Freya looked round to find Satish, so that she could tell him that she couldn't carry on doing this. She had no idea how to help with these problems and she was feeling faint in the heat of the midday sun.

A gang of small boys came walking towards her. As they got closer, she heard them calling out, '*Mimi, memsahib*'. The girl who was helping her said, 'Come, please madam, they no good.'

Freya tried to walk faster, but the gang of boys danced round her. One of them pushed an old silver photo frame in her face. It was a faded photograph of a white child wearing a bonnet, sitting in a large old-fashioned pram.

'You buy?' they said and pushed the picture close to her face. Freya turned her head away, waved her arms and tried to push them away. She accidentally hit one of the boys across the face and she heard him shout angrily. People came out of their huts and stood watching.

One of the boys tugged her hair, another pulled at her dress. She was getting more and more agitated when Satish appeared from a banana *shamba* and shouted at them as they ran away.

'I'm so sorry,' Satish said, 'it's not usually like this. We had better go.'

Then, suddenly, a man dressed in rags, his eyes bloodshot, was running towards Satish, swaying as if he was drunk, and shouting, '*Mahindi, kwenda, kwenda*'. A man and two women held him back as he screamed and struggled.

Freya ran to the Land Rover and frantically pulled on the locked door. She turned and an old woman grabbed her arm. She stared closely at Freya's face. There were beads of sweat at the sides of the woman's nose. Freya could smell cassava on her breath. The woman's arms were scarred and blotted with white scald marks. Freya guessed that they were caused by endlessly carrying large pots of food and water from the fires in the yard to her hut.

'You got children?' the woman asked.

Freya tried to pull away but the woman tightened her grip.

'No, please,' Freya said, leaning away from her.

'Don't be scared. Get some, or he'll leave you.'

Freya looked round anxiously for Satish but he had disappeared.

'Do you want money?' Freya said as she struggled to open the clip on her bag.

'*Chi, chi*', the woman said and wiped her brow with a soiled piece of rag. 'Come back and I'll give you the medicine. Then you give me money.'

Satish appeared alongside two old men and there were sounds of a man screaming in the distance as if he was being beaten. Satish's hands were trembling and large patches of sweat now covered his blue safari suit. As they drove off, people ran after them, waving and shouting, until they reached the main road.

Why had the woman said that? How did she know that Freya was afraid of getting pregnant? Had she imagined the whole thing? She turned and looked at Satish. He seemed calm in spite of everything that had just happened.

'What did that man say to you?' Freya said.

'Asians, go,' he said.

'Why did he say that? They know you always try to help them,' Freya said. 'Was he a madman?'

'You can't really blame him,' Satish said. 'Amin has told them that the Asians have sabotaged the economy and caused the shortages. Now that people think that we are leaving, they are happy and can't wait to see us go. Amin keeps saying that we are black Jews. They think that after we've gone, they will all drive around in big Mercedes cars. Even if some of them know it's not true, they're too frightened to say so.'

'That's terrible,' Freya said.

'Well, some of it is our fault,' Satish said. 'You British brought workers from India here years ago to help build the railways. And since then, people have come here from Pakistan and Bangladesh and other places. But it's easier to lump us all together and call us Asians, just like you're all *msungus*.'

'But why is it your fault?' she continued.

'Some Asians have made a lot of money on the backs of Africans. Like you all did with slavery and colonialism.'

Freya was surprised at being blamed for something she hadn't thought much about before.

'But some of us are not all that well off,' Satish said. 'We might own a small shop or small business or do a government job. But you know how it is; everyone seems to need someone to look down on. And they say we don't mix much. But then who does? In the end, everyone keeps to their own group, tribe, whatever. That's how they feel safe.'

'Some of these jumped-up Asians have probably got it coming to them,' Don had said at the dinner party.

Freya's father had worked at the Post Office. He didn't talk about work much but one day he had said, 'These Indian postmen are decent chaps but they're a bit lazy.' She had wanted to argue with him but she knew it was no use.

'Trouble is,' Satish said, 'when things go wrong, people always need someone to blame and they usually pick on a group of people who they think don't really belong, even if they've lived there all their lives. Many of us were born here. This is our home.'

'Are you scared?' Freya asked.

'Of course. I hope it all blows over and Amin doesn't do what he's threatening to do. I'm just glad my wife isn't here. She went to the UK a few months ago, and she is waiting to see how things are before she comes back. It's just me and Adam now.'

Adam didn't sound like an Asian name to her, but she said nothing.

Freya's black hair had grown longer and her skin was tanned. She might be mistaken for one of the women from the Goan community who wore western dress. She suddenly felt sick with fear. How you look, the colour of your skin, could change your world, could mean life or death.

As if he had sensed what she was thinking, Satish said, 'Don't worry, he won't touch the *msungus.*'

In her mind's eye, Freya saw the sad face of the woman they had spoken to. 'I was wondering,' she said, trying to hide the tremble in her voice, 'can bilharzia cause miscarriage?'

'Yes,' he said, 'it can, why do you ask?'

'Just a woman we spoke to, she'd lost a baby.'

'Yes, it's a terrible thing.'

She looked away so that he couldn't see her tears.

'I'm sorry that you are upset. Unfortunately, there are a lot of unpleasant things happening. I saw that woman talking to you. She's called Miriam. Don't take any notice of her. She's a bit unhinged. They blame her for her husband's death and some people say she's a witch. As far as I can tell, he just died of malaria.'

'The men you were talking to looked angry. What were they saying?' Freya asked.

'It's one of the project villages. They are annoyed about the fish ponds they are digging. They say that they think they are causing more cases of bilharzia. They want some compensation.'

Freya touched her neck and something felt strange. 'Oh no, it's gone,' she said.

Satish turned to look at her and then put his foot hard on the brake as a goat ran into the road.

'My gold chain has gone. Those children must have taken it when they were dancing around me with that photo.' Roger had given her the chain just before he left for Uganda. There had been no time for an engagement, or money for an engagement ring, and the wedding ring had been simple and inexpensive. The gold chain had seemed like a gift that Roger had given her to say sorry, a promise that things would be better in their new life.

'It's probably on its way to Kampala to be sold now. Well, at least someone might get something from it,' Satish said.

She had hoped they would get back before Roger came home from work. But as they drove through the gate of the bungalow she saw Roger standing on the driveway with Jock by his side.

'Please don't tell him that we have been to a village,' Freya said.

'Look, I don't want to get caught up with things between you and your husband,' Satish said.

She knew he was right. It would be unfair to involve him. She would tell Roger where they had been.

'I'm sorry, we're late but…' she said.

Before she could say any more, Satish interrupted. 'Sorry we are a bit late getting back. We had a lot of people coming into the office today and my assistant wasn't there, so Freya agreed to stay on a bit. We couldn't get through on the project phone to let you know that we would be late. You must be Roger; pleased to meet you.'

He put out his hand for Roger to take. Roger's face was pink and his lips were tight but he shook Satish's hand and said 'Thank you' before he called Jock to heel and walked back to the house.

Freya turned to mouth 'Thank you' to Satish but he was staring at Keziah. She was taking the washing off the line at the back of the house. She stopped and stared back at them.

'Is that your house girl?' he asked.

'Yes,' Freya said, wondering why he had asked. But Satish said nothing and just climbed back into the Land Rover and drove off.

In the living room, Roger was opening the post.

'I was a bit worried. I think he's taking advantage. You are only a volunteer,' Roger said as he pulled her towards him and kissed her. There were wrinkles on Roger's pink forehead. They reminded her of one of the turnips her dad had grown in the garden of the prefab they had moved to after the war. He gently stroked her neck and she saw a puzzled expression on his face.

'Where is your necklace?' he said.

She had been brought up to tell the truth. There had always been little white lies. She had told lies about her pregnancy all the time until everyone had found out. Was she getting into the habit of telling lies? Once you had told one, it got easier.

'Oh, I took it off this morning and must have forgotten to put it back on. I expect it's in the bedroom somewhere. I'll check in a moment,' Freya said.

'Shall we go there now?' Roger said as he led her down the corridor to the bedroom. He didn't ask again about the necklace.

TEN

Freya and Oketch crawled through the hot, noisy traffic on their way out of Kampala. Freya had bought shiny coloured silk material from a shop on the Kampala Road and she was looking forward to getting home so that she could lay out the paper dress patterns that her mother had sent her. One of the project wives who had decided to go back to England had given Freya her old Singer sewing machine. Roger seemed pleased that she had found something to keep her occupied.

Freya suddenly remembered that she had forgotten to buy chicken while she was in town. Keziah had asked to have the evening off and Freya was excited to think that she would be able to take charge of the kitchen and show Roger that she was serious about learning to cook. She planned to make the lemon chicken dish that Simon, Mavis' cook, often served at their dinner parties. Roger always said that it was delicious.

Working at the charity felt more normal than the strange life of the project and it made her feel more relaxed and settled. Perhaps this evening would be the time to tell Roger that she had decided to stop taking the pill. After supper, they could go to bed early and make love without worrying about Keziah being around somewhere.

'Oh, I'm sorry,' Freya said to Oketch. 'Please, can we turn around and go back to the supermarket?' As usual, Oketch did as he was asked without questioning or complaining.

They crawled back to the centre of town and finally stopped outside the supermarket where the better-off people shopped. Freya prepared herself for the sudden, noisy blast of cold air-conditioning and the smell of carbolic soap and cheese. Then she saw the sign.

WE REGRET BUT WE WILL
BE CLOSED TODAY

The only other alternative was the market. But she was nervous of the crowds of people pushing, shouting and nudging, and she always felt nauseous from the smells of dung, sweat and dust.

She was disappointed that it would have to be omelette and coleslaw for supper. Then she looked across the street and saw the blue, yellow and red shop sign that said Colbey Butcher. She knew that the shop had been owned many years before by a European called Mr Colbey. There was a story that a neighbour had murdered him by poisoning his beef steak in revenge for his having slept with his wife. And people joked that the turkeys he sold every Christmas were really vultures.

A faded old photo of Kampala Road with people in

Victorian clothes hung at an odd angle on the open shop door. A long queue spilled out onto the street. Uniformed house servants, policemen, soldiers, nurses and workmen queued alongside women with babies on their backs and smartly dressed teachers and government office workers. A beggar with one leg crawled beside the queue, holding his bowl out for scraps of food.

She was nervous about going into the shop but she crossed the road and stood at the back of the line. She smelled dried blood and watched the flies buzzing around the meat that hung from hooks above the counter or lay on the counter slabs. She felt sick and tried to stop herself from retching.

The butcher, a large man wearing a bloodstained overall, looked in Freya's direction and tilted his head slightly to the right as if beckoning her forward. She was embarrassed and pretended that she hadn't seen him, worried that the other people standing patiently in line would get angry if she jumped the queue.

The queue moved slowly and the heat made her feel faint. A woman offered her some water from a tin mug. She put the cup to her lips and pretended to drink so as not to offend the woman.

Then she heard a loud voice behind her.

'Freya, what are you doing standing there in the queue?'

The voice was familiar. She turned around and was astonished to see that it was Mavis, the last person she had expected to see in the shop.

'Don't look so surprised. I always come here myself, instead of sending Simon. I like to make sure I get the best stuff and the best price.' She smiled at the butcher and he laughed. It was almost as if she was flirting with him.

'This is Felix,' Mavis said. 'I've known him since he was a young man. He used to come to the house with his father, selling vegetables.'

'Hello, Madam Mavis, what is it that you need today?' the butcher said.

Mavis moved quickly to the front of the queue and Freya heard her say in a loud voice, 'I'll take some of that meat for the dogs and can you give me some boys' meat?' Boys' meat was what people called the cheap, poor-quality meat that was only slightly better than the meat sold for dogs. Felix smiled and carried on chopping and hacking at the dead flesh.

'Of course,' he said, 'anything for my best customer. And what about your friend? She seems shy.'

'You don't need to stand in the queue,' Mavis shouted and beckoned to her. Freya moved slowly forward to the counter, past the line of waiting people. She thought she could hear people whispering '*msungus, mahindis*'. A man raised his hand and shook his fist at her before another man pulled the hand down.

'Amin has been telling them we're all going soon and they think they can do as they like now,' Mavis said.

Freya wanted to escape from the shop as soon as she could. She asked for a small chicken and Felix took one from the slab. He wrapped it in newspaper and handed it to her.

As they walked out of the shop, Mavis said, 'Is that girl still with you?'

Why couldn't Mavis leave things alone? She was like

the *chenzi* dog that sat outside the shop, growling as it gnawed on its bone.

'Everything is fine now,' Freya said.

'Are you sure?' Mavis asked.

What did she mean? Did she know something?

Before Freya could answer, Mavis said, 'You look tired. I expect it's that thing at the charity that you are doing.'

Where was Oketch with the Land Rover? She wanted to get away from Mavis.

'I can give you a lift,' Mavis said.

'Thank you,' Freya said. 'But we have to go back to the material shop.' Lying was beginning to feel easy.

'I'm not sure that these charity things do much good,' Mavis said. 'They just stop people standing on their own two feet. It's the same with the politics. They wanted independence and now look at what a mess they've got themselves into.'

Freya spotted the Land Rover and waved at Oketch.

'The men have a hard life out here. The most important thing is to be there for them,' Mavis said.

Freya looked at Mavis and wondered if she was wearing a wig. The curls were so neat and tight. She had an urge to pull at her hair, to see if it would come off, leaving her head bald and shiny.

Oketch was standing outside the Land Rover, waiting for her. She wished Satish were there so that she could have told him about Mavis and the butcher's queue and how embarrassed she had felt. What made people like Mavis think that they were superior to other people?

When she was a child, they had told her to be wary of

foreigners, to cross the road if she saw a black person, to be careful of the Polish and Italian prisoners of war who spoke strange foreign languages.

It was strange that here the *msungus*, who were the foreigners, thought that it was their right to jump queues, to be in charge. It wasn't surprising that Amin could easily persuade people that the only way they could get the things they wanted was to get rid of the Asians.

Satish would know the answer. He had studied social anthropology. She had thought that was something to do with studying animals. But he had said it was about looking at the different ways people behaved in different cultures. There was nothing strange or irrational in the way anyone behaved. Everything had an explanation. Things people did weren't just primitive or stupid.

She turned and looked at Oketch and saw that his cheeks were heavily marked with what looked like an even row of scars. She wondered what was the explanation for the scars. But it was too complicated a question to ask him.

'Do you think Amin will do things to the *msungus*?' she asked.

Oketch said nothing and she wondered if he had understood. Then he sniffed and said, 'Only God knows.' There was an old Bible on the dashboard.

There was a silence and then he said, 'I see Memsahib Mavis. She a good woman. Always give money for school fees. Let me use Land Rover take children to hospital.' Freya was surprised. Perhaps there was a side to Mavis she had never really seen?

As they drove into the driveway of the house, she saw

that Roger's car wasn't there. He had left a note on the table.

Gone to town to meet an old school friend who is passing through on his way back to South Africa. Probably back late. Don't wait up for me. Lock the door properly.

There was nothing she could learn from looking outside to see if there was a light on in the servants' quarters. But she couldn't stop herself. Everything was dark outside. Keziah had either gone somewhere or she was asleep in her house.

She took the chicken out of the brown paper bag and tried not to think about the times when Keziah might have accidentally brushed against Roger as they passed each other in the hallway or the kitchen. Her hand trembled as she tried to cut the chicken into pieces. The knife slipped and cut her hand and the blood stained her face as she tried to wipe away her tears. She had no idea how to cut a chicken properly and so she gathered the half-cut pieces into a bundle, put them in a bag and pushed them into the freezer compartment of the fridge.

It was like a rerun of the night after the dinner party. She could hear Mavis asking if everything was okay with their girl. She drank three glasses of gin and tonic and felt sick and giddy before she fell into bed.

She dreamed about the small cat that followed her, scratching at her heels. It needed feeding but something stopped her from doing it. The cat at home was just called 'Cat'. It slept in the outhouse, amongst the rusty bikes and garden tools.

ELEVEN

Roger's side of the bed was empty. Freya had been disturbed during the night when he had climbed carefully into the bed. She wanted to ask him where he had been but instead she pretended to be asleep and had lain awake until dawn, listening to his breathing.

There was a knock on the door. Keziah brought in tea and put it on the bedside table. Freya could never get used to the morning tea ritual. She heard Keziah moving quietly around the room and as she opened her eyes Freya saw her opening the drawer where they kept the papers and odds and ends that didn't have a place anywhere else.

'What are you doing?' Freya asked.

'*Bwana* ask me to look for a key.'

'No, not now, please,' Freya said.

Keziah shut the draw and walked out of the room. Freya was shaking as she jumped out of bed and put on her dressing gown. She went to the drawer and opened it slowly as if afraid of what she might find, yet not knowing what she was looking for. The sudden musty smell of paper and oddments nauseated her. There were no keys, just old letters, bills and other oddments.

And where were her father's old bicycle clips? After he had died, they had given most of his stuff away, apart from his stamp album. The bicycle clips had been a reminder of how he used to get up at four in the morning, trying not to disturb them as he put on his Post Office uniform before he cycled to the sorting office. She had kept them in a drawer and came across them when she was packing to leave for Uganda. It had been easy to push them down the side of the suitcase.

Freya needed to find them. They were a reminder of her life, of who she was before she came to Uganda. She rummaged around in the draw. Perhaps Keziah had thought they were some kind of jewellery or something she could sell in the market.

Freya sat on the bed and looked across at the open wardrobe mirror. Her black hair was tangled and wet with sweat. She saw a flat-breasted, pallid woman with a sad face. She smelled of bedclothes.

Keziah was always neatly dressed and smelling of lavender soap and talcum powder. That was the smell of old ladies at home. But here it was the smell of sex. What did Roger see when he looked at Keziah? A young girl with large breasts and a shapely bottom who could do everything: cook, clean, make him laugh. If something broke in the kitchen, she would run to her house and bring back some kind of tool that could fix whatever needed fixing.

Freya got dressed slowly and went to the kitchen. Roger was repairing something, his fingers stained with oil.

'I thought you'd be gone by now,' she said.

He didn't look up. 'Yes, I should be halfway to Mbale by now but this damn gasket has gone.'

Freya tried to keep calm. 'Where were you last night?' she said.

'Meeting an old friend from South Africa, I told you.'

'I didn't know you knew anyone from there,' she said.

There was an oil stain on his bleached white shirt. He looked down at it and cursed.

'Just someone I used to go to school with. They emigrated there ten years ago.'

'So why is he here?'

Roger hunched his broad shoulders, as he always did when something annoyed him.

'I can't talk about it now. I've got to leave in a few minutes.'

'Where's Keziah?' Freya said.

'She's gone to have her tea. She seemed upset.'

'I'm the one who should be upset. She was in the bedroom looking for something without asking me.'

'Is that all? It's my fault. I asked her if she could look for the spare key to the cupboard where I keep some of the tools. I don't know why it's gone missing. I told her to try not to disturb you. Did you say something to her?'

'I don't like her wandering around in my bedroom before I'm properly awake.'

'You're being ridiculous,' Roger said.

'And I can't find my dad's bicycle clips.'

'You can't possibly think that she would take those?'

Freya didn't answer.

'I really don't understand why you can't get on with her. She does everything we ask her to do.'

'I just feel as if it's her house and that I don't belong here.'

'You are being stupid,' Roger said.

'I don't think she likes me.' Freya could hear herself sounding more and more childish but she couldn't stop. 'And she pretends she can't understand what I'm asking her to do.'

She followed him into the kitchen and watched him washing his hands.

'Look, I'm late already. The traffic will be building up around Kitante,' he said, picking up his things and slamming the veranda door as he left.

Freya sat for a few minutes listening to the sound of Keziah noisily rattling the breakfast crockery as she washed up. Then she took a shower, hoping that the flowing water might help to calm her down. She dressed carefully in one of the dresses she usually wore in the afternoons. Already the colours of the dress were fading from the vigorous daily washes and the hot drying sun.

She was still angry and she didn't know what to do about it. Things couldn't go on like this. Then she made up her mind. She knew what to do. Keziah had to go. She shivered with fear. She had never done anything before that would change someone else's life. She wasn't really sure how to sack someone, or what the consequences might be. At home, when people lost their jobs, they went on strike. There were trades unions to help people. Who would help Keziah? She had said she had a man. Freya knew that she had to stop thinking about these things, if she wanted to make Keziah disappear.

She called out to Keziah, '*Kuja hapa*', pleased that at last she felt confident enough to use a few words of Swahili. Keziah appeared from the kitchen, holding a drying-up cloth in her hand.

'Sit down, please,' Freya said.

Keziah looked surprised. 'No understand,' she said as she sat tentatively on one of the dining room chairs. The only time she ever sat down in the house was on the small stool in the corner of the kitchen.

'Please, no,' Freya said; 'over there on the sofa.' The two women sat facing each other. There was a long silence as Freya struggled to find the words that they could both understand. Then, as the words came out, they sounded harsh and cruel. 'You go. I want you to go,' Freya said.

The sunlight shone in and Keziah squinted. She shook her head but said nothing for a few seconds.

'Why? I do my work. No trouble.'

Freya had never looked directly at Keziah's face before. The look that you gave a house servant couldn't be the same as that you gave to anyone else. A familiar look would break the rules, allow an intimacy that could be dangerous, implying that you had let them have the upper hand. Now she saw the face of a woman who was just as scared and anxious as she was.

'You don't like me?' Keziah asked.

'This morning in the bedroom, you took something.'

Keziah looked confused and then angry. 'You say I thief?' she said.

Freya trembled. It was turning into an argument, with both of them confused about what the other was saying.

'No … not a thief. You go now. I'll write a reference in your book,' Freya said.

Freya saw the anger in Keziah's eyes. She tried to look away but Keziah stood up and came closer to her so that she could smell her breath.

'The *bwana*. You told him. What he say?' Keziah said.

Freya hadn't thought about what she would tell Roger. It would need another lie. She could say that Keziah had left to go to her village because her mother was ill and didn't know when she would be back. House servants disappeared all the time saying their relatives were sick.

'It doesn't matter what he says. I'm telling you to go.'

'I want to ask the *bwana*,' Keziah said.

Freya wanted to say, 'Just go, or I'll call the *askari*.' But she knew it would be a false threat. The *askaris* were Keziah's friends and they would just laugh at her, thinking she was just another crazy memsahib. She knew she was losing control of the situation.

'Just go and I'll say nothing. I'll give you wages for three months.'

Keziah moved forward to sit on the edge of the settee and sat upright on the chair. She stroked her belly carefully.

'It will be no good. No one will want me now,' Keziah said.

Then, with a sudden flash of understanding, Freya saw the bulge in Keziah's stomach. Her heart lurched. She felt angry. She didn't know if it was with herself or with Keziah. It was an anger that made her want to strike Keziah across the face, just as her mother had done to her when she had finally had the courage to tell her she was pregnant.

There was a long silence. The man who sold the bananas walked past the window, carrying the thick green bunches on his head. He knocked on the door.

'No, not today,' Freya shouted angrily, then turned back to Keziah. 'You can go to your home. To your village?'

'We don't all have village. Kampala is my home.'

'Who is the father?'

It was an intrusive thing to say but Freya couldn't stop herself, she needed to know. Keziah looked away and there was a long silence. There was the sound of babies crying and *ayahs* laughing and chatting as they took the *msungu* children on their daily walk to the rest house.

'Is it your man?' Freya asked.

'He no want me if I have no money. He beat me, kill me.'

Violence was everywhere, an accepted part of life. The daily reports in the newspapers, in small, almost hidden columns, described revenge killings with whole families and villages being brutally killed with large knives they called *pangas*. Did she really want this for Keziah?

There was a long silence. Then Keziah started sobbing loudly.

Freya didn't know what to do. Her mother had gradually calmed down when she had found out that she was pregnant, saying they would work something out. But there was nothing to work out with Keziah. She was clearly afraid of what might happen to her and the child if she had no job or people to look after her. Freya needed Keziah to leave, but not like this. She was trying to be strong but inside she was crumbling.

'All right, you can stay,' Freya said. It sounded feeble, like a kind of surrender.

Keziah got up and walked towards the kitchen door. Then she stopped and turned to Freya and said, 'Can you help me?'

Freya was silent. She wanted her to go.

'I need money,' Keziah said.

'What for?'

'Want to get rid of it.'

Freya's head throbbed with the start of a migraine. An image of the blood of her miscarriage flashed through her mind. The guilt rushed back. Had she caused the miscarriage herself by trying to 'get rid of it', by drinking gin and sitting in a hot bath? They had said it couldn't be that. It was just an old wives' tale. But how could she ever be sure that it hadn't been her fault?

The babies she had seen in the village always seemed to have someone to care for them.

'You have a mother, aunt, someone who could help with a baby?'

'I don't want baby. Want some more schooling. I want to get a job. A waitress. A government job. Even if someone take the baby, I have to pay them,' Keziah said.

A woman in the village had sat crying in a pool of blood. Satish said women took medicine made out of chillies, or just used a stick when they wanted to abort. If you had money, you could always find someone at the hospital or in a private practice who would do it for you. A lot of women died.

She could hear Mavis' voice. *Keziah is trouble. Get rid of her. I did warn you.* She began to calculate. Keziah was probably four months pregnant. She had been working at the house for about that time. Roger could be the father.

The room began to spin. Was it somehow her fault that Keziah had become pregnant? She knew at that moment that she couldn't be responsible for the death of another baby.

Freya hardly knew what she was saying.

'I'll give you money. But you must not get rid of it.'

Keziah shook her head. 'No understand.'

'Baby. Keep it inside!' Freya shouted, reaching out to touch Keziah's stomach.

'You crazy?' Keziah said as she moved away.

'It's not right. To kill a child,' Freya said. Outside in the garden she saw Jimmy looking towards the house. Had he heard them arguing?

Keziah shook her head. 'This baby no good for me.'

Freya tried to speak quietly.

'The money; it would be enough for you to go to the Technical College, enough to pay Comfort's school fees.'

There was a long silence. Keziah stared straight ahead without looking at Freya. Then she bent her head and put her hands together in front of her face as if she was praying.

Freya unlocked the desk drawer and took out some notes.

'Please take this, I'll give you more later,' Freya begged.

Keziah sat in silence for what seemed like an age to Freya and then nodded. She snatched the money from the table and went back into the kitchen.

Freya felt faint. She couldn't explain to herself what she had done or why she had done it. She didn't even know if Keziah would keep to the agreement. But it was as if some kind of cloud was lifting. She had taken control of things.

*

When Roger came back from work, Keziah brought in the tea and cakes as usual. She said something in Swahili to Roger. Freya was afraid of what she might be saying.

'She says we need more flour,' he said.

After Keziah had gone, Freya said, as calmly as she could, 'It seems she's pregnant.'

'How do you know?' he said.

'She asked me for money for a new uniform. She said they were all getting too small for her. Then I noticed that her stomach was getting bigger. So I just asked her. She pretended she didn't understand at first but then she told me.'

Roger was looking through the window with his back to Freya. His neck was flushed and striped with marks. He slowly turned to face Freya.

'Thought she might be,' he said and passed a blue airmail letter to her. 'It's from your mother.'

'Why didn't you say anything?'

'These women are always having babies,' he said without looking at her. 'It won't make any difference. She'll probably try and get rid of it.'

'Yes, she said she wanted to,' Freya said as she carefully opened the letter. 'I gave her some money so that she could keep it and find someone to adopt it.'

He turned and faced her.

'Why are you getting involved? This charity thing is giving you the wrong ideas.'

She said nothing. The kitchen door closed suddenly. Perhaps Keziah had been listening.

'Anyway, I don't have time to talk about it. I have to go to a meeting at the office. Bobby will be here in a couple of weeks.'

She was tired of hearing about Bobby. Everyone was making such a fuss about his visit. She felt exhausted. She picked up the letter from her mother and read it.

Dear Freya

I hope you and Roger are getting on all right in that place and settling down. We are getting worried because we keep hearing about Uganda all the time on the radio and it doesn't sound very safe. That Amin sounds like a madman. We hope all those Asians won't be coming. The country isn't big enough and it'll just mean more trouble everywhere. Anyway the good news is that Derek and Frances have decided to get married in the Autumn. I don't expect you will be able to come back so he'll be disappointed. I don't suppose you can buy wedding presents out there so I'm sure if you send a postal order that will be fine.

Try to keep safe and write often.
Love
Mum

Her mother and the old life were already in a time and a world she hardly recognised. Could a place turn you into someone else? Would things ever be the same again? She looked at herself in the bathroom mirror, pulled her face and squinted so that she looked like an old woman. What would her life be like between now and then?

She sat on the bed and tried to calm herself. She remembered with a jolt that it was the day they paid Jimmy. She opened the drawer to look for the spare cash she always left there, and hastily shifted the papers around. Then she saw the bicycle clips. They had been there all the time. She had been a fool. Instead of getting rid of Keziah, she had bound herself more tightly to her. She touched the bicycle clips and began to sob. For her dead father, for the dead baby, for the confusion she felt about everything.

She heard Jimmy calling '*Hodi*' and knocking on the door. She wiped her eyes and fumbled for her sunglasses. Perhaps she had been selfish, always thinking about herself. Life wasn't easy for Roger either. He had to keep in with all these people, go to work every day. She didn't have to do anything.

She had almost forgotten why she had liked him when she had first met him. How he had looked neat and clean in his hacking jacket and cord twill trousers. How he didn't care that she was shy, and always asked if it was okay before he kissed her or fondled her breast. How polite he was to her mother.

She wasn't sure exactly how she had become pregnant, only that his promise to carefully pull out before he came hadn't worked. It wasn't his fault that he had felt just as confused and anxious as she had. The fuss was all about her. No one had asked him what he felt.

She would have to put this thing with Keziah behind her. She would have to try to make a go of things.

Jimmy was standing by the closed veranda door. She opened it and gave him the money.

'*Bado haitoshi,*' he said and laughed.
After he had gone she looked up what it meant.
'Not enough,' it said.

TWELVE

The invitation said:

All project staff and their families are invited to lunch at Don and Mavis' house on Saturday, April 8th. The lunch is an opportunity to meet Bobby Fleming, the project supervisor. We do hope you can come. Dress smart casual.

There would be no excuse for not going. Everyone was expected to be there so that Bobby could get a good impression of how things were progressing.

Being a project wife, Freya thought, was like the small porcelain shepherdess permanently attached to the tree trunk. Perhaps she had broken it on purpose.

'Bobby was an agricultural officer here in the early sixties. I'm sure you'll get on with him. Some of the houseboys remember him from then and he'll probably want to ask you how you are getting on and settling in,' Don had said.

Why would someone so important have any interest in her? She knew very little about what the project was doing. There was always talk about machinery, crops, varieties of fish, corruption, politics. But not much about the people they were supposed to be helping.

*

The project men were standing around in the garden in small groups. She guessed that they were talking about work. The men glanced round from time to time, as if they were hoping to catch Bobby's attention. The wives sat together, laughing and chatting.

Bobby was a bald, slightly plump, short man. He was wearing a shirt with rolled-up sleeves and a tie. His trousers were crumpled as if he'd just got off a plane. Did he ever stay long enough in one place to get his washing done? It must have been difficult for him to remember which project he was visiting.

'Come on, everyone, time to eat,' Mavis called out. She would have spent all morning fussing around and supervising Simon as he prepared the food. A very large pot of chicken curry set in the centre of the table, surrounded by small plates of chopped bananas, nuts, raisins, cucumbers, tomatoes and mounds of different homemade chutneys. People had lent their house servants to help Simon serve the food and replenish the drinks.

Keziah carried a tray of food to the group of project men. They laughed and joked with her. Freya wondered if the men had noticed the bulge in Keziah's stomach. Roger spoke to Keziah as if to steer her away from the men, and Freya felt the old pangs of jealousy.

Freya was holding a glass of beer. It suddenly slipped from her grasp and fell onto the concrete veranda floor. The glass shattered and the beer splashed all over her shiny, flower-patterned silk dress which she had made on the sewing machine the day before. She stood up and cried out. People turned and stared at her. Simon came rushing towards her and said, 'Sorry madam' as he picked up the pieces of glass.

Roger stopped talking to Keziah and walked quickly across the garden.

'How did you manage to do that?' he said.

Freya tried to mop the wetness with her handkerchief.

'I'll have to go home and change.'

'You can't go home now. Bobby likes to meet the new wives.' He looked around and lowered his voice. 'You didn't do it on purpose, did you?'

'No, of course not.'

'I didn't want to mention it,' Roger said, as he patted the pocket where he kept his cigarettes, 'but people are saying things.'

'Like what?' Freya had no idea what he was talking about.

'I know it's nonsense, really. But I overheard someone say that they think you're a bit stuck up and that you don't want to mix with people.'

It was as if she had been kicked in the stomach. People had said that about her when she was a child. It was because she was shy, always afraid to speak first.

'I know you find things difficult, but just relax, be

yourself. Try and talk to them. And there is something else.'

It was getting worse. She wanted to put her hands over her cars.

'Don said to me the other day that he'd heard you were getting a bit pro-African. He made it sound like a bit of a joke but I think he was giving me a sort of warning.'

Pro-African was what people said about the lecturers at the university, the expatriate school teachers and the VSOs. She was astonished that anyone would say that about her.

'Why did he say that?'

'Seems the other day at that birthday party at the rest house, you told Phil's wife that you didn't think people should call Africans the *watu* as it was a kind of insult, just lumping everyone together.' Freya remembered. She had drunk too much, plucked up courage and said it. Maybe she should have kept quiet?

'Don said he thought you might be spending too much time with these charity people. Going a bit native, asked me to take it up with you.'

The drunken laughter was getting louder. One or two of the project men were trying to get Bobby's attention before the party was over. One of the wives glanced in Freya's direction and then turned away. The wetness had seeped through to her pants. She wanted to leave, to get away from everyone.

'I think I should go. I feel unwell. Perhaps it's malaria coming on,' Freya said.

'No, you can't. It would look odd. People would notice.'

Don and Bobby were walking towards them. Bobby was looking around as if he was trying to find someone interesting to talk to.

'Roger, come and meet Bobby. Roger is our project engineer,' Don said. Bobby shook Roger's hand firmly. Then, as if it was an afterthought, Don said, 'Oh, and that's Freya, his wife.' Bobby looked at Freya and nodded. He had eyes like Jock, the Labrador.

The three men pulled up their chairs and sat together at a small card table, eating their curries and opening beer cans. Freya knew she should make an effort to join the laughing group of wives and children at the other side of the garden. She moved her chair so that the sun could dry her wet dress. The heat made her sleepy and she closed her eyes and drifted into a dream. A black dog chewed angrily on the head of a white rag doll. She woke suddenly, coughing from the dust that had caught in her throat. The men turned and looked at her for a moment.

Bobby's voice was cracked, as if he smoked too much.

'I'm sorry there's been such a delay with the Caterpillars. It's just so damn difficult to get things out of the port in Mombasa. Then, of course, it takes ages to get the stuff up here. I suppose if we have to give them something to help them on their way, that's the price we have to pay.'

He looked bored. He probably had the same conversations wherever he visited. He lit a cigarette.

'Let's relax a bit. Must say it is good to be here. Economy at home is in a terrible state. Awful unemployment problems. Ireland doesn't get any better. You chaps are better off here for as long as you can stay. Let's hope this Asian thing doesn't get out of hand.'

He looked at Freya as if noticing her for the first time. 'Sorry, my dear, we've been neglecting you. So, Freda...?'

The look in his eyes reminded her of a boy at school who sat by her at the back of the class in the last year of primary school. He had once tried to put his hand on her breast when the teacher was facing the blackboard.

'What is it that you do, my dear, to fill the time? Can't be easy. Got to keep out of mischief, eh? But there are kids, I expect?'

She could see the men's anxious faces behind him. She was almost the same height as Bobby and she met his eyes for a moment. He looked away from her as if he was bored and in search of someone else to talk to.

'No, I don't have children, not yet. But yes, I ... work,' Freya said.

Bobby laid his hand on her arm. It felt clammy.

'Work? My wife didn't. Preferred to stay at home to supervise things. But it was different then, before independence. What sort of work?'

Did he really want to know the answer?

'I volunteer at a small charity. We help people in rural villages.' Freya hoped that would be enough, that he would move on to talk to someone else.

'Oh, that could be good for us, eh, Roger? She can keep an eye on what's going on to see where we can help a bit with things to keep people on our side. Very important for the project.'

There were gunshots in the distance. Bobby's face twitched and his eyes looked momentarily scared.

'Don't worry, it's nothing,' Don said. 'We get it all the time. It's probably thieves. The police shoot first, then ask questions afterwards. It's been getting a bit worse lately. Everyone's edgy.'

Bobby patted his shirt pocket, took out a cigarette packet and passed it round.

'I've been talking to the people at the High Commission. They don't think Amin will go through with it. He's making a lot of threats on the World Service. Probably needs a sweetener from the British Government. It'll all blow over. Anyway they're pretty certain that there's no danger to you people. He won't dare touch you.'

Freya's head was throbbing. She looked across the garden, through the red, purple and orange bougainvillaea bushes and frangipani trees with their large white flowers to the servants' quarters at the back of the house. She saw a small child sitting in a patch of dirt outside the building. He was playing with toys made of old wire, twisted into shapes that mimicked the toy cars and lorries that the expatriate children played with, broke and then tossed to the bottom of the play box. She thought about the sounds of Comfort coughing in the night, even though the measles were over.

Maybe she was 'pro-African'. It suddenly felt like a good thing to be. Then she heard a voice that didn't sound like hers, saying, 'Actually, people in the villages have been telling us they are worried.'

'What about?' Bobby said. He was frowning and his bald head was pink from the sun. He moved closer towards her until she was aware of a strange smell on his breath. Roger and Don were two shadowy figures behind him.

'They are worried about the dams and the fish ponds,' she said.

'They should be happy. They'll get electricity and some of them will get a bit of income, if they can bother to get out of bed. You can never please the *watu*. Don't let them play on your feelings, my dear.'

There was a stain on his crisp khaki shirt. He turned away from her and looked at his watch. There was relief on Don's and Roger's faces. Bobby began shaking peoples' hands as if he was about to leave.

'So good to have met you,' Roger said. She felt his arm around her shoulder as if he was trying to move her away.

'Good to have met you, Roger,' Bobby said. 'Give me a call and let me know how things go with the machinery. We always need good engineers. There are lots of things coming up all the time.'

He turned to Freya. 'Nice to meet you, my dear, I hope all goes well with you. Can take a bit of time to settle down.'

He put out his hand for Freya to shake but she didn't take it. She had to say something before he left.

'I wanted to say that the people are scared that the fish ponds and the dams will make the bilharzia worse.' It felt as if she had blurted it out.

'Nonsense. No evidence of that. Besides, they're used to it. It's in the lakes, rivers, everywhere. Some of them are immune.'

'But we shouldn't be making things worse,' Freya said.

'Well, you can't stand in the way of progress. They will just have to keep the children away from them. This is all about education and hygiene. I'm sure your charity, or whatever it is, can do that sort of thing with people.'

Everyone was watching them.

'People are going to protest,' she said, although she had no idea if that was true.

'Well then, you are in a good place to stop them.' Bobby's suntanned, wrinkled face was red with anger. Behind him, Don was frowning and stroking his moustache. He followed Bobby and they moved to the far end of the garden.

Roger lit a cigarette. 'What is wrong with you?' he said. 'Are you ill? Let's hope they thought that, for God's sake.'

'I wanted him to know. I thought he might be able to help.'

'And what was he supposed to do?'

'I read that you can do things, like putting certain plants in the water, to control the snails, or you can use chemicals.'

She could see that Roger was trying to control his temper. 'Yes, of course, there are risks. But they're worth it, if they get more fish to eat, more protein. You can't get involved with these things that you know nothing about.'

She was trembling, but it felt good to be speaking out.

The house servants were chatting and taking away the plates of half-finished food, clearing away the rubbish that had been dropped and picking up the empty drink cans. She wondered what they were talking about. Were they waiting and hoping for the *mafuta mingi*, the money and the cars that Amin would give them when the Asians left?

Bobby was talking to Keziah. He laughed as he put his hand on her arm. He was the kind of man who thought he could handle people, whoever they were. The kind of man, like her Uncle Ron, who thought all women were just there for him to flirt with.

There was a long silence on their way home in the car. Then Roger said, 'I still don't understand why you thought you had to say something to him. He was virtually offering me another job, when this contract is over.'

She remembered how she had felt about the banana trees the day she had arrived. She knew now what was behind the trees. There was just a big gap, which strangers like her had to fill as best they could. Maybe she was beginning to see how that hole might be filled. But it wouldn't be easy.

She thought about the life ahead of her. They would probably have to move to a different country every two years or so, leaving the friends they had made and needing to make new ones quickly to replace them. The expatriates would always more or less think the same, united in stopping the *watu* – or whatever they were called – from gaining an upper hand.

'I thought he might want to know how people feel about the project.'

Roger was staring straight ahead. The roads were dangerous at night. A huge lorry passed them with only one headlight on.

'Do you really want to keep doing this kind of job for the rest of your life?' she asked quietly.

'Someone has to pay the bills. And I can't see you doing that. And what's this stuff about the people protesting?'

'Just something I heard, that's all.' Perhaps she should talk to Satish about how people could … organise, or whatever it was called, so that they could tell Don what they were worried about. But Satish would probably say that was political and the charity didn't want to get involved.

'Where's Keziah?' Freya said. 'I thought we were giving her a lift home.'

'She's gone with Bobby,' Roger said. 'Apparently he knew her when she was a small girl. Her father used to work for Bobby as a houseboy.'

Roger turned and looked at her, taking his eyes off the road for a moment.

'Look, I know you mean well. Actually, I was quite proud of the way you stood up to Bobby. It's true that we don't always think about the people when we're supposed to be doing things to help them in the long run. It's just the way things are and I can't afford to upset people. And Bobby is a pompous twit. Did you notice he's got a funny smell, like rotten cheese?'

Freya laughed. For a moment, it felt like the time when they were first going out together, when, cocooned inside his Mini, they would laugh at Roger's imitations of her mother's favourite sayings.

'It's just that I have to work with these people. And even if I don't always agree with them, I can't say anything. I'm too junior.'

He put his hand on her thigh. The dress material was still damp from the spilled beer. But she pushed it away and said, 'I think you should concentrate on driving.'

THIRTEEN

Freya was sitting on the veranda. She picked up the *Uganda Argus*, half afraid to read the stories about Idi Amin and his threats. She saw the date on the paper. Her period should have started a few days before. Had she forgotten to take her pill?

She breathed deeply and tried to calm down. It would be better this time. There would be no shouting or screaming. Her mother would be pleased, but disappointed that she was so far away for the birth. Freya would have to ask her to send baby clothes, toys and books. At last, there would be something to talk about with the other wives.

A group of the *ayahs*, dressed in pink and blue cotton dresses and scarves, walked past the gate, laughing and chatting. They carried the *msungu* children on their backs, tightly wrapped African style, or pushed them in prams and pushchairs. They went every day to the garden of the project rest house. Blankets would be placed on the ground under the mango tree and toys scattered around. They would all come back around lunchtime, the children clutching the avocados or mangoes they had collected from beneath the trees, their faces stained with mulberry juice. For a moment she dared to see the child in her mind's eye. She or he would be blond like all the other *msungu* children, their hair bleached almost white by the sun.

Jock barked loudly and disturbed her daydreams. She looked up from the veranda and saw Mavis walking down the driveway. It was too late to go into the house, to tell Keziah to say she was still asleep.

It must be something important, as Mavis hardly ever went anywhere uninvited. She was wearing her tennis shorts and shirt. Varicose veins ran up and down her thin legs. She stopped in front of the veranda, panting slightly as if out of breath. Milton came running up the drive and sat down beside her.

Freya stood up, embarrassed that she was still wearing the faded cotton shift that she wore around the house.

'Mavis, this is a surprise. I'll get some coffee,' she said.

'No, thank you,' Mavis said. Her face was without make-up. Freya thought that the slight bulge at the top of her spine looked more curved than usual. Perhaps she was older than she had first thought.

'Tea, then?' Freya said.

'I don't want anything. I have something to say and then I'll go.'

The headmistress at Freya's school would catch people out for doing something they hadn't realised was wrong. They had all hated her.

'Don has asked me to speak to you about the other day at the lunch party. He is very upset. He has just had a phone call from Bobby. He said that he might have to do another monitoring visit quite soon, as things don't seem to be quite as they should be.'

Freya pictured the headmistress again, and remembered that they had called her an evil old bitch.

Keziah appeared at the door. 'You want coffee?' she asked.

'No, not now,' Freya said sharply.

Mavis sat on a veranda chair and began fanning herself with a Japanese fan.

'I was just saying what people have told me. The children are sick and dying. I thought he might want to know,' Freya said.

'There are all sorts of reasons why they are dying. You can't blame everything on the project. You can't wear your heart on your sleeve all the time. If you keep on saying these things, you won't have any friends.'

Freya tried to fight back unexpected tears. Mavis put her hand on her arm and Freya pushed it away.

'I'm sorry. I didn't mean to upset you. It's just that things are hard enough for Don, trying to keep this project on track,' Mavis said. Her face was pale with red blotches and her eyes were heavy. Perhaps she hadn't slept, or maybe the tennis hadn't gone well.

'Look, I do know what it's like when you are new to a place,' Mavis said.

The change in her voice disturbed Freya. She prayed that Keziah would call her and give her an excuse to stop the conversation.

'When I came here twenty years ago, it was because I had a career in the civil service,' Mavis went on. 'I was what they called a Woman Administrative Officer, a sort of District Commissioner. Before the war, only men were allowed to do these jobs. But afterwards, when there was a shortage of men, they opened it up to women recruits.'

Freya didn't want to hear about the old days. Her mother was always talking about the war, about rationing and how people had to make do with what they could get. She thought about the District Commissioner in *Things Fall Apart*. The people in the village had blamed him for the death of the man who hanged himself. But that was a long time ago.

'I was only twenty-six but I was in charge of a whole district. You know: giving out licences, rationing things, hearing court cases, all sorts of things. I loved the work.' She stopped and looked away. 'I knew the wives were often jealous of me. A single woman is always a bit of a threat.'

Freya had an image of a young Mavis surrounded by men who looked like Bobby, while their wives stared angrily from a distance.

'I travelled up-country a lot. I spoke the local languages, mixed with all sorts of people and ate food with them in their huts. I even...' She stopped suddenly as if she realised she had said too much.

'Then I met Don. He was a young agricultural officer and we got married. So I had to resign, of course.'

Mavis touched her lacquered hair.

'So, you see, I know it's hard not being able to do anything; to work, I mean. To give up ... your freedom. But we don't really have any choice. Life is hard for the men. They need us to support them. And with all this stuff with Amin, we all have to stick together.'

'So you understand why I said what I said to Bobby,' Freya said.

Mavis turned away so that Freya couldn't see her face.

'The main thing to remember about Bobby is that he is the boss, and none of us can afford to upset him. You have to make allowances for him. He is old school. He has been quite bitter since independence.'

Freya felt a sudden sharp pain in her stomach.

'And did you have children?' she asked.

Mavis looked away again. The back of her neck was flushed. There was a pause.

'No. We wanted them, but it didn't happen. Don has a son by his first wife, but we have never seen much of him. He's grown up now.'

The air felt humid. A thunderstorm was probably on its way. Mavis irritated her, but maybe that was unfair. She was the only woman who talked to her about anything that mattered, but she was still afraid to confide in her.

'It's just that I can't seem to get on with the others,' Freya said. 'I have nothing in common with them. I could never play games. And I can't talk about what they talk about.'

There was a flash of lightning.

'I really should go before the storm comes,' Mavis said. 'No matter how long I live in Africa I can never get over my fear of these storms.' She stood up to leave. 'Look, I know it's difficult but you just have to learn to settle in, make the best of things. They don't renew contracts for men whose wives cause trouble.'

Mavis had changed suddenly, gone back to being her old self.

'It's not too late, you can send a letter to Don apologising and explaining that you didn't know what you were saying, that you were ill. Then, maybe he can sort things out with Bobby.'

There was another sharp pain in her stomach, so sharp that Freya had to stop herself from crying out.

'Please can you go,' Freya shouted as the pain got worse.

Mavis' face was red with anger.

'Please don't speak to me like that. I came here to try and help you but I'm not sure that you want to be helped.'

Mavis stood up to leave. 'I have to say we all hoped that Roger would pull his socks up when you came.'

'What do you mean?'

'No one could understand what was going on,' Mavis said.

What was going on? What did Mavis mean? The door opened behind her and Keziah stood there.

'You call, Memsahib?' she said. Freya shook her head. Mavis looked at Keziah as if noticing her growing belly for the first time.

'Oh, I see,' she said.

Keziah slammed the door as she went back inside.

'You should have got rid of her. I did warn you,' Mavis said.

There was a loud clap of thunder and Mavis looked scared. Milton growled at a stray dog that was attacking him. Mavis picked up a large stone and threw it at the stray dog, which ran away whimpering.

'I have to go,' Mavis said. She walked down the drive, patting and comforting the Alsatian as she went. Freya went inside the house and sat down in the chair. Keziah came into the lounge from the kitchen.

'You okay?' It was the first time that Keziah had asked her about how she felt. Freya didn't know how to respond. She tried to make things normal again, to hide the trembling in her voice.

'Some tea, please. And ... dust that table over there, you always forget.'

Keziah looked annoyed, but took a cloth from her pocket and began dusting.

There was another sharp pain in her stomach and then she felt the familiar warm flow of liquid between her legs. Was it another child seeping away from her, or just a late period? A woman could never know for sure.

The house felt claustrophobic. Mavis' voice was still in her head repeating *what was going on*. Everyone would soon know that Keziah was pregnant and they would draw their own conclusions. If only she had sacked Keziah, she would have gone, disappeared by now.

Freya had to get out of the house, away from having to look at this woman and her growing belly.

The second-hand Hillman Imp that Roger had bought so that she could learn to drive stood on the driveway. Roger had given her a few driving lessons but she was still afraid of driving on the dangerous, potholed roads, littered with overturned burnt-out cars and lorries.

But how would anyone know that she hadn't passed her driving test? The roads were full of crazy drivers. She opened the door of the car and climbed into the driving seat. She sat for a few minutes. She switched the engine on. Then she gradually crawled forward, pressing her foot hard on the ancient clutch. She drove down the driveway and onto the project road. She stalled the car a couple of times before she reached the project gate. For a moment, she was afraid that the *askaris* would stop her but they hardly looked at her as they waved her through. She drove slowly down the *murram* road, trying not to hit the bumps too hard and looking out for people who might dart unexpectedly in front of the car. A small goat jumped into the road and she jammed on the brakes. Her hands trembled as she gripped the steering wheel.

She had no idea what she would do when she reached Kampala. When she got near to the outskirts of town, the traffic slowed down, horns sounded loudly and people dodged in and out of the traffic. Two young men peered closely into the car, shouted something and banged on the windscreen. She was terrified but she was trapped by the traffic all round her. She couldn't turn around and go home, not yet. Then she spotted a sign to the market. The other wives went there. Why shouldn't she?

She parked in the big muddy area outside the market. She could hear Mavis' voice saying, *reputation, what was going on*, echoing in her head. The air was filled with the smells of rotting fruit, shit, and petrol fumes from the taxis that waited at the edge of the market. The taxis were slung low on their chassis through years of manoeuvring along the potholed roads. Taxi drivers leaned against their cars, smoking and chatting.

The market was bustling. She walked carefully on the muddy ground. Something soft and wet squished underneath her foot. She was wearing flip-flops and a layer of thin, green slime had covered her pink-painted big toe.

Goats wandered around, nibbling at the almost invisible strands of grass in the otherwise bare, dusty earth. Chickens lay as if dead under the stalls. People stared at her as she made her way towards the fruit and vegetable stalls. She was still amazed by the shiny green and red peppers, avocados, eggplants, bunches of dark green, large-leafed spinach, breadfruit, mulberries and small, yellow, lantern-shaped pockets of gooseberries. At home, they had mainly eaten potatoes, carrots, cauliflowers, cabbage, apples and pears, and her father's beloved runner beans and broccoli tops. Bananas were still a treat for people who could remember the shortages in the war. Freya reached out to touch a tomato and jumped from the sting of a red chilli accidentally dropped in the middle of the pile.

Brightly dressed market women called out to her, 'Come buy cheap'. Men were standing idly by the stalls. Others were sitting on the floor playing a game called *mweso*, deftly scooping black banana seeds into the holes of a wooden board. They looked at her for a second or two and then got back to the game.

She walked past the meat stalls, scared of the vultures that sat above them, waiting to swoop down on the discarded pieces of flesh. The *chenzy* dogs growled over the bones.

A man lurched towards her and she could smell the *waragi* on his breath. He was waving a ruler. She was wearing a green and white striped dress. It came just above her knee. The man knelt in front of her, blocking her way.

'Let me measure the mini,' he said and laughed. Freya was too terrified to move. What was wrong with her dress? She looked around to find an escape from the market.

Then a woman in a red patterned dress with a matching scarf pulled her arm, shouted at the man and pushed him so that he fell over on to the ground.

'Madam, come buy some cloth, very nice for you, to cover the mini,' the woman said as she led Freya towards her stall which was piled high with brightly coloured rolls of cloth.

Freya trembled as she touched a roll of smooth, shiny fabric.

'You want?' the woman said. People were still staring at her. The man was still waving the ruler and laughing. She didn't know what to do. She shouldn't have come here.

'How much?' Freya asked.

'Eight shillings.'

Freya opened the purse from the belt she wore round her waist and took out a note. The woman smiled and handed the cloth to her, then gave her some coins as change, whispering, 'Put on, quick, please, these men are not good.' A small crowd had gathered to watch. The woman shouted at them and they ran away.

Freya took the cloth and walked to a place behind the stall, hoping that people wouldn't see her. Then she unravelled it and wrapped it around her waist. Was she in a dream? She pinched herself and suddenly thought about the money she had given the woman. She had been cheated. She hadn't given her the right change.

She looked round for the woman and saw her laughing. At me, she thought, at my stupidity, a *msungu* fool, easy to dupe.

'I think you gave me the wrong change,' she said.

'No, madam, you mistake.'

'Give me my change,' she said.

The woman was tall and there was a row of scars on her forehead like those on Keziah's. She heard Mavis saying *reputation* again and she had a sudden image of Roger making love to a naked Keziah. It was as if she had lost control of her mind and body. She raised her hand to hit the woman across the face.

Then she felt someone grab her arm. She turned and saw that it was a man. She tried to scream but no sound came out. The man took his arm away and whispered, 'Go home now, this is no place for you.' His accent was different from the accent she heard when Ugandans spoke their precise, careful English. Where had she heard it before? At home on the buses, at the local hospital. It was West Indian.

A crowd had formed around her.

'Just check in your purse,' the man said softly.

She opened it and saw the twenty-shilling note that she thought she had given the woman was still there. She had given the woman a ten-shilling note and the change was correct. Tears were streaming down her face. She took the note out of her purse and carefully tore it into pieces, then threw it as if scattering ashes. As the pieces landed, they stuck in the shit that covered the ground of the market.

'You need to go home now. You'll get hurt,' the man said. He was wearing cricket whites like those her father wore every Sunday during the summer months. They were speckled with the brown dust of the market. She looked up and met his slightly bloodshot eyes and saw pain, fear and concern in them.

'Where is your car?' he said.

She struggled to remember.

'Outside the market. I think I saw a mosque nearby. It's a grey and blue Hillman Imp.'

'I'll find it,' he said. 'Just keep walking.'

A group of small children followed them as they left the market. They searched around in the densely packed car park. She tried the key in two cars that she thought might be hers before they spotted the right one. She recognised Jock's tatty old blanket in the back seat.

The car door was stuck and she struggled to open it. One of the children called out, '*Mahindi*'. A policeman came towards them. He stopped and said something to the man and she thought she heard the word 'licence'. The door still refused to open. She heard them laughing and then the policeman walked away.

'What did he say?' she asked.

'Oh, just that he saw my picture in the *Uganda Argus* and wanted to tell me I was welcome.'

She wanted to ask him why the policeman had said that. Then the car door opened. As she clambered into the car, she knocked her leg so hard that it began to bleed. He took out a handkerchief and gave it to her.

'Take this. Will you be okay getting home?' he asked.

'I'm really sorry. I don't know what happened. I lost my mind for a moment.'

'You should try and see a doctor,' he said.

'I'm fine. I'm not ill.'

She struggled to start the engine.

'You want help?' he said.

'No, thank you. It will be okay.'

'It ain't easy being a stranger; you take care.'

She drove away from the market trying to remember how to get back to the main road. There were no signposts and all the roads looked the same. She was too scared to stop the car and ask someone. She was about to turn around to go back to the market when she spotted a sign to Bugelere.

Tears streamed down her face as she drove along the road. What had the man meant about being a stranger? Don, Mavis and the others always talked about the Africans and the Asians as if they were the strangers. The *msungus* were the people who thought they were there by right. Did the man think that they were both strangers?

When she got back to the house, she sat in the car for a few minutes, too exhausted to move. Roger was talking to Jimmy as he watered the peppers and courgettes in the vegetable patch. He looked up and walked quickly towards her as she got out of the car.

'What on earth are you doing?' he asked.

Telling him the truth would just make things more difficult.

'I just thought I'd practise a bit on my own.'

'You shouldn't do that. But I suppose as long as you don't go off the project road it's okay. What's wrong with your leg?'

'Nothing, I just banged it on the car as I got in.'

She began sobbing. Roger tried to put his arms around her but she pushed him away. Jimmy was watching them.

'What's the matter?'

'I just don't feel well.'

Her legs were wobbly and she thought that she might faint. Roger called for Keziah and together they supported her and took her to the bedroom. She heard them talking quietly outside the door and then Roger gave her some tablets and she fell into a deep sleep.

*

Over the following weeks, Freya was often unwell with headaches and fever. Roger said she should go to the hospital. But she made the excuse that it was probably malaria and said she would take some chloroquine. She frequently had nightmares about her mother standing by her bedside, dressed in a nurse's uniform and shouting and screaming that she was a wicked girl.

She hardly ever went beyond the house or the garden any more or talked to any of the project people. She thought that Keziah was watching her all the time like a prison warder.

Mavis and Don had held a lunch party for the project manager from Kitante and they hadn't invited Roger and Freya. Mavis had apologised to her, saying that it had been a mistake and that the invitation must have gone astray.

'I'm not so sure about that,' Roger had said. She knew that it was probably because of the incident with Bobby.

One morning, as she walked along the project road in the blazing hot sun after dropping off something she had borrowed from Mavis, she had suddenly felt confused about which bungalow she lived in. She had turned into the driveway of the house next door and heard children shouting and screaming. Then a toddler had run towards her and thrown a mango which landed at her feet, the orange flesh oozing out from the green skin.

She had screamed and the child's mother had come running out of the house to see what was happening, As if from nowhere, Keziah had appeared.

'She make a mistake. Not well,' Keziah had said. Then Freya had slowly followed Keziah back to the house. When she got home, everything had become clear again. But she had lost all memory of what had happened. An hour or so of her life had gone missing.

'Don't tell *bwana*,' she said to Keziah. When Roger came home later that day, she heard them talking in the kitchen. She waited for him to come into the living room, ready to explain that it was just like the sleepwalking she had done as a child. But he had said nothing.

Satish phoned the project office and left messages asking what had happened to her. She ignored them. She wanted to forget the charity. It had once felt as if the charity would be an answer to her problems but it had only made her more confused. Whatever she could offer, it was just small and pointless.

FOURTEEN

Freya was woken from her afternoon sleep by the sound of a car outside. She jumped up quickly, smoothed down her clothes and combed her hair. She peeped through the bedroom curtains and saw that it was Satish. She decided to stay in the bedroom in the hope that he would go away. It was too late. Keziah knocked on the door and then gently opened it when Freya didn't answer.

Satish was sitting in the living room. He was wearing a shiny grey tailored suit instead of his usual safari jacket. As soon as she saw him, she knew that she had missed him.

'I had to go to the High Commission to sign off the latest small grant they are giving us, so I thought I'd better look smart. How are you? We miss you at the office,' Satish said.

'I just haven't been well for some time,' Freya said. She wanted to explain the strangeness of her illness to him but she couldn't find the words. Just sitting looking at him suddenly made her start to feel better.

'I came to ask you if you would like to come to the village with me on Saturday but I can see you aren't really up to it.'

He looked anxious, as if he might have said the wrong thing.

'But maybe it's better for you to just rest for a while,' he said.

She knew he was right but as he stood up to leave, she said, 'I think it would be all right. I am feeling a bit better every day.'

'Are you sure?' he said. 'It's just that someone has donated some old sewing machines and I want to give them to the women. Maybe you could come along and talk to them?'

She knew that Satish was trying to help her and that there would be nothing she could tell the women that they didn't already know. But the thought of the village made her suddenly feel better. It would be an escape from the house and the project compound.

'Yes, thank you. I'd like to come,' she said.

There was no point in telling Roger that she was going to the village again. He would say she was too ill and that it was a ridiculous idea, as well as a dangerous one.

After dinner that night, she said, as lightly as she could, 'I'm going to Kampala on Saturday to meet one of the wives from the High Commission for lunch at the Chinese restaurant.'

He pulled her towards him and kissed her.

'That's good that you're making an effort. I know it's not easy for you.'

FIFTEEN

Oketch gave Freya a lift to the charity office and she asked him to pick her up later. She knew he wouldn't say anything to anyone.

As Satish drove along the road to the village, Freya's headache gradually disappeared and her vision became clearer. The windows were open and red dust stung her eyes but the breeze on her face soothed her. They passed fields of cassava, banana and plantain and she watched people working in the fields. Keziah occasionally made dishes of *posho*, maize meal porridge, or of cassava for them to try.

'I really don't like cassava,' she said. 'It's tasteless.'

'That is all some people can afford to eat,' Satish said. 'That's why the children get those fat bellies and red hair. It's a disease called kwashiorkor.'

'Yes, of course,' Freya said, embarrassed at her own thoughtlessness. 'Are people pleased with the well we funded?' she asked, wanting to change the subject.

'People are happy with it but they have to make sure it doesn't keep breaking down. We gave them some tools but they have all gone missing.'

Freya gradually felt more relaxed. Being driven by someone inside the safety of a vehicle always felt good. A goat ran into the road. Satish changed gear suddenly and his hand brushed against her knee. He said sorry but a flicker of excitement went through her. She thought that she might like it to happen again.

As they drove into the village, people looked scared and ran away into their huts. Then someone called out, '*Mahindi, msungu*' and the villagers gradually reappeared.

'Everyone's a bit nervous these days,' Satish said as he took the sewing machines out of the back of the Land Rover. An old woman, wearing a stained white tee shirt with Amin's face on it, and a red scarf, shook her head, waved her arms and laughed as she pretended to drive a car.

'She says she doesn't want a sewing machine. She'd rather have a hoe or a tractor,' Satish said as he mopped his brow. 'The project is giving the men fertiliser and seeds so that they can grow cash crops. But the women have to work twice as hard now, helping with that as well as growing food crops for their families.'

More women quickly gathered around them, talking and shouting.

'They are saying that the well isn't working again and that we should have given the tools to them, not to the men,' Satish said.

Freya thought she could suggest to Roger that the project should work a bit more with the women and talk to them about what they wanted. But she could still hear Bobby's voice telling her to keep out of things she didn't understand.

The women moved away, chatting amongst themselves. They sounded sad and angry. Two men picked up the sewing machines.

'We can go now,' Satish said.

She had thought Satish wanted her to talk to the women and help them to use the sewing machines. But he seemed eager to leave. Perhaps he had asked her to come with him because he felt sorry for her, or maybe because he just liked her company.

As they walked back to the Land Rover, an old woman wearing ragged clothes, her legs bent and twisted, followed them. Was it the same woman – Miriam – who had spoken to her the first time that she had visited the village?

'You need a baby, I give you medicine,' the woman said.

What did she know and how did she know it? Freya began to walk faster but the woman kept up with them, hobbling along and using the gnarled branch of a tree as a walking stick. Freya looked straight ahead and walked faster but the woman kept touching her arm and pulling on the sleeve of her dress.

Freya felt panic rising inside her. She turned round to face the woman and screamed, 'Go away, leave me alone.' The woman shook her head and raised the branch as if she was about to strike her. Then an old man stepped between them, took her arm and gently led her away. Children laughed and jumped around, clapping their hands.

They got into the Land Rover and drove off. Freya was shaking uncontrollably.

'Breathe deeply,' Satish said. 'Don't worry, some days are like that.'

She wanted him to touch her or put his arms around her.

Satish switched on the car radio. It took her a few seconds before she realised that it was Amin speaking. He was talking about expelling the Asians and asking the British to do something. Satish shook his head and gasped quietly.

'What is it?' she said.

'It's all getting worse,' he said. 'I really don't know what we are going to do.'

People walking along the sides of the road carried portable radios on their shoulders. They stopped and cheered as if pleased at what they were hearing.

Freya searched for something to say. 'Maybe it will be all right. Don says Amin wants money from the UK and he's sure Edward Heath will pay up because they don't want...'

'The Asians coming to Britain in great hordes?' Satish interrupted. It scared her to see him so angry.

'No. I didn't mean...' she said. 'But yes, I suppose you are right.'

He drove faster. But it was the time of the day when cars and buses were crowded with people going home from work and the traffic came to a sudden halt. Further down the road, she could see that there was a large crowd standing round something. Satish told her to make sure the doors were locked. Four men came towards them, shouting, '*Mafuta mingi*'.

People knocked on the sides of the vehicle and peered

in through the windows. Satish gestured at them to go away but they just laughed. Then they began pushing and rocking the Land Rover. Freya tried to open the door to get out.

'No!' Satish said. She could smell his sweat. 'Whatever you do, don't get out.' More faces appeared at the window, knocking on the glass. For a second, she thought she might die. Then the traffic started again and they moved forward slowly. Horns were blowing loudly and a policeman struggled to direct the traffic past the group of people.

'It's probably a dead goat or chicken,' Satish said. 'They will be arguing over who it belongs to, or dividing up the meat, or something.'

As they drove slowly past the crowd, Freya tried to see what they were looking at. Then she saw a limb, a leg with a crumpled white blood-stained sock. She began to feel strange, as if she didn't know where she was. It was like the day when she had lost her memory and the day in the market.

Then she remembered that Roger had said that he had to go into town some time that day. Her heart began to beat faster, and sweat dripped from her neck. She reached for the door handle; as usual, it was stiff and difficult to open.

'What are you doing?' Satish shouted.

Satish tried to lock all the doors. But before he could do it, she had pushed the door open. The cars and lorries behind her blared their horns as she walked slowly towards the crowd. An old man raised his hand, wagging a finger at her. It must be her skirt again. She should have worn trousers. Two women laughed and said, 'Ee, madam.' Then a young man in tight cotton trousers and a tee shirt with *mafuta mingi* written on it shouted, 'You woman, you a disgrace.' Another young man in school uniform tried to stop him, saying that he should leave her alone.

'Let me through,' she said, 'it's my husband.'

She heard laughter from the crowd.

Then she saw that it wasn't a body after all, just a dog with a bloodstained piece of cloth tied round its leg. Two young men grabbed her arms and pulled her away.

'Stop that,' Satish said, appearing behind her. The crowd looked angrily towards him but he made his way through them.

'Get in the car, quick, and let's go, now,' he said.

He said nothing on the way home, occasionally glancing at her as if to make sure she was all right. She didn't know what to say and closed her eyes, pretending to be asleep. Satish usually just dropped her at the end of the drive and left her. But today he took her to the front door and she ran into the house, crying.

Through the window, she saw Satish talking to Roger. Were they arguing? Then Satish got into the Land Rover and slammed the door. She heard the brakes screech as he drove off.

'What did you say to him? It's not his fault,' Freya sobbed.

'He told me what happened. I said it was irresponsible taking you to those places. You said you wouldn't go there any more,' Roger said.

'I thought it was you, that you were dead.'

'You're ill,' he said. He tried to put his arm around her but she pushed him away.

Keziah stood in the kitchen doorway. 'You want something?' she said. 'I help her?'

Roger nodded and turned away as if he didn't know what to do.

'Get her away from me,' Freya screamed. 'Everything is her fault.'

Roger indicated to Keziah that she should lead Freya away to the bedroom. She tried to push Keziah away but then stopped struggling. She lay on the bed and sobbed until she fell asleep.

SIXTEEN

When Freya woke the next morning, she started crying again. It was silent crying with uncontrollable tears. She couldn't understand what was happening to her.

Roger came into the bedroom. His face was tight, red and blotchy, as it always was when he'd had an argument with an *askari* or when he was frustrated with a car problem that he couldn't fix.

'Please tell me what it is. I can't help you if you don't,' he said.

When she didn't answer, he lay on the bed beside her and tried to stroke her arm but she turned away from him and buried her head in the pillow.

After he had gone, Keziah came in with milky tea and slices of sweet white bread and jam.

'Drink, eat, you sick,' she said. Freya sipped the tea, took a bite of the bread, and then pushed it away. Her tears stopped. Keziah smiled at her. Freya thought for a moment that Keziah might be the only person who had some understanding of how you could be lost and swamped with a fear of the unknown.

After that she fell into a deep sleep and when she woke, Mavis was standing like a ghost at the end of the bed.

'Go away!' Freya shouted.

Mavis' face turned pale and she backed away from the bed. Freya's mother's face had the same look when she had finally told her that she was pregnant.

'It's no use, Roger. She is ill,' Mavis said.

Later that day, Freya heard Don and Roger talking outside in the hallway.

'I'll have a word with Tom Witherspoon; he's the Superintendent up at the mission hospital. I've known him for years,' Don said.

'I'm not going,' Freya shouted. Hospitals were places of blood and death and bossy nurses.

Keziah came in and offered her a pill and a glass of water.

'No, take it away,' Freya said.

'Take it or bad things will happen,' Keziah said.

Like a naughty child, Freya swallowed the pill. As she drifted off to sleep, she heard Roger say to Keziah, 'Good girl.' His voice was soft. He never spoke to her like that. They've poisoned me, she thought, as the darkness came.

When she woke, she was in the back seat of the car sitting next to Keziah. Roger was driving. She couldn't remember getting into the car. They had brought her to the mission hospital on the hill, an old colonial building with wide verandas and well-kept gardens. Why hadn't they taken her to Mulago Hospital with its modern white walls? No one there would know who she was. She tried to open the car door but Keziah grabbed her wrist. It was the first time that Freya had been touched by her. Keziah's hands were dry and cracked like those of an old woman.

They drove through the hospital grounds and she saw a kind of camp with makeshift shelters. Women with huge bellies were sitting around in the garden, their legs stretched out in front of them. Small children ran around or sucked from their mothers' swollen breasts. Other women were washing clothes or preparing food.

Before she could ask, Keziah said, 'They come from far. They wait here until baby comes.'

'You will come here?' Freya said.

'Tsh, no. No need. I go to the local midwife. It cost less.'

A nurse met them at the door and led Freya to her private room. The yellow paint on the walls was peeling. A vase of flowers stood on a small wooden cabinet. Did the nurse know how sinful she had been? Would they punish her? Roger and Keziah followed, but as soon as she was in bed, Roger waved at her as if he was leaving a child on the first day at nursery and they both left.

Then the nurse gave her more pills and she fell into a deep sleep.

*

After that, Freya slept all the time. She would wake briefly to the smell of latrines and disinfectant and then quickly fall asleep again. She thought that she saw Roger standing by her bedside but it might have been a dream.

When she finally woke properly, they told her that she had been at the hospital for three days. A tall, white doctor, who reminded her of Don, asked her endless questions until she sobbed uncontrollably and then told him about the miscarriage.

Roger brought flowers picked from Mavis' garden. He stood awkwardly by the bed and held her hand, stroked it, and told her that the project people had invited him to dinner almost every night.

'A bachelor again?' she said. He laughed nervously.

'You'll soon be back to normal again. Mavis says that she'll make sure you are okay when you get back home.'

On the fifth day, she woke feeling better as if she had been walking through a patch of dense fog and then suddenly come into bright sunlight. The nurses propped her up in bed and she ate a plateful of *tilapia* and chips. The doctor came to see her and told her that they weren't entirely sure what it was but it was probably a kind of nervous breakdown caused by the miscarriage. He said that she would most likely recover fully when she started a family. It was easier for Freya to nod in agreement. The image of the dead dog in the road floated into her mind. Was it something to do with that? They would think she was mad if she said that.

She spent some time every day sitting in the chair by her bed and then began gently walking around the hospital grounds. She began to think that the women's camp seemed like a happy place, with women laughing and helping each other with their new babies.

On the sixth day, there was a knock on the door of her room and a nurse came in, followed by Satish. He was smartly dressed in a white short-sleeved shirt and tie and carrying a book and a small wooden box.

'He says he knows you,' the nurse said.

'Yes,' Freya said, 'he's a … friend from work.'

'I was worried about you. I tried calling the project office but no one answered the phone,' Satish said. The door opened suddenly and he looked round anxiously but it was just the cleaner coming in to remove the dead flowers.

'It's okay,' Freya said. 'Roger doesn't come until after work.'

'I really don't understand why you're here,' Satish said.

'I just couldn't stop crying and I didn't know why. They say it's a sort of nervous breakdown and some kind of temporary memory loss thing.'

'I find that all hard to believe. It could have been the malaria pills; they can affect people in all sorts of ways.'

They were silent. Freya felt awkward and vulnerable, dressed in her nightclothes. But she was glad he was there. There were sounds of people talking softly and of the bleeping of hospital machines. There were distant noises of women crying out with the pain of birth contractions. The women shouted '*Eee mama*' repeatedly. Would she cry out for her mother if she ever got to experience childbirth? She turned away from Satish so that he wouldn't see the tears in her eyes.

'I'm sorry,' he said, 'so sorry to upset you. I should go.'

She didn't want him to leave. He was the only person she could really talk to. The only person who didn't judge her or blame her.

'No, don't go,' she said. 'It's not the malaria pills. They think they know what it is. I got pregnant. Before we got married.'

'Well, that happens everywhere, all the time. Even my youngest sister. She was just seventeen so we sent her to Kenya and when it was born she left the child with her aunt.' He paused. 'What happened … to the baby?'

'I had a miscarriage at four months.'

'Oh I'm sorry.'

'I think it was my fault,' Freya said.

Satish looked away from her. She was afraid that she had said too much. She hardly knew him.

'Of course it wasn't your fault,' he said softly.

A nurse put her head round the door. 'Remember, visitors are only allowed for half an hour,' she said.

'You mustn't blame yourself for anything. Just get well. I should go now and let you sleep.'

'I tried to get rid of it at two months. I sat in a hot bath and drank some gin.'

'I don't suppose that caused it.'

She didn't know if he was religious or even what his religion was, but he reminded her of a priest.

'I'm just so confused all the time. Roger is different, not the person I knew before I came here. I don't agree with the things the project people say but I'm supposed to just keep quiet. And I can't escape from them. And there is no one I can talk to … except you.'

She wanted to tell him about Keziah's baby and the money she had given her, about her suspicions of Roger and Keziah and about the strange, mixed-up feelings she had for her, but she knew she had already said too much.

She could see that he was embarrassed. He put his finger down the front of his shirt collar and tried to loosen it. She thought he might leave and wanted to stop him.

'Look, you are still very young,' he said. 'This is what happens when you sort of ... grow up. I mean that in a good way. If you had stayed in England, you might never have had to think about these things. But at least now you have to confront things, decide what you really believe and stick with it, even though it might be difficult.'

He stood up to leave. Freya was scared that she might not see him again.

'What is happening with the expulsion?' she asked, not really wanting to hear the answer.

'Nothing is definite yet. But we know it's coming.'

'What will you do?'

'I'm a British citizen so I have the right to go to the UK and settle there. It's not the same for all of us. Some Asians took out Ugandan citizenship at independence so they will have to sort out what that means if they are threatened with expulsion. We'll all probably have to go sooner or later. It won't be safe to stay here.'

Freya closed her eyes. She felt guilty that she had forgotten what was going on outside. At night she could hear the sound of gunshots and screams in the distance. But illness made you think only of yourself.

'Safe?' Freya said, her heart beating faster. 'What do you mean?'

'I don't want to worry you,' he said. 'But maybe you should know, so that you can make sure you're careful. It's my wife's niece. She's at Makerere, and the other night she and her roommate, a *muganda* girl, were attacked by two men.'

'Attacked?'

'Well, raped.'

'Oh God, that's awful.' Freya thought about the large, jolly man who had so recently visited the project. People said he sometimes directed the traffic on the Kampala Road. Surely the British could get him to stop his people doing things like that?

'I'm sorry. I shouldn't have told you. You're supposed to be resting.'

She tried to think of other things to say, to keep him there.

'What about the charity?'

'I'm trying to work out what to do in future. That young VSO teacher, Sam, is thinking about leaving. His parents are worried about him.'

Freya remembered how enthusiastic Sam had been at the dinner party.

'The doctors, everyone, have said I have to rest,' she said. 'I think they think the charity work might be upsetting me.'

'I guessed that,' he said. 'Never mind, you must just focus on getting well'. Satish took out his handkerchief and wiped his brow. His white shirt was stained with sweat marks.

'Oh I forgot,' he said. 'I didn't know what to bring you. So I've brought you a chess set. It belonged to my mother. The pieces are made of ivory and we don't know how old they are. But we can't take everything with us. So I thought of you. The pieces are so beautiful, they might make you more interested in playing.'

He handed the box to her and she started to cry.

'Oh, I'm sorry. Please, don't. Here, take this book as well. It will help you learn more about the moves.'

She was still crying.

'Don't, please,' he said. 'I'd better go or they'll think I'm causing trouble.'

He walked towards the door.

Freya thought about what he'd said about growing up. She had been letting everyone treat her like a child.

'Please,' she said. 'I've decided that I'm going to help you with the charity when I get better.'

'Look, don't be hasty, just take things easy for a while.'

'There is something I wanted to ask you. Do you know my house girl, Keziah?' she asked, half afraid of what he might say.

He looked surprised.

'No. She reminded me of someone from the village who asked me for a job some time back. But it wasn't the same person. Look, I'd better go,' he said.

She heard his footsteps outside the room and the voice of someone muttering '*mahindi*' in the corridor outside.

SEVENTEEN

Freya took the ivory chess pieces out of the carved wooden box and laid them out on the shiny board. They were so much nicer than the plastic chess set they had brought from home. Roger had taught her to play but he had quickly become bored after beating her so easily.

The book that Satish had given her was open. Concentrating on learning new moves was a good way to help her forget her illness.

Jock ran in, barking and wagging his tail, scattering the chess pieces all over the floor. As Freya picked them up, she saw Comfort watching her from the kitchen doorway.

'I help you?' Comfort said, and Freya nodded.

Comfort knelt down by the low table, carefully picked up the pieces and began setting them out on the board.

'You know how to play?' Freya said.

'We learn at school.'

Keziah came from the kitchen, holding a broom, and shouted something at Comfort, who stood up quickly.

'It's all right. I asked her to help me,' Freya said.

Keziah shrugged her shoulders and began sweeping the floor.

Comfort set up the pieces and then said, 'We play?' Freya hesitated and looked at Keziah, who nodded and smiled. Keziah watched them play and gave occasional instructions to Comfort. At times they sounded as if they were arguing. But after a few moves it was checkmate and Freya was beaten. Was there anything that Keziah couldn't do? Had she played chess with Roger during those evenings when he had been alone?

It was a Wednesday morning. 'Shouldn't Comfort be at school?' Freya asked.

'She's still sick,' Keziah said.

She didn't seem sick. She wasn't coughing any more. Keziah bent over to pick up a newspaper that had fallen to the floor. She winced and clutched her back.

Then Freya remembered that, the evening before, she had watched Keziah leave the house dressed in a loose-fitting, cream-coloured silk shift dress and red high-heeled shoes. The dress had reminded her of one she had seen in a small dress shop in town owned by a French woman. It stocked expensive dresses with labels that said *Made in South Africa*.

'You had some new clothes. I saw you in them last night,' Freya said.

Keziah stopped her dusting and stared at Freya. She grabbed Comfort's hand and pulled her up from where she had been kneeling at the table. The chess pieces scattered around the floor.

'You think I used the school fees money you gave me for the dress?'

Keziah pulled on Comfort's hand and walked towards the door.

'We go,' she said.

Freya knew that the tables had been turned on her, that she had lost control. But wasn't this what she really wanted? For Keziah to leave, to disappear? She knew now that giving Keziah the money so that she wouldn't have an abortion had all been part of her illness. She was recovering now. It didn't matter any more what Keziah did.

Keziah was standing by the door holding Comfort's hand. She was clutching her belly as if she was in pain. Soon there would be a real baby. Freya knew at that moment that she couldn't let another baby slip away from her. She looked directly into Keziah's eyes, holding them as if they were unexpected lovers. Keziah started to walk away.

'Please, no, don't go,' Freya said.

'I go. You don't like me.'

'I can't do the housework … not by myself.' It was a stupid thing to say.

'You don't like my work. Always complaining.'

'No, I'm sorry,' Freya said. 'The baby, what will happen?'

Keziah looked angry. 'Baby not yours. My business.'

'Don't go, please,' Freya said again.

Keziah stood and stared at Freya for a moment and then said, 'I stay, for the *bwana*.'

Then she ran out of the house before coming back with a large bag. She dropped it on the floor at Freya's feet. Freya opened it and saw the cream silk dress inside.

'See. Take it back to Memsahib Alice; she give me because it didn't fit her,' Keziah said.

Alice was one of the project wives who had recently gone back to the UK.

'No, you keep it,' Freya said.

Keziah picked up the bag and said, 'And see this,' pushing a letter into Freya's hand. The letter was from the school. It was addressed to parents and guardians. It said the school was closing for two weeks because there was an outbreak of measles and many of the teachers were ill.

'I'm sorry,' Freya said.

Keziah took out the duster that she kept in her pocket and started to dust the coffee table. Freya wanted to tell her to stop but she was afraid that it would lead to another argument. Keziah went over to the radio, looked at Freya as if to get her agreement and then switched it on. There was the usual music for a few minutes and then the newsreader said:

Idi Amin Dada has today announced a decree prohibiting miniskirts, hot pants and maxi dresses with a V-shaped split. Skirts must be no shorter than three inches above the knee.

Keziah said 'Eeeeeh,' and shook her head. Freya could hardly believe what she was hearing. She would have to search through her wardrobe to find the offending skirts and dresses. She suddenly felt scared. That's how the Asians must feel now, always being watched so that they could be punished for things they weren't aware of doing. And why were women being punished for what they wore? *Be careful. Men can't control themselves*, her mother used to say when she went out in her miniskirt.

EIGHTEEN

2 JUNE

Freya searched through her wardrobe to find something suitable to wear to the reception at the British High Commission. It was a regular monthly event but Roger and Freya hadn't been invited before. People had to wait their turn.

'Do I really have to go?' she asked.

'I'm sure it will be okay,' Roger said. 'You can wear what you like inside the High Commission compound.'

'No, it's not that. I just find these parties difficult.'

Roger lit a cigarette. 'Look, I know you've been unwell. But you've really got to pull yourself together,' he said.

She had never been sure what that meant. All she knew was that she still couldn't control the rapid heartbeat and the sudden migraines.

'You don't know what it feels like,' she said.

'That's the point. I can't understand what *it* is.'

He turned his back on her and blew smoke in the air.

'I have been thinking,' he said. 'Things seem to be getting more uncertain. Perhaps you should go home. I have to stay and work out the contract. But I might be able to fly back after six months if we can afford it.'

Freya's stomach sank at the thought of her mother's grey, pebbledash, semi-detached council house. She could smell the stink of pee in the outhouse. It was summer in England now but the rain and the gloomy winter days always came round too quickly.

They listened to the BBC World Service every day. There were strikes, power cuts, trouble with the IRA. The people that were interviewed in the streets said that they didn't want the Asians to come to the UK, that there were too many people already in the overcrowded country. They didn't say that they were afraid that the UK would be swamped by coloured people but she knew that's what her mother would think. And if she tried to explain what it was really like for the Asians, or what she had learned from being in Uganda, her mother would just turn a deaf ear and say, *Well, you're home now, so you can forget that stuff.*

People would think she was a failure if she went home. Separation from your husband was risky. The war had shown that. There were so many broken marriages and illegitimate children. Her mother would say, *Stop moaning, just get on with it. You never could stick at anything for long.*

She knew then that she didn't want to leave the vibrant colours, the sudden beautiful sunrises and sunsets, the noise and smells of life in the villages. But there was something more, something that she had to stay for. She hardly dared admit it to herself. She couldn't leave without seeing Keziah's baby, without knowing that it was alive and well.

'No, no,' she said. 'I don't want to go home, not yet.'

Roger put his arms round her and said, 'Well, let's see how things go.'

She took another dress out of the wardrobe and then put it back. The illness had made her lose weight. Maybe the dark blue linen sheath dress with the cutout shamrock motif below the neck would fit her now. She pulled it on. It was the right length. It felt tight but it made her breasts look good. Instead of pulling her hair into a ponytail, she let it fall down her back. She had brought white shoes with thin spiked heels with her but she had never worn them. She hesitated before putting them on. She would be taller than Roger if she wore them. They felt uncomfortable at first but as she walked around in them they gradually made her feel better, as if she was more in charge of things.

'You look good,' Roger said and tried to touch her breast. She laughed and pushed him away.

*

As they drove through the gates of the High Commission, Freya saw a crowd of people standing about chatting in the garden and around the pool. Fairy lights hung from the trees. A few women wore dresses that looked as if they had let the hems down. Others wore brightly coloured and patterned caftan dresses or long skirts made of local material. Amin had also banned the wearing of wigs. Women who usually wore wigs looked strange with their wispy, straightened hair. Groups of Asian women stood together, apart from everyone else. There was noise and laughter, and music playing in the background, but the atmosphere felt tense.

Male servants, dressed in long white *kangas* and red *fezes,* moved skilfully between the guests offering small, beautifully presented plates of sausages, pineapple and olives on sticks, Scotch eggs, anchovies on toast, and trays of drinks.

The High Commissioner, a tall, slim man with grey hair, made a speech thanking them for coming.

'I suppose he can't say much. You never know who is here,' Don said.

An African man put his arm round Don's shoulders and said, 'You people shouldn't be scared. Idi Amin Dada wants you all to stay here to help our people. He loves the Queen, you know.'

Don laughed politely. After the man had gone, Don said, 'He's an MP from the North, big friend of Amin, so we have to put up with it.' Then he said to Roger, 'That chap from the High Commission, with the bald head and glasses, wants to talk to you about something.'

'That's strange, I've never met him before. Suppose I'd better go and see what he wants,' Roger said.

Freya watched Roger making his way towards the man, shaking hands and occasionally laughing with people. Freya wondered what they would be talking about. Roger was usually rude about the people from the High Commission, saying that they had no idea what life was really like for people who were doing real jobs.

Freya's feet were hurting in her new high heels and there was nowhere to sit down. She felt self-conscious standing by herself and she searched around for someone to talk to. But she couldn't see anyone close by that she recognised and she had always been shy of introducing herself to someone she didn't know.

She suddenly spotted Satish in the distance. He was standing in the middle of a large group of what appeared to be largely Asian men. They were all wearing matching blazers with gold insignia on their pockets as if they were part of some kind of sports team. She desperately wanted to talk to him and wondered how she could break into the group without drawing attention to herself. Then she spotted a tall man in the middle of the group, and realised she had seen him somewhere before. Maybe he had visited the charity?

Then she remembered. He was the West Indian man in the cricket whites who had rescued her in the market and then helped her find her car. She wanted to forget about that day. She panicked, terrified that he would recognise her, and tried to think of an excuse to leave. Suddenly Roger was standing in front of her. He looked preoccupied by something and lit a cigarette.

'That was strange,' he said.

'What did he want to talk to you about?' Freya said, trying not to stare at the man.

He looked as if he was about to tell her and then apparently changed his mind.

'Oh, nothing really. Just something to do with work,' he said.

Over his shoulder, Freya saw the man from the market walking towards them. She simply had to think of an excuse to leave.

'I'm sorry. I'm trying but my head is pounding. I really think I have to go home,' she said.

'All right, just give me a minute or so to sort things out and we'll go.'

But it was too late. The man was standing in front of them. He reached out to shake Roger's hand. Roger looked wary, hesitated and then took his hand.

'I don't think we've been introduced,' the man said. 'My name is Wensley … Wensley Barnes, pleased to meet you.'

'Good to meet you, Wensley,' Roger said, sounding more relaxed as he heard the man's accent. 'Wensley Barnes, did you say? Wensley, *the* Wensley Barnes. The one who's…?'

'Been playing for Surrey, yes.'

'Oh, I'm so sorry. I just didn't realise. My God, I was at the ground when you had that last stand of fifty-seven. It was amazing. Look, let me get you a drink.'

'Thanks. Sure. Something soft,' Wensley said.

'This is my wife, Freya,' Roger said. He looked at her as if to say, *Just stay for a few minutes and talk to him.*

Roger made his way through the groups of people to the drinks table.

'Nice to meet you,' she said, praying that he had forgotten. 'But I have to go and talk to someone.' But Satish was nowhere to be seen.

'No need to go,' Wensley said. 'I won't say anything. It's just between the two of us.'

Freya blushed and hoped her suntan would hide it.

'Are you all right now?' he asked.

'Yes, thank you. I don't usually behave like that. Something made me angry and I couldn't help myself.'

'We all get like that sometimes. Things are not easy nowadays, what with all this stuff going on.'

'I thought for a moment that the woman in the market was someone else.'

'Don't worry, it's over,' he said.

'I was ill. I spent some time in hospital after that. In fact I had ten days there.'

'You look well now,' he said. His voice was comforting and she looked up and met his eyes. Even in her high-heeled shoes, she only came up to his chin. She was glad that she had chosen to wear the dark blue dress.

'They said it was a ... a nervous breakdown,' she said, ashamed to admit it.

'Be careful with that stuff. They said the same to me in your lovely country when I tried to punch one of the Warwickshire team. He just kept taunting me on the pitch, calling me names till I couldn't stand it any more. They wanted to send me home but they agreed to let me stay if I had a few days' treatment. So I went along with it. If you don't behave like they think you should, they say you're ill.'

She could guess what name they had called him. He smelled of aftershave and soap. Their eyes met again and then he turned away as if he was leaving. Freya had a sudden desperate need to stop him from going. She just wanted to talk to him. She couldn't remember ever feeling like this before. She struggled to find something to say.

'What about your drink? Roger will be here in a moment,' she said. 'And I wanted to ask you about something that you said in the market.'

'Fire away,' he said. He looked directly at her so that their eyes met again. Was he laughing at her? She looked away.

'You said that it wasn't easy being a stranger. What did you mean?'

'Don't expect too much. You ain't never gonna belong here. I just keep my head down. Try to do what's right without upsetting too many people. But you have to take control. Don't let them tell you what's right or wrong. Decide for yourself.' There was a small pinkish mark on his cheek. Perhaps a cricket ball had hit him. She imagined him fiercely hurling a ball at a batsman. Wensley looked at his watch and she tried to think of ways to stop him walking away.

'Have you been here long?'

'No, just a few months.'

'Where are you from?' She hesitated, afraid that she might have said the wrong thing. 'I mean, where were you born?'

'Dominica, but I've been to so many places; not sure where I'm from any more.'

'Dominica?' She had no idea where that might be.

'Not everyone's heard of it. It's very small, beautiful, mountains, rivers, everything; green all the time.'

'You miss it?'

'Of course. Homesickness, it's a funny thing, like something heavy in the pit of your stomach. Couldn't stand the cold in England. Can't stand the politics here.'

The noise of everyone in the garden talking had turned into a dull babble. His shirt was bleached white and there was a slight protrusion over the belted trousers. She had an urge to raise her hand and press her palm against his stomach.

'What are you doing here?' Freya was afraid that she was asking too many questions.

'I came to play with this cricket team, the guys over there. All Asians except me. I was due to go back but then one of Amin's ministers saw me one day and asked me to give him some coaching.'

'Did you want to do that?'

'No, but there wasn't much choice. He's very close to Amin. Just hope they won't stop me leaving in September.'

'Are those things true, the things they say he does to people?'

'I don't say nothing. It ain't safe. I just do what I'm asked.'

She heard Roger's voice behind her.

'Wensley, there you are. Look, I've just had an idea. I think the High Commissioner has a bit of cash in a sports fund. Maybe we could pay you to come to the project to coach the project team for a few hours a week. What do you think?'

Roger's red hair was thinning at the front and his face was puffy. The day before a group of small boys had called out, '*Zeru*, give us money,' when his truck pulled up. She knew that *zeru* was a name given to Africans who were born with bleached white skin and red hair. They were called albinos and taunted and called ghosts. She had read that people sometimes murdered them because they believed that their body parts brought good luck.

A cigarette hung from the corner of Roger's mouth. Wensley shook Roger's hand. 'It's a deal, man,' he said, laughing, then turned to Freya, made a mock bow and said, 'And madam, hear you later.'

He had long legs and he walked away with a self-confident stride. It was probably something to do with being a cricketer. Her dad always said that cricket was all about showing that you were in charge, fooling the other side.

She suddenly felt lighter, happier. Some kind of cloud had been lifted. If this man, Wensley, was going to visit the project from time to time, maybe she would see him again.

'Just a moment,' Roger said, 'I'll go and thank the High Commissioner, and then we can go home.'

Freya watched as he walked across the garden and then stopped and spoke to Satish for a few minutes. Satish waved and walked towards her.

'It's good to see you looking well and happy,' he said.

'Yes, I'm much better.' She hesitated. 'What was Roger saying to you?'

'He said that you weren't really well enough to work any more, and I said that I understood, and anyway we'd probably be closing down soon.'

Freya looked round to make sure no one was nearby. 'I can still help you with things if you want,' she said.

'I think you should talk to Roger first.'

'I don't need to tell him.'

'I don't really think…'

Freya interrupted him. 'It will help keep me … sane. I just feel dead, cooped up and trapped in the house all day.'

Satish looked around, as if afraid that someone might be listening. 'There are some spare parts for the well that I have to take to the village on Sunday morning. You could come with me. That woman Miriam keeps asking about you. I don't know why.'

Freya had forgotten about her and what she had said, and her heart beat faster for a second.

'I can't come on Sunday. We have to go to a lunch party,' she said. 'But if things change I'll let you know.'

On the way back in the car, Roger was more relaxed than usual. 'You seem better,' he said.

'Yes, this thing comes and goes. I just never know.'

'It was good to meet that cricketer,' Roger said.

'Yes,' she said, 'he seemed nice. You didn't tell me properly what the man from the High Commission wanted to talk to you about?'

'Oh, nothing much,' Roger said. 'He asked for my help with something. But it's all a bit complicated.'

She was busy running the conversation with Wensley through in her head again and didn't want to be disturbed, so she just said, 'Oh, that's good.'

'I said I'd meet him and some other people on Sunday for lunch in town. You don't mind, do you?'

Freya smiled to herself. 'But what about Don and Mavis' lunch party?'

'You'll have to do that on your own,' Roger said.

'That's okay,' she said, and put her hand on his leg so that it rested close to his groin. He laughed and said, 'I know what you want but you'll have to wait until we're home. Do you ever think about what we used to do in the Mini?'

'Yes,' she said as her hand moved closer.

NINETEEN

Freya met Satish at the project gate and hoped that no one was watching her as she climbed into the Land Rover. The day before she had sent a note to Mavis, saying that she wouldn't be able to come to the Sunday lunch party as she was still feeling unwell.

It felt good to be driving along the road through the countryside. The traffic gradually got less. People were walking along the road dressed in their best clothes, on their way to church.

'Are you sure this is okay?' Satish said. 'I feel bad about Roger not knowing.'

'It'll be fine,' she said. 'He's very busy these days. He's always away.'

'So you haven't been married long?'

'Only since last October.'

'Still the honeymoon period,' Satish laughed.

There hadn't been a proper honeymoon. They had stayed for two nights in a local hotel. They were finally free to make love without feeling guilty and Roger had been keen to make up for lost time. But she had turned away from him, afraid that it might hurt the baby. She had lain awake most of the night wondering if marriage had been the right thing to do. But no one had given her any other choice.

'I hadn't thought of it like that,' she said, trying to remember what she had told Satish when he had visited her in hospital. 'And what about you?'

'Oh, seven years. A friend of my parents from India introduced us. You people would call it arranged. But it's not a bad idea. Other people can often be the best judges of who is suited to who. And love is something that grows, rather than something that happens right away.'

Marrying Roger had been like an arranged marriage. No one had asked either of them if that was what they had really wanted. In films and books, falling in love was like being struck by a bolt of lightning. She hadn't known Roger long enough for the bolt to strike. She had needed a steady boyfriend and he was nice, quite good-looking and dressed well. Her mother had always liked him and was impressed that he had a steady job and sometimes picked her up from the house in his father's car.

Freya needed to change the subject. Talking about Roger was making her feel guilty.

They drove slowly into the village, trying not to hit the people who were walking haphazardly towards the old wooden church. The men were dressed in tight-fitting, shiny black suits. Some women wore *busutis*, long dresses with pinched tight waists and wide padded shoulders. People said it was 'traditional' dress, but she knew it had been introduced by missionaries many years ago to cover the women up, to stop them going into the church with bare breasts.

'Oh, of course it's church day,' Satish said. 'I'll have to wait until church is over before I can deliver the sewing machines into safe hands. They'll need to lock them away.'

'Can we go inside the church?' Freya said, curious to see if it was anything like church at home.

'You can if you want. I'll wait outside.'

Inside the church, people were packed tightly together on benches, chatting and laughing. Children played and babies cried. There weren't enough hymn books to go round, and those who had managed to get one stared intently at the open pages. It looked as if the old men had got hold of most of the hymn books. She recognised some of them. They were wearing the used spectacles which they had snatched from the big basket that Satish and Freya had brought to the village some weeks before. The old men wanted the spectacles so that they could learn to read the Bible and be saved, before they died and joined the ancestors.

Freya remembered the Sunday school of her childhood and the snotty-nosed, badly dressed children from the Dr Barnardo's home who would file in every Sunday and then kick the backs of the seats in front of them. She had always been scared of them.

When she had suspected she might be pregnant, she had gone to the local church and sat in the empty pews and cried. The vicar had seen her and tried to find out what was troubling her, but she couldn't tell him. The next time she had seen him was at the wedding. She had prayed that he wouldn't notice the small bump under her blue broderie anglaise dress.

People in Uganda had so many things to pray for. Enough food to eat, good harvests, good health, babies who would live long enough to be recognised as real people, safety from cattle raiders and soldiers. She felt relieved and guilty that she didn't have to pray for those things.

Satish had told her that even though people went to church, they still made sacrifices to the ancestors, killing chickens, cattle, goats and sheep. The missionaries had brought their God, but people still kept the old ones as well.

Satish knew about these things. He had studied social anthropology at Makerere and had wanted to be a teacher. But after he had carried out fieldwork in a village, living for a month in a small thatched-roofed village house, he had decided that setting up a charity would be a more useful thing to do.

The priest was a short white man with a bald head. People walked around the church, greeting each other as if they were in the market. They chatted noisily so that Freya struggled to hear what the priest was saying. She thought his accent might be South African.

She heard him say, 'living in difficult times ... people arrested'.

He was telling them to turn to God and not to witchcraft. Satish had explained to her that witchcraft wasn't just crazy, ignorant superstition. It got worse when things were changing quickly, when things divided people and turned them against each other. This made people suspicious of each other and increased the accusations of witchcraft that people made against each other.

After the blessing and the loud Amen, people left the church, pushing and shoving as they went out. The priest shook hands with everyone. A tall, light brown woman, probably his wife, stood by his side.

Outside the church, she found Satish sitting on the ground drinking a bottle of Coca-Cola. He gestured with his head that they should leave.

The priest and his wife walked towards them.

'Welcome', the priest said. 'I'm very sorry about what is happening to the Asians. Things are going from bad to worse very quickly. Nowhere is safe, not even in the church. Amin's people are everywhere, listening to what we say.'

'Any news of the Bishop?' Satish said.

The priest sighed and shook his head. 'He has completely disappeared. We are beginning to fear the worst. I hate to leave these people but we don't really have a choice. We don't know where we will go. We can't live together as a couple in South Africa.'

Freya knew that it was bad to buy South African apples, or sherry or cigarettes. That's why she had been surprised to see the *Made in South Africa* dress labels in the French dress shop in town. She remembered her father complaining about the noisy anti-apartheid protests at cricket and rugby matches. She hadn't thought much about what it might be like to live there, not to be able to live with the person you loved.

Don had said, *I'm not against mixed marriages, it's just that they never work out. Too many cultural differences. Then there are the children. They can have a hard time if they have to go back to the UK.* Mavis had looked embarrassed and tried to change the subject.

Someone pulled on Freya's sleeve. She turned and saw that it was Miriam. She smelled of carbolic soap. She was talking rapidly in Luganda. The priest waved his hands at her, as if swatting away a fly, and she moved back.

'What is she saying?' Freya said.

'She says you look sad and she thinks she might be able to help you. I've told her we have to go.'

Miriam's eyes were bloodshot. She wore a wrap stained with food and dirt and a wrinkled and torn grey tee shirt. Her hair was knotted in spikes. Satish had called her an old woman but Freya knew she might be only forty or so.

'I should speak to her,' Freya said.

Satish touched her arm as if to stop her.

'I really don't think it's a good idea. She is a medicine woman and those people are often a bit unhinged.'

'I'll just be a minute,' Freya said. She followed the woman to a large shady breadfruit tree and they sat down. A small girl dressed in a checked cotton school uniform stood nearby.

'I translate. You give me money,' the girl said in careful, precise English.

The woman spoke in Luganda for what seemed like a long time, gesturing with her arms as she spoke. A crowd of people gathered round. Some of them were laughing. Freya could see the priest and Satish watching anxiously.

When she stopped talking, the woman dropped her head and held her hands clasped together in her lap.

'She says she has seen you when you come here with the *mahindi* man. But he's not your husband. She thinks you look sad. You are not happy with your husband. And you are barren.'

How did the woman know this? Her mother believed in fortune tellers and sometimes went to the Spiritualist Church. But didn't all these people work in the same way? They guessed, or used some kind of intuition? Weren't most women unhappy with their husbands in one way or another? The woman could have guessed that she didn't have children. This was all nonsense. She glanced towards Satish.

'Come on,' he shouted. 'Let's go.' She could tell that he was getting worried.

The woman began talking again and waving her arms. She pointed her finger at Freya and walked towards her as if she was about to jab her with it.

'Tell her I have to leave,' Freya said.

'She says something bad has happened to you. She can see a dead baby. She can see blood everywhere, all the time.'

Freya's heart began beating rapidly. How did she know? Was it just another wild guess?

'She says you can be happy if you get a baby. She has herbs to give you. Then the baby will come and stay inside you. The husband will be happy and not leave you for another woman.'

The old woman was so thin that her bones stuck out sharply. Her skin was dry and cracked and her eyes were bloodshot. Maybe if Freya bought the herbs, it would help the woman to buy some food.

'How much does she want?' Freya said.

The woman smiled and said a figure Freya knew would buy the roof of a small house.

'Tell her that's too much.'

When they had agreed a price, the woman gave her a small newspaper packet and Freya put it quickly into her pocket. She was relieved when she saw that Satish was talking to someone and hadn't seen what she had done.

As they walked towards the Land Rover, Freya felt a sharp pain as someone pulled on her earlobe and wrenched off her clip-on earring. The old woman shouted at two young boys, raising her arm as if to hit them as they ran off laughing.

Then someone shouted, '*Mafuta mingi,*' and laughed.

'It's all right,' Satish said. 'Just keep walking.' Freya touched her ear and saw that there was blood on her hands.

They climbed into the Land Rover and drove off.

'We try to help them and that's what we get in return,' Freya said. It sounded like something that Mavis would say.

'Life's not always what you think it will be. There aren't any natural rules about anything,' Satish said. 'And what was all that stuff with that woman about? What did she want?'

'She wanted me to buy something. In the end, I just gave her money.'

'You should be careful. Better to give your money to the charity fund – then we can make sure it goes to the right people.'

'Yes, of course, you're right.'

The dust drifting in from the open window made her sneeze. She reached in her pocket for a handkerchief and felt the small newspaper packet.

Satish dropped her off. Keziah didn't work on a Sunday and Freya was relieved that she would be on her own in the house until Roger got back. She was exhausted. She sank into the armchair and took the newspaper packet carefully out of her pocket and put it on the coffee table.

She had been stupid to buy it. But perhaps she would just try the herbs? It couldn't do any harm. Was she supposed to mix them with water? How would they taste? She remembered the vile-tasting Steedman's Powders of her childhood. Her mother would force her to take them with jam on a spoon. Sometimes she vomited.

What if the herbs worked? It was surely worth a try. She jumped when she heard footsteps on the veranda.

'Hello, dear, are you all right?' a voice called out.

Mavis stood at the door.

'Yes,' Freya said, trying to pull herself together. 'I'm feeling better now, thank you.'

'I'm sorry that you missed the lunch. I thought I'd come and check on you as Roger is away. Well, do take care. You don't want to go back into that hospital again, do you?'

'It must have been something I ate. I'm fine now,' Freya said, hoping that she would go away.

'You've been through a lot. It's not easy. But I'm sure you'll settle soon, now that you have given up that charity thing.'

The kitchen door opened and Keziah came in. Why was she here on her day off? She was wearing a wrap around her bulging stomach and a pink blouse that Freya had thrown out for the rubbish. When she saw Mavis, she went back into the kitchen.

'You should ask her to knock before she comes in,' Mavis said. She sat down in the armchair. 'Does anyone know who the father is?' Before Freya could answer, Mavis continued, 'Someone at the bar, I suppose?'

'The bar?' Freya said.

'Didn't you know? Don and the others have seen her in the Paradise Bar. You should have got rid of her by now. She won't be much use once the baby has arrived.'

Freya knew the bar. They had stopped there one day when there was a puncture on the car. She had felt awkward sitting sipping her Coca-Cola while watching the bar girls drinking with the red-faced, sweaty white men who treated the place like their own home, chatting to the barman and occasionally taking drinks for themselves from the fridge.

'Well, I'll leave you now,' Mavis said. 'We're going into town to see a film. Would you like to come with us, dear?'

Freya made the excuse that she thought she might have already seen the film some years ago and Mavis left.

Keziah came back into the room.

'It's Sunday,' Freya said.

'They bought the gas bottle. I fixed it. You nearly out of gas.'

'Oh. Thank you,' Freya said.

'You want something?'

Freya shook her head.

'Okay, I go.'

'The Memsahib Mavis, she said you have another job.' Freya had blurted it out. She should have kept quiet. She didn't really want to know the answer.

'No understand. Job?'

'At the Paradise Bar?'

Keziah made *chee chee* noises and frowned. 'Go there to meet friends.'

Then she put her hands on her hips, puckered her lips, and said, 'Stupid old woman.' She looked at the coffee table and moved to pick up the small packet that Freya had left there.

'Who give you?' Keziah said. Before Freya could answer, Keziah picked up the packet, felt it and smelled at it.

'A woman at the village,' Freya said.

'What for?'

'To help me get a baby.'

'She cheated you. You take this, you get ill, die maybe.'

Freya stood up, moved closer to Keziah and grasped her wrist. It was thin and her skin felt smooth.

'Give it to me,' Freya said.

'No,' Keziah said. 'I tell *bwana*.'

Freya let go of her wrist. Keziah put the packet in her apron pocket.

'You won't tell him?' Freya said.

After Keziah had gone out of the room, she began to cry.

TWENTY

Freya drove slowly down the *murram* road until she reached the main road. She had passed her driving test a few days before and it was the first time that she had driven alone into town since the argument with the market woman. She was nervous but it was an adventure.

She began to drive faster, exhilarated by the challenge of weaving in and out of the chaotic traffic. She grew more confident about using the horn all the time and about accelerating fast and overtaking when she wasn't quite sure what was coming from the opposite direction.

She had made sure that the only jewellery she was wearing was her wedding ring. And she had carefully checked the length of her skirt. It was easy to forget that the police and the army were watching women all the time, eager to chastise them or, worse, assault them.

Satish had sent a message asking her to meet him at the café above the church bookshop in Kampala.

An army roadblock lay ahead. She slowed, breathed deeply to calm her nerves. They usually waved *msungu* women through without stopping them. She would do as they asked and everything would be okay.

She stopped the car and wound down the window. A soldier pointed his gun at her. She held her breath, trying not to move. He was just a young boy, about the same age as Jimmy the gardener. His uniform was too big for him and the sleeves covered his hands. His face was sweating and his eyes were dark and scared.

'Open boot,' he said. Freya trembled as she got out of the car. She opened the boot. It was empty except for the spare tyre and a spanner. The boy looked around as if to see if anyone might be listening and then whispered, 'You give me money.'

One of the older soldiers shouted something at him and the boy quickly closed the boot and said, 'You go, madam.'

Freya got back in the car, feeling shaken. She knew she should drive off as quickly as she could before they changed their minds. The boy stood to attention and saluted. His wrist was thin and childlike. Freya beckoned to him. He looked puzzled but came to the car window. She made sure the other soldier wasn't looking and then handed him a five-shilling note. He snatched it and ran back to his post.

There were two more roadblocks before she reached Kampala. Terrified Asians and Africans stood waiting by the side of the road as the soldiers searched through their cars, occasionally scattering things out into the road and then ordering them to pick everything up. But they waved her through at each one.

She parked the car carefully outside the bookshop, pleased that an important part of the driving test had been the ability to reverse park between four steel poles without touching them.

As she got out of the car, a man wearing ragged shorts and a tee shirt which had *mafuta mingi* on the front came towards her with a tin cup.

'You give me money,' he said. He smelled of *waragi* and his eyes were bloodshot. Another man was leaning against the wall, smoking and watching.

Don't give money to beggars, Don always said. She didn't know if it was guilt or fear but she opened her purse and gave him a coin. She heard the man tutting as if it wasn't enough as she started to climb the stairs to the café. It was a favourite meeting place for expats, Asians and better-off Africans and she prayed that Mavis or any other of the project wives wouldn't be there.

Only two tables were occupied. Satish and a small, thin child were seated at one of them at the far end of the balcony. She knew that he had a child but he rarely talked about his family.

'This is Adam, my son,' Satish said.

Freya tried to hide her surprise. The child was African. She smiled and said, 'Hello, Adam, I'm Freya.' Adam shook his head and picked up a book from his small bag of toys and crayons.

'Are you all right?' Satish said. 'You look exhausted.'

'It was awful driving in today,' she said, deciding not to tell him about the young soldier and the money. Adam took some red, blue and yellow Lego pieces from his bag. He pulled at Satish's sleeve to get his attention.

'It's strange, isn't it?' Freya said. 'They – the soldiers – try to frighten you, to be tough, but really they're scared themselves and they still have that fear–respect or something for the *msungus*.'

'Don't be so sure,' Satish said. 'It won't last for ever. We thought it would be the same for us.'

He was silent for a moment.

'You don't know what it's like going out and not knowing if you'll be assaulted or shot. My wife's sister had her necklace snatched from her throat and her rings torn from her fingers the other day. She's traumatised and won't leave the house now. People have died.'

There was an awkward silence. Freya didn't know what to say.

'I stay at home as much as I can these days,' Satish said. 'But I had to come into town today to go to the High Commission to sort out some paperwork.'

'So you will have to leave soon?' Freya said quietly.

'It's only a matter of time before he says we all have to go.'

Freya still couldn't believe that it would happen. It was such a big thing to imagine, telling thousands of people that they had to leave the country just because of their race.

Adam dropped his Lego bricks on the floor and began crying. Satish put him on his lap and tried to comfort him. Freya touched the child's thin arm and stroked it.

'I expect you're wondering?' Satish said.

Freya looked away, unsure of what to say.

'How old is he?'

'Three, we think. His mother died in childbirth. They said it was punishment for something that she had done and that she was a witch. No one wanted the child. I was afraid that they might drown him. He is a bit slow talking and we're not sure how much he understands. It's the trauma he's been through.'

Adam got down from his chair and sat on the floor playing with his Lego. Freya thought of the kittens her Aunty Eileen had regularly drowned.

Satish lowered his voice. 'So I decided to take him. My wife was a bit unsure about it. I think she thought someone would come from the village and eventually take him back. Our *ayah* has pretty much looked after him. But I think of him as my son now.'

Freya thought fleetingly about what would happen to the child in England. There was still so much colour prejudice.

'The problem is that we intended to adopt him but never got round to doing it. It would have been so complicated getting the village headman to sign papers and all that stuff. Now, of course, they won't want to let him into the UK without the proper paperwork.'

'I'm really sorry,' Freya said. 'I hope you can sort things out for him. If you can't, what will happen?'

'Well, that's what I wanted to talk to you about. Do you happen to know anyone who is working at the High Commission in the visa section?'

Freya knew that the High Commission was taking on extra people to help with processing papers. One of the project wives called Rosemary had already started there. But she hardly knew her.

'I don't know. I'm not sure. I'll ask.' Freya felt nervous about getting involved.

There was a sudden noise from downstairs. People were shouting and screaming. A man appeared at the top of the stairs, holding a knife. It was the man Freya had seen talking to the beggar downstairs. Satish pulled Adam close to him and stood up to move away. A security guard came to the top of the stairs, grabbed the man roughly and dragged him away.

For a moment, Freya couldn't breathe. Satish looked terrified.

'So that's what it's like for us,' he said.

Freya was scared. She wanted to escape, to make the journey back while the sun was at its hottest and the soldiers were more likely to be sleeping after a heavy lunch.

'We can't let them win,' Satish said and beckoned to the waiter to bring more coffee. Adam played with his toy car. 'I'm sorry. I shouldn't have asked you to come here. It's really better and safer to stay at home unless you have to travel. Anyway, what will you do now?'

'Well, nothing. They seem to think things will settle down and everything will just carry on...' Freya hesitated, choosing her words carefully. 'I mean, Amin might change his mind about the expulsion. The British Government is doing what it can.'

'We know the British don't want us,' Satish said.

Freya didn't know what to say.

'And are you happy staying here?' Satish said.

She was afraid to say how she really felt. But it would be a relief to tell someone who she knew wouldn't judge her.

'I came here not knowing what to expect. I just wanted to make a go of things with Roger, to try to be a wife, to forget the ... bad start. I suppose I thought it would be like being at home, but with servants and hot weather.

And life would just move forward in a sort of straight line, that I would just settle down to married life, like everyone else.'

Freya lowered her voice and looked around to see if anyone might be listening. The café was still empty apart from a waiter who sat at a corner table reading a book.

'It's just that I don't think I know where I belong any more. When I think about my mother's house, it all seems so far away, as if that's the foreign country. But I know that I can never really fit in with the project people. And when I'm in the village I feel like a total stranger, and I know that nothing I do will make the slightest bit of difference to anybody. But there's something here that excites me, that makes me feel as if I'll wake up one day and know what it is and where I belong.'

Satish frowned. Freya was afraid that she had said something wrong and that he was offended.

'I'm sorry, I'm being selfish,' she said.

'Well, at least you have a choice,' he said. She could hear the irritation in his voice. 'How do you think I feel about belonging anywhere? My grandparents were born in India. I was born here and now I'm being shunted off to England, the great motherland. I've never even seen snow!'

He reached out and stroked Adam's hair as he sat on the floor.

'I'm sorry,' she said.

'Maybe it's no good just always doing what other people want you to do or trying to please them. In the end, you have to do and say what you believe is right,' Satish said.

She looked at him and met his eyes. His face was very handsome with its even features, dark eyes and thick eyebrows. It would be good to be married to someone like him, someone who would always understand what she was feeling. He held her eyes for a moment and then nodded as if he knew what she was thinking. Adam pulled on his sleeve and started crying. Satish picked the boy up, sat him on his lap and gave him a drink of milk from a plastic cup.

'Look, I think we'll have to go soon. He's getting fractious.'

She was suddenly afraid that she might never see him again.

Satish began gathering the toys from the floor and packing the small holdall. Then he looked at her again and met her gaze, but this time his eyes had lost the softness.

'I think that there is more to you than just being a woman who is going to spend her life being someone's wife or the mother of children,' he said.

No one had ever said anything like that to her before. Her mother, the teachers at school had told her *you're not academic, you don't really want a career, you'll soon be getting married.*

Satish hesitated.

'There is something I have to ask you. I need someone to come in to help sort things out. And after we have left, maybe you could just let me know how things are going from time to time. Some people think we might all be back when this nonsense is over. I don't really believe that, but we can hope.'

The café was still empty. Was this what Kampala would look like in a few months' time? Would all the restaurants, cafés and shops where the expatriates, the Asians and the better-off Africans liked to meet and socialise become deserted and closed? Or would they soon be filled with Ugandans happy to have seen the back of the colonialists?

Adam began crying. Satish stood up and continued packing away the books and toys.

The view from the rooftop café was startling. The hills that surrounded the city were outlined against the intense blue sky. There were mosques, temples and cathedrals on top of the hills, and brown roofs and greenery as far as the eye could see. In a small forest area nearby, the trees were covered with thick, heavy curtains of black bats.

'What do you want me to do?' Freya asked.

'Open the office twice a week and sort through the post and the bills. If you can, help with anything that people want. Prudence knows what to do. If you could help her sometimes.'

'Roger, the others. They won't want me to do anything that will be dangerous,' Freya said.

'Don't worry, I can see now that it would be difficult for you. It was a crazy idea,' Satish said.

Books by Wilbur Smith, John Updike and Barbara Cartland sat alongside orange-coloured paperbacks by African authors. She saw the names Chinua Achebe and Ngūgī wa Thiong'o. She had read some of them. There wasn't just one story about Africa. East and West, South and North. Each part of Africa was different. They were stories of life in villages, of struggles to survive, of fights against colonialism and corruption, and stories about sex and death and revenge. She wanted time to read more, to find out more about things that she didn't understand.

'Actually, I don't think I really care what Roger and the others say. So yes, I'd really like to do that.'

'Thank you,' Satish said.

She was relieved that she would have the chance to see him again.

'And, of course, I'll ask someone if they can help with the paperwork for Adam.'

*

When Roger came back from work that evening, he was in a good mood. They sat down to dinner and he told her that Bobby had decided that he didn't need to make another visit as everything was going well at the project. He had sent a letter thanking Roger for sorting out his transport issues.

'And how was the drive into town? Did you manage to get there and back without bumping into anything?' He laughed as he put his arms around her and kissed her.

'It was fine; there were one or two roadblocks but there wasn't a problem,' she said as lightly as she could.

'You're getting to know the ropes like an old-timer,' he said as he pulled her closer. 'Maybe an early night tonight?'

'Actually, I went to meet Satish at the bookshop.'

Roger loosened his grip.

'I thought you'd finished with that stuff. I know it's hard for the Asians but you should be careful about meeting up with people.'

'He's … a friend,' she said. 'I've agreed to help with the charity when he leaves … just occasionally.'

'You could have asked me first. It's not safe. I don't think Don will agree.'

'What has it got to do with Don?' She could feel the anger coming back. They had given her exercises at the mission hospital to help her keep calm. Women weren't supposed to be angry. She knew that it made her ugly.

'Don is an old stick-in-the-mud colonialist,' she said.

Roger's face turned red.

'Why didn't you say you were going to meet him?'

'Because I knew you would be like this. And there is something else. I've been twice to the village with him.'

Roger sighed. 'You're getting good at lying, aren't you?'

'I wouldn't have to lie if you could understand how I feel about things.'

'Well, I've tried but it's difficult. I'm only trying to help you … fit in.'

He walked out of the door and she heard the car engine.

She waited until ten o'clock and then went to bed. She tossed and turned restlessly, waiting for him to come home. Then around midnight she woke and heard the sound of the spare room door closing.

TWENTY-ONE

Freya woke the next morning at six o'clock to the sound of men's voices outside. Don's old Land Rover was parked outside the front of the house. She went out onto the veranda and watched Roger, Don and a man called Mark packing fishing rods, boxes of beer and soft drinks, folding chairs, Tilley lamps, paraffin stoves and other things into the back of the vehicle. They reminded her of boy scouts in their baggy shorts and matching khaki shirts.

Mavis was standing in the driveway watching them. Simon, the cook, stood by her side, waiting to offer his services for whatever might be needed. Mavis waved to Freya.

'Are you sure you should be doing this? You know what the High Commission said about going up-country,' Mavis said to Don.

'Oh, them; it's their job to be overcautious. We are only going for the day. We'll be back by sunset,' Don said.

Freya tried to catch Roger's eye, to show that she wanted to make up with him, to say she was sorry. She went up to him and offered her cheek for a kiss but he turned away from her.

'Where are you going? Why didn't you tell me you were going fishing?' she whispered but he didn't answer.

*

At dusk, Keziah came in and began drawing the curtains. Freya wished she would leave them open so that she could watch the sun go down with its strange suddenness. But she still found it difficult to ask her to change her daily routine.

There was a sound of gunshots in the distance. Freya jumped up and rushed to the window. 'What's that?' she said.

Keziah finished pulling the curtains together.

'Police, army. Shooting thieves,' she said. 'I finish now?'

'Yes, of course.' Freya was usually relieved when she left in the evening, but the sound of gunshots had scared her. She comforted herself with the thought that the men would be back soon. Everyone knew that it was dangerous to be out on the road after dark. Huge trucks drove haphazardly without lights. Thieves hijacked cars and robbed drivers at gunpoint. Drunken soldiers stopped and searched people at army roadblocks.

When Roger got back, she would try to make it up with him. Maybe she had been unreasonable. He was only trying to protect her from danger.

Suddenly the lights went out and the noisy fridge went silent. Damn, it was another power cut. This was happening more and more frequently. No one knew why.

Freya moved around in the dark, looking for candles. Keziah must have put them in another drawer. She jumped as the door opened and she saw Keziah in the doorway, carrying a Tilley lamp.

'You want?' she asked. Freya nodded and took the lamp from her.

'I stay?' Keziah said. 'You scared?'

Freya nodded, ashamed to show her fear of being alone.

'I go to my house and wait,' Keziah said as she shut the door.

If Roger had been there, they would have given up waiting for the electricity to come back and gone to bed early. But she felt she should wait up for him to come back.

Freya sat for a while, hoping that the room would suddenly blaze with light. But the electricity might be off for hours. She lit some candles and searched for something to read. She couldn't find the Agatha Christie story that she had been reading. There was a pile of old magazines that she had brought from the rest house. She picked up the one on top and glanced at it. The title page said:

TRANSITION
DOES AMERICA LOVE AFRICA?

She opened it and saw that it was produced by the university and dated 1966. Don always said that the expats at Makerere thought that they were better than everyone else and were too fond of mixing with the locals, and taking drugs.

She flicked through the pages. It was not the sort of thing that she usually read. She jumped at the sound of another gunshot. This time it was followed by a loud scream. She tried to distract herself by turning the pages of the magazine and she saw names that she had never heard of before. Paul Theroux and Ali Mazrui.

She started to read an article by someone called John Pepper Clark. It was about poetry and how it was often just spoken rather than written down, and then passed on to people who couldn't read. There was an article about a theatre group that travelled around the country. That sounded like a good idea. People in the villages often didn't even have a radio.

Someone called Conor Cruise O'Brien had written a letter about white people being brutally murdered in the Congo. She had read in the newspapers about trouble in the Congo but it all seemed a long way away. The letter said:

The safety of Europeans in Africa depends on the group reputation they have established for themselves in particular areas.

What kind of reputation had Don and all the other *msungus* established in Uganda? If it wasn't good, what might happen to them if the British didn't do what Amin wanted? She shuddered with fear. It was already eight o'clock and she listened anxiously, hoping to hear the sound of a car drawing up outside.

The programme for a play called *The Road* by Wole Soyinka was lying on the coffee table. They had seen the play a few weeks before. Roger preferred to go to a film at one of the cinemas on the Kampala Road but Freya had always liked the small theatre at home and had persuaded him to go to the National Theatre in Kampala. It had been built in 1959 as a place of entertainment for the Europeans. But now there were plays of all sorts and audiences of all kinds. Freya thought that it was a happy and relaxed sort of place. The audience would shout at the actors, or cry out or moan when something exciting happened.

Roger had fallen asleep in the middle of the play and she had tried to explain things to him in the car going home. But she was unsure herself about the disturbing story of the Nigerian Professor and the drivers who tried to run over dogs as sacrifices to the gods. It had brought back dark memories of the dead dog in the road and her illness.

Jock barked and growled outside. It was probably a stray cat or dog, or even one of the lizards he loved to chase. She listened for the sound of the *askari* but everything was eerily silent. She called for Keziah but there was no answer.

There was a knock on the mosquito door. There had been no sound of a car drawing up outside. Her heart beat faster. Then a voice called '*Hodi*', quietly. A figure stood in the doorway but it was too dark to see who it was.

'What do you want?' she said. 'The *bwana*'s not here. Come back tomorrow.'

'I'm sorry if I've scared you,' the voice said. She recognised the accent. It was him. The man from the market and the High Commissioner's party. She still felt too scared to open the door, afraid that she might have made a mistake.

'What do you want? Roger isn't here. They have said I shouldn't answer the door to strangers.'

'Yes,' he said. 'I remember that's what you said we were. I'm Wensley, in case you've forgotten.'

She suddenly felt foolish that she had let her stupid fears get the better of her.

'I'm sorry. Of course,' she said and slowly unlocked the door. 'Please come in.'

He was dressed in a blue tracksuit. It showed off his broad shoulders and made his legs look longer than she remembered. He wore a matching baseball cap.

The dog whimpered and then lay down panting on the darkened veranda.

'Your dog doesn't seem very pleased to see me.'

'No, no,' Freya said. 'He's always like that with visitors. He's harmless.'

Wensley met her eyes, smiled and lifted one eyebrow.

'Really? All visitors?'

Freya was embarrassed. The lights suddenly came back on. Freya switched off the Tilley lamp. Her old dress was stained with dirt marks from trying to find things in the dark. Her hair was tangled and uncombed and her face shiny and without make-up.

'Look, I'm sorry if I scared you. I didn't want to disturb you. I've been at cricket practice with the team and I was having something to eat with them when I heard about the curfew,' he said.

'Curfew?'

'Yes, it was on the radio. No one should be out after sunset.'

'What's happening?'

'There are rumours of invasions from Tanzania.'

'Invasions? Who would invade?' she said.

'Obote, the old president, and his supporters.'

'Do you think it's true?'

'Well, it was terrible out there this afternoon. There were army roadblocks everywhere. They were pulling people out of their cars and searching for anything they could get their hands on.'

He looked around, as if he was expecting someone to come into the room.

'I just don't know how I'm going to get back into town tonight. You and your husband are the only people I really know here.'

'Roger went fishing with the others this morning. I was expecting them back by now. Do you think something has happened to them?'

Wensley pulled on his fingers until they clicked.

'I wouldn't think so. I'm sure they can take care of themselves.' He took off his baseball cap. 'I don't really know what I'm going to do. Is there anywhere I could stay?'

She knew what Mavis would say. *You can't really trust any of them, dear, even the educated ones.* All Freya knew about this man was that he had seemed to understand what she was feeling and had wanted to help her. Did it matter what Mavis thought? She felt a glimmer of excitement at the idea of doing something that Mavis might disapprove of. And she was afraid of being alone in the house.

He put his cap back on.

'I understand, it's difficult for you, a woman on your own.'

'Please, it's okay. You can't go out there now. You can stay here. We've got a spare room for visitors.'

'Look, I could ask your house girl if I could stay in her house.'

'No, stay here, please.'

'Well, if you're sure? Thanks,' he said and sat down carefully in the chair, as if afraid that he might damage something. The silence was awkward and she wasn't sure what to say to him.

He looked around the room and fixed his gaze on a statue, carved from a single piece of wood.

'Is that a *makonde* from Tanzania?' he asked.

'Yes, we got it from someone who came to the door.' The statue's face was rather like his. He smiled at her. She hoped he hadn't read her thoughts. It might not be the right thing to even think, let alone say. It was so difficult to know. She tried not to stare at him. He was handsome, like someone in the movies. Sidney Poitier perhaps? She had been excited by the story of the mixed-race couple in *Guess Who's Coming to Dinner*.

She blushed, stumbling over what to say next.

'I'll get some tea. Or … maybe something else?' she asked.

He laughed. 'Tea will be fine. I spent some time in England, remember?'

The kitchen door opened and Keziah stood in the doorway. She had changed from her usual faded blue uniform dress and pink plastic shoes into a loose-fitting shiny red dress and the Indian sandals that she wore when she had a day off.

Wesley said something to her in Swahili. Freya didn't

understand what he was saying, but it was as if they already knew each other. Keziah said, '*Ndio,*' and went back into the kitchen.

He got up, said 'Excuse me' and followed Keziah into the kitchen. She could hear them talking. A few minutes later, he came back.

'What is it? Do you know her?' Freya said.

'I sometimes pass her on the project road when I'm visiting for coaching. I didn't know she worked here. I just wanted to make sure that she understood about the curfew. She asked me to tell you things aren't safe and you should be careful and make sure you lock up. She has left some cold food in the kitchen.'

'Surely she's not going anywhere. Is she?'

'Seems she knows people in the army and so she's not scared of the curfew.'

Keziah opened the door, carrying a tray of tea.

'You want anything else?' she asked.

'No, please go,' Freya said.

Keziah closed the kitchen door with a bang.

Wensley sat down on the low chair, his long legs bent awkwardly. She poured the tea and gave him a cup. He held it in both hands and leaned back against the cushions for a couple of seconds and then closed his eyes so that she was afraid that he might drop the cup. But he opened his eyes and picked up a book lying on the coffee table.

'Oh, *The Road*. I saw it at the National Theatre,' he said and then laughed. 'Don't look so surprised. You think I'm not the sort of person to go there. I went to school, you know. Best one on the island. We read Dickens, Thackeray, the lot. I could have been a teacher if it wasn't for the cricket.'

She felt embarrassed again. 'No, I mean, not everyone likes the theatre,' she said. 'Roger hates it.'

'Be careful, you're digging yourself in deeper. Kill us a dog, Kotonu.' He laughed again.

'Yes, I remember,' Freya said. 'They kept saying that. I didn't really understand what it was all about.'

'Well, this guy, Kotonu, he's the one who has given up driving because of all the terrible accidents. But the other drivers can't understand why because the gods need sacrifices, people killed on the roads by accident, or dogs killed deliberately. They say it's about colonialism.'

Her heart beat faster. Was the dead dog she had seen on the road a sacrifice? She thought about the blood of the miscarriage. Was that some kind of sacrifice? They had said in Sunday school that bad things happening might be a punishment for something you had done. She didn't know what she was supposed to think about colonialism. When Don and the others talked about it, it sounded like a good thing. She would look for something in the bookshop next time she was there.

Wensley mopped his brow. There were large sweat marks staining his tracksuit.

'Do you mind if I just get a wash?' he said.

'Please use the bathroom.' She hesitated and then said, 'Perhaps you would like a shower before we eat?'

'Are you sure?' he said.

'Of course. I can get you one of Roger's tee shirts and a wrap, if you like?'

'That would be good, thanks,' he said.

Freya suddenly felt as if things were hurtling somewhere unknown.

She fetched cold chicken and coleslaw from the kitchen.

After his shower, Wensley came into the living room wearing the wrap and the tee shirt. His shoulders were broad. There were small drops of water on his dark skin. She wanted to touch him, to check that he was real. It was as if she finally knew what handsomeness meant. Roger and the few other boyfriends she had known had been quite good-looking. That was usually enough. Being well dressed, polite to her mother or having some access to a car always seemed more important.

They sat down to eat. He ate holding his knife between his thumb and first finger, something her mother would have smacked her for when she was a child. She offered him a *waragi* and tonic, and then poured herself a glass and gulped it down.

Once, after a few drinks at one of the dinner parties, she had heard herself nervously saying that it was strange that so few Africans came to the project houses. There had been a brief moment's silence until Mavis had said they had tried from time to time, but people had always turned down invitations. *They don't really want to mix. And the men don't want to bring their wives. You'd be surprised; some of them don't know how to hold a knife and fork properly*, she had said.

Wensley ate in silence. Freya struggled to find something to talk about. Her father would have known. He would have loved the chance to talk to a county cricketer.

'You were in England? When was that?' Freya asked, trying to break the awkward silence.

'Couple of years back, only for a year.'

'Did you like it?'

'Yes, I suppose so. Cricket was good. My teammates were fine. Lodged with an old couple in digs. It was just a small house in a terrace. I had the box room. They were good to me. But they always asked me to go out when their friends came round.'

'That's horrible,' Freya said. Her mother occasionally took in lodgers, usually single women. *You never know with men*, she always said.

Wensley met Freya's eyes and his cheeks tightened.

'Well, they weren't as bad as those idiots who called me names in the street.' He stopped eating and left his knife and fork at angles on the plate instead of neatly together.

'I take no notice. Sticks and stones. Name-calling on the pitch and off. I just get on with it. No good dwellin' on things.'

She wasn't sure what to say, afraid she would get herself into a deeper mess. The *waragi* was making her feel lighter in the head.

'There's this TV programme, *Till Death Us Do part*. It makes fun of this old man who is … prejudiced.' She said the word carefully, hoping he wouldn't be offended. Maybe it was a mistake to have mentioned it? She was light-headed with the drink.

'Oh yes,' he said. 'I watched it with the people I lodged with. Wilfred, that was his name. He used to laugh when the old man called people *nig nog*. I just think it made him feel better. You know, he was all right with me. I was a cricketer, so not really like the other coloured people, as he called them. He liked watching that programme because he thought the old man was like him and that made it okay.'

'Yes, but some people watch it because they think he's ridiculous and old-fashioned. The world's changing,' she said, feeling happy that she had made this clear to him. She poured herself another gin and tonic.

'Oh yes,' he said again. 'So what about all this stuff with the Asians? Saw this big advertisement they printed in the *Argus* the other day, came from the council in Leicester telling the Asians not to settle there.'

'I suppose some people are just afraid of all those people coming at once. There won't be enough houses, or hospitals, or …'

He looked angry and she stopped.

'So you people don't mind us keeping the hospitals and buses going for years and years, or making money out of us when we were slaves, but when we want to come to your beautiful country, you make all kinds of excuses to keep us out.'

She felt ashamed that she hadn't seen it like that before. The gin was making her a bit dizzy. Everyone was against her even when she was only trying to say the right things. She stood up and swayed slightly. He looked alarmed and held on to her.

'You all right?'

She nodded and they both sat down.

He poured himself another glass of *waragi* and tonic and offered her one. She took it. She knew she should stop drinking before she made a complete fool of herself.

'I really want to ask you something,' she said.

'Go ahead.'

'Do you think we should be here? It's ten years since independence and all these white people are still doing all these jobs. I mean, do you think this project is doing any good? Nothing seems to make much difference. Everyone just seems to hate someone else.'

She could feel herself becoming more excited. Perhaps she had already said too much, talked about things she knew nothing about. Then she looked up and saw that his eyes were closed. Thank goodness, he hadn't heard what she was saying.

Wensley opened his eyes. 'Sorry. I didn't mean to be rude. I wasn't asleep. But it's been a long day. What were you saying?'

She tidied away the dinner plates. He followed her into the kitchen. He started to wash the plates.

'No need to do that. Keziah will do them tomorrow.'

'You seem to find her difficult?'

Freya wondered why he thought that. He had probably guessed from the way they spoke to each other. She wanted to tell him everything; about her miscarriage and the pact that she had made with Keziah about keeping the baby. He might know how to help her to understand things that she couldn't understand herself.

'I never had a house servant before. I don't always know how to treat her.'

'Like a real person, for a start,' he said. She heard the anger in his voice. She knew then what he thought of her and she didn't want to leave it like that. The night air suddenly felt colder than usual.

'Look, do you mind if I go to bed? I'm really tired. I'll leave as early as I can tomorrow,' Wensley said.

They stood up and faced each other. The room was spinning. She saw his eyes were bloodshot but they softened. Roger and the others might still be back any minute. But she didn't care. Did she even like Roger any more?

She moved towards him, put her arms round him, and rested her head on his chest. He gently lifted his arms and held her to him. She moved her head upwards and looked into his eyes, wanting to kiss him.

He met her eyes for a moment and then turned and took his arms away.

'No,' he said.

'I'm sorry,' she said, on the verge of tears.

'No need to be. You're tired and a bit drunk. Lock up properly before you go to bed.'

TWENTY-TWO

Freya woke with a splitting headache. She could hear someone moving about. Was it Roger? When she woke properly, she remembered with a start that Wensley was staying. What had she said to him last night? She felt hot and embarrassed as she remembered putting her arms around him.

What had happened to Roger and the others? They must have decided that it was too late to drive back before the curfew started and found a rest house somewhere. They would have lots of stories to tell. Would Roger still be annoyed with her? She would have to make a special effort. She would tell Keziah to take the evening off and she would cook his favourite steak with Béarnaise sauce.

There was a sound of running water in the shower room. She didn't want Wensley to see her in her nightclothes and she hurriedly pulled on an old cotton dress.

In the kitchen, she took out the packet of cornflakes from the cupboard. It said *Kellogg's* on the side but the flakes were soft and slightly musty tasting, not like the crisp cereal at home. A lot of things were like that. The label on the outside would be familiar. But whatever was inside would have a different or unfamiliar taste or texture.

The pawpaw in the fridge was turning dark orange and mushy. They said it could be used as meat tenderiser. It made her think of the rotting corpses that they swerved to avoid on the road at night.

Eggs; yes, eggs would be safer.

Wensley came into the kitchen still wearing the wrap and the tee shirt. She thought again how handsome he was and she suspected he might know it. She tried not to meet his eyes. It was awkward, being trapped in the small kitchen with someone she hardly knew. He smelled of Roger's aftershave. She suddenly wanted to touch him again, to run her finger down his muscular upper arm.

'Are you okay?' he said lightly.

She prayed that he had forgotten anything she might have said or done the night before.

'I should have said that I don't eat breakfast, so please don't bother getting me anything, juice will be fine.'

She carefully folded the top of the cornflake packet.

'Last night, I was ...'

Before she could finish he looked at her, lifted his index finger and moved it towards her lips so that it was close but not touching. She wanted to touch his finger, to lick it with her tongue. What was happening to her? She had to pull herself together.

'I'll go and get changed,' he said.

She made some tea and took it to the dining room table. She looked through the window and saw someone walking past the hedge that separated the house from the road. The woman turned into the driveway. It was Mavis. She was wearing the faded denim skirt and yellow shirt that she usually wore in the morning while she organised the servants' routines for the day. She hardly ever walked around the project compound.

She pushed open the veranda door without knocking. Her hair was tangled and uncombed. Her eyes were small and tearful.

'Have you heard anything?' Mavis said, sounding out of breath. 'Where are they? I'm getting scared. It was bad enough last night not knowing what was happening.'

Freya wanted to tell her to go away. But she felt sorry for her. She looked vulnerable without Don by her side. Freya suddenly felt strong and in charge of the situation.

'I am sure they will be okay. They know how to look after themselves. They would have found somewhere to stay,' Freya said.

Mavis sat down heavily in the wooden armchair. Freya tried to think of an excuse, a way of getting her to leave before she saw Wensley.

There was a sudden screech of brakes outside. The project Land Rover pulled onto the drive. Oketch, who was usually calm in all circumstances, looked agitated.

'Memsahib, memsahib, the *bwana*, the others, they're in Makindye Prison.'

Freya found it hard to register what he was saying. She recognised the name of the prison. Mavis' face went white. She trembled as she clutched at the chair and made a sobbing noise.

'Oh no,' she screamed. 'That place is terrible. People die in there.'

Freya was afraid that Mavis might faint.

'It must be a mistake,' Freya said. 'He probably means they are at the police station.'

'No, no,' Oketch said. 'In big prison.'

'No!' Mavis screamed.

Wensley came in from the kitchen. 'What's goin' on?' he asked.

Oketch waved his arms and spoke to him in rapid Swahili.

Mavis stopped crying and stared at Wensley. He returned her gaze but she quickly looked away as he offered her his hand to shake.

'This is Mavis,' Freya said.

'I'm Wensley; pleased to meet you. Look, don't upset yourselves. They can't have come to much harm. Someone probably just wants to give them a bit of a fright.'

'What are we going to do?' Mavis began crying again.

Wensley turned to Freya and met her eyes. 'I think I know someone who might be able to help. At least it's worth a try,' he said.

Freya thought she understood what he meant.

'Really, could you?'

'Your driver says he can take me there.'

Freya could feel Mavis looking at them. Only project staff were allowed to have lifts in the Land Rover. Oketch often picked up his friends but there was nothing much that anyone could do to stop him. So mostly they turned a blind eye.

'That's fine,' Freya said.

'Thank you for the hospitality,' Wensley said to Freya as he climbed into the Land Rover.

Keziah appeared from behind the house. She was wearing the clothes that she had worn the night before. She ran over and gave Wensley what looked like a letter. Mavis looked at Freya as if to say, *What is she up to now?*

After they had gone, Mavis followed Freya into the house, sat down and lit a cigarette.

'Who is he going to see? What did he mean?' she said.

'He does cricket coaching with one of Amin's ministers. He's probably going to ask him what's happening and to see if he can help get them out of the prison.'

Mavis began crying again. 'I'm so worried about Don. He doesn't have his blood pressure tablets. He hasn't been well since the last bout of malaria.' Then she stopped crying. 'What was that man doing here, anyway?'

'He stayed here for the night. He'd been coaching the students and he couldn't get back because of the curfew.'

'Was that wise?' Mavis asked. It was as if she had forgotten her distress about Don. The ash from her cigarette was dropping onto the floor. Freya got up and pushed an ashtray towards her.

'I mean, you know how people talk. He could have gone to the rest house or even stayed in the quarters.'

Freya tried to control her anger. Why was there a need to explain anything to Mavis?

'Perhaps you should go and wait at your house,' Freya said.

Mavis looked tearful and vulnerable again.

'I'm so sorry, I didn't mean anything. He's a West Indian, isn't he? He's different … from the others, I suppose?'

Freya imagined her falling to the floor and shattering into pieces like the porcelain shepherdess. But she saw something strange and unexpected in Mavis' eyes, as if she wanted to say something that was hidden deep, and unsayable. Then Mavis' face became hard again.

'I'm so worried. Don hates being on his own. I hope they're all together, wherever they are.'

Roger would probably be all right, Freya thought. He was tougher than the others. He was used to long journeys on his own. He had told her about some of the rat-infested rest houses he had stayed in, and how he had bribed his way out of roadblocks that had threatened to keep him held up for hours. He would know how to deal with all this.

Mavis sank into the chair. She looked old and tired without her make-up and her carefully pressed clothes. Keziah came into the room. She had changed into her uniform. She picked up the broom and made tutting noises when she saw the cigarette ash on the floor by the sofa. Freya wanted to ask her what she had given to Wensley. Instead she said, 'No, leave it, you can do it later.'

'Not good for the *bwana*,' Keziah said and left the room. Through the window, Freya watched as she sat on the floor outside her house, her legs stretched in front of her so that the bulge of her belly was more pronounced.

Simon, Mavis' cook, walked up the driveway. When she saw him, Mavis looked relieved. He said something to her in Swahili in a gentle voice.

Simon had worked for Mavis for ten years. Everyone said that he worked longer hours than any of the other house servants. They could often be heard shouting and arguing with each other like an old married couple.

There was a story that some years ago there had been a big argument when Mavis had accused Simon of stealing rice. He had been angry and annoyed and had left the house to go back to his village. But after a few days, Mavis had found life so difficult that she had asked Oketch to take her to the village. His house was one of the biggest in the village with a tin roof and a large *shamba*, so it was thought he hadn't really needed to work as a houseboy. At first, he had refused to let Mavis come into the house. But then, gradually, he agreed to speak to her, saying he would only come back if she told everyone on the project that he was not a thief. When they got back Mavis found the rice at the back of a cupboard.

'I'll go home now and wait. There's nothing we can do,' Mavis said wearily. As they walked away, Simon stayed close to her as if to make sure that she didn't slip in the puddles in the driveway.

After they had gone, Freya was relieved to be on her own. She switched on the radio. The sound of the BBC World Service was always comforting. She wasn't listening properly to the calm, soothing male voice. Then she heard the word 'prison' and the newsreader said that two British journalists had disappeared. Armed police had arrested them at their hotel and they hadn't been seen since. It was believed that they might be in the notorious Makindye Prison. She began to shake with fear.

*

Around four o'clock, the men came back. They climbed carefully out of the Land Rover, shaky and dishevelled and stiff-limbed. Mavis must have seen the vehicle from her house because she had followed it, half running down the driveway. She put her hand to her mouth as if to stifle a scream, and ran towards Don. She tried to put her arms around him but he pushed her away, saying, 'Leave me.' His clothes were torn and smeared with dirt and dark red crusts of blood.

'What have they done to you?' Mavis asked. She was in tears as she followed closely behind him. He limped slowly back to the Land Rover.

'I just want to get home,' he said as he struggled to climb into the vehicle. Mavis tried to make sure he didn't fall backwards. 'How could they do this?' Mavis asked as she followed him into the Land Rover.

Roger was like a stranger. His clothes were crumpled and dirty and his pale, freckled face was covered with red blotches. His red hair was matted and the whites of his eyes were yellow. He rushed inside the house, sank into the sofa and bowed his head in his hands. He scratched at the raw mosquito bites that were scattered all over his pale arms and legs.

'Can I get you something?' It sounded like a trivial question but she didn't know what else to say to him.

'Whisky,' he said.

She poured a full tumbler and he gulped it as if it were a glass of water.

'Would you like something to eat?' she said, still feeling helpless.

'I haven't eaten anything but beans and filthy water since yesterday. I can still taste and smell that place and I think I'd throw up if I ate anything now. I think I've got a fever. It must be malaria. That stinking place was full of mosquitos.'

Freya struggled to find something to say.

'It must have been awful,' she said.

'Awful?' He tried to laugh but it became a cough. 'I need some sleep.'

'What happened?' she enquired, unsure of whether she really wanted to hear the answer.

'I can't … I don't want to talk about it.'

Freya remembered the nice district nurse who had visited her after the miscarriage. She had said, *Try and talk about it, dear. It might help you to get over it.*

He took his head out of his hands and looked at her. There were tears staining his face. She had never seen him cry before and she didn't know what to do. She tried to touch his arm but he brushed her away.

'I don't know where to start. There isn't a word to describe that place,' he said.

'Maybe you should try.'

'I can still hear the screams of the poor buggers they were beating up. It sounded as if a lot of them didn't make it. At least we are alive.'

Freya reached out to hold his hand and he grasped it tightly.

'We were about an hour's drive away when they stopped us at a roadblock. We thought it was just the usual thing. At worst, we'd have to give them a few shillings and they'd let us through the barrier. But they kept us there for two hours. Then more soldiers arrived and screamed at us to get into their van. Don got angry and told them that they couldn't do this to us and that he would be contacting the High Commission.'

Roger stopped for a moment as if he couldn't go on.

'Then one of the soldiers slapped Don across the face. I could see the soldier was frightened and he smelled of booze. I hardly dared look at Don but when I did I saw that he had taken it without flinching. Don said we should do what they told us to do.

'Then the soldier screamed that it was on the President's orders. Every European out on the streets had to be taken to Makindye. Even then, we didn't believe they would do it.

'They bundled us into a police van. There were no windows so we didn't know where they were taking us. Even then, we thought that they might be just trying to frighten us. When we got to the prison, they pointed their guns at our heads and, honestly, I thought that was it. But they just laughed and tied our hands behind our backs and made us sit on the floor. When we tried to break free, they pulled and pushed us around. That's how our clothes got torn.

'Then they took us to the guard room and made us take off our shoes and sit on the floor. They pointed their guns at us again and I could see that Don and Mark were terrified.'

He stopped talking, pulled out a blood-spattered handkerchief and wiped his eyes.

'They took us into this room. Men were lying all over the floor, pressed together like sacks. It was like a terrible nightmare. They gave us a filthy blanket each and pushed us onto the floor. All night we could hear the sounds of screams and groaning. I can still smell the stench of latrines and fear.'

There was a knock on the door and Roger jumped and began trembling. She had never seen him frightened like

211

this before. He usually acted as if he was in charge, as if he didn't want to show any weakness. Now he was dependent on her to reassure him, make him feel better, like a child lost in a supermarket. There was another knock. It was Jimmy.

'Tap not working, hose no good,' he said.

'Tell him to go away,' Roger shouted. He was suddenly back to his old self.

Jimmy walked away and she watched him turn the tap on. There was nothing wrong with it. She heard him shout something to someone and they both laughed.

'I'm going to sack him. He does nothing,' Roger said.

'So how did you get out in the end?'

'They kept asking us a lot of stupid questions, as if we were spies or something. I was so scared I thought they would torture us. Then all of a sudden they stopped and told us we could go. One of them said to tell the Queen that Idi Amin Dada loves her like his own mother.'

Freya tried to touch him to comfort him, but he pushed her away angrily.

'Well, you're home now,' she said. 'Everything will be all right.'

'You don't understand how awful it was,' he shouted. 'These people are bastards, there's no getting away from it.'

He lit a cigarette and closed his eyes as he drew on it.

'We could hear the sounds of clubs hitting skulls.'

Freya wanted to put her fingers in her ears.

'They make prisoners execute each other. They shatter the skull of the man in the front by hitting his head with a twenty-pound hammer.'

He was trembling and she felt sick.

'They make people lie down and then the first man is forced to get up at gunpoint and has to smash the skull of the man in front.'

'Stop it!' Freya cried. 'I can't bear it.'

'Whatever they say, no one's safe.'

She put her arms round him and he sobbed. Then he stopped and looked into her eyes. It was as if he had become a completely different person.

'I'm sorry. It must have been awful for you as well, not knowing what had happened. Were you scared?'

An image flashed through her mind of Wensley standing in the doorway, the towel wrapped around his waist. She blushed and guiltily turned away from Roger.

'We heard about the curfew. We were worried but we thought you had probably decided to stay in a rest house somewhere. The phones were all down so we couldn't call the High Commission, and we daren't leave the compound.'

She thought that she had better say something, to get it out of the way before he found out from someone else.

'I think it may have been Wensley, the cricket coach, who helped to get you out,' she said.

'What's he got to do with it?'

'He said he would ask the minister who he coaches if he could help.'

'Who told you that?'

'He stayed here … last night.'

'What?'

'He couldn't leave because of the curfew and he had nowhere else to go.'

'Why here? Couldn't he have stayed at the students' place?'

'I didn't think.'

'No, you don't ever think. You know what they're all like. They'll be gossiping.'

She knew he was right. 'I thought you liked him,' she said. The lights began flashing in the corners of her eyes.

'I don't really know anything about him.'

'I think I'm getting a migraine,' Freya said and began to cry. She didn't know if it was guilt or just the stress of hearing Roger's story and seeing him so changed.

'Stop. You'll make yourself ill again. I'm sorry. I suppose you only did what you thought was best. No one needs to know. He's gone now.'

He winced in pain as he got up from the settee. He tried to pull her towards him. He smelled of sweat, blood and urine, and she turned her head away. She would wait until he was feeling better before she told him that Mavis had seen Wensley and knew that he had stayed the night.

'I know. I stink. I need a shower and I just need some sleep. Where is Keziah?'

'Why?'

'Some food would be nice.'

'I don't know. She hasn't been around since this morning; I suppose she's scared like everyone else,' Freya said.

'After I've had a shower, maybe you could lie down with me?'

She was surprised at his neediness. She let him put his arms around her and she rested her head on his shoulder.

Roger stroked her hair.

'When I thought that we might all be killed, all I could think about was you and if you would be okay. Coming here can't have been easy for you. I've been so busy with work. But I can try and change.'

He hesitated.

'I think we should try a bit harder for the baby.'

She could see by the look in his eyes that the idea excited him. She wanted to say that she had changed her mind about getting pregnant when everything was so chaotic. But she decided to wait until he was feeling better.

As they kissed, she remembered something and pulled away from him.

'I'll check that everything is okay in the shower room for you,' she said.

The smell of Roger's aftershave lingered in the shower, where Wensley must have used it.

She opened the window wider. The towel that Wensley had used was lying on the floor and she hurriedly moved it and hung it on a peg on the wall.

Roger came into the room and put his arms around her. He sniffed and his face looked puzzled. Before he could say anything, she said, 'Shall I get in the shower with you?'

He looked surprised and nodded. She had seen people do it in the movies, but it always looked awkward. Roger pulled her to him and kissed her. They gradually undressed each other and got into the shower, where she gently washed his cuts. After the first clumsy efforts, he entered her and the sensation she felt was like something gathering in her body so that she felt she would explode. It was a new and frightening feeling. She knew what it was because she had read about it in books. She just hadn't expected it to happen like this. As she came, she looked at the towel Wensley had used.

After that, Roger wanted to have sex all the time. She sometimes thought it was as if he was using it to forget what had happened. He was usually gentle and considerate but occasionally he drove into her so hard and frantically that it felt as if it was punishment.

They even had sex when she was having her period. At first she had turned away from him, as she always did at this time of the month. But then she had said, 'Why not?' They had carefully laid an old towel on the bed. She had relaxed and it had felt particularly good and she came twice.

Roger didn't ask if she was taking the pill. It didn't seem to matter to him any more.

TWENTY-THREE

The morning sun that came through the gap in the curtains was so bright that Freya had to shield her eyes. She looked at her watch. It was eight o'clock. The tea should have arrived. Where was Keziah?

The night before, Roger had suggested using the Polaroid camera. At first she had been shocked and embarrassed. She thought about the magazine she had found hidden at the back of a cupboard in the outhouse, where her father sat patiently mending the bicycles or peeling the onions for pickling.

But Roger had gently persuaded her that it wouldn't do anyone any harm. It was just between the two of them. Then, gradually and guiltily, she had enjoyed the excitement it created.

As she thought about the photographs, she felt foolish. She fumbled to open the bedside drawer. She would have to cut them up and throw them away or burn them before anyone saw them.

She dressed quickly and went to the kitchen, opened the drawer, took out a pair of scissors and laid them on the table. Through the kitchen window, she saw three tied bundles of fading cloth placed on the ground. Keziah stood beside them dressed in a wrap and a shiny red blouse. Her huge belly bulged through the skirt. She looked across at Freya and then turned away. Freya opened the kitchen door and called to her.

'Where are you going?'

'Somewhere. Till the baby come.'

Freya had known this would happen but she had stopped thinking about Keziah and the baby after Roger had come back from the prison. She was trying to hold on to something that was slipping away from her.

'When will you come back?'

Keziah shrugged her shoulders. 'Not coming back. Work finished. The *bwana* give me money and say it finish.'

Roger had said nothing about this. The old jealousy came back. If Keziah went, it would be like getting rid of a ghost in a haunted house. But didn't she want to be haunted? She felt panic rising. She might never get to see the baby. She felt the pain between her legs, the sensation of something slipping away.

'It will be better for the baby if you stay here. It's nearer the hospital.' Freya's voice was cracking and her throat was dry.

'The hospital is too much money. Local midwife is better.'

Keziah picked up the bundles. She swung one up onto her head and carried the other two. Freya watched her walk down the driveway. The colours of the garden were fading. A taxi drew up, Keziah got in and it drove away.

After she had gone, Freya sat in the living room. It reminded her of how she had felt after her father had died of a heart attack. She and her mother had gone out to the shops and left him listening to the test match on the radio. When they got back, he was dead. Now she wanted to grieve but she didn't know how or why.

There was a film of dust on the coffee table. She would have to start cleaning the house herself now. Did the house really need to be swept, dusted and polished every day? Her mother did housework as something to fill the time. It was her way of controlling everyone, of exhausting herself or of making everyone else feel guilty while she pushed the Hoover around their idle feet.

Did they really need a new houseboy or house girl? She could do the housework herself. The other wives would probably think that she was making some kind of statement, showing that she was superior to them. But she didn't care what they thought any more.

'She's gone,' Freya said when Roger came back from work.

'Yes, I know.'

'She said you gave her money.'

'You have to give these people something when they leave. It's a sort of pension.'

She was too tired to argue, to ask him why he hadn't said anything to her.

'Keziah said you told her it was finished and that she shouldn't come back.'

'Oh, she probably misunderstood what I was saying,' he said.

He turned away from her and she saw that the back of his neck was pink. Was he lying?

'I think it's better if she doesn't come back,' he said. 'You've always found her difficult. And she'll find it hard to work with a baby.'

She wanted to scream at him, to say that he shouldn't do these things without asking her. Instead, she said, 'I've decided I can do the housework myself.'

'Don't be ridiculous.' He cursed under his breath as he searched through his briefcase for something. 'You'll make yourself ill again.'

Freya didn't answer but went into the kitchen to make tea. The kitchen was hers now, to do as she liked. She looked at the scissors that she had left on the kitchen table and thought about the photos. Now that Keziah was gone, they would be able to have sex any time, in any place.

She took the tea into the living room. Roger was holding an opened envelope and a letter in his hand. He was standing by the door as if ready to leave.

'I have to go to town. I'll be back before dark,' he said.

'What for?'

'I just found the letter. It's from the High Commission. I have to go and meet someone. It's too complicated to explain.'

After he had left, she took the scissors to the bedroom. She opened the drawer to find the photographs. There was no one around now who might find them. She didn't need to destroy them. She lay on the bed. There was something else she could try. After all, no one could interrupt her now. She had found a book called *The Female Eunuch* in a second-hand bookshop. She kept it in her underwear drawer alongside the pills. She would check what it said about doing it.

*

Washing the clothes every day was the worst part of the housework. They had to be left to soak in the bath and then hauled out into the garden to be hung on the line. Everything had to be carefully ironed to get rid of the *tumbu* fly eggs that might have been laid in the wet washing. If they got into your skin they could be painful and itchy.

So many things in the tropics were just ready and waiting to invade your body. If you didn't keep your feet properly covered, you could get jiggers, caused by a flea that buried itself in your toes, then laid its eggs in a tiny sac and caused unbearable itching.

When Freya had had her first jigger, she had tried to remove it herself with a needle, carefully following the instructions in the book, but she had ended up with a bloody mess oozing from her toe. Keziah had watched, taken the needle from Freya and then, kneeling at her feet, studiously and carefully picked at the sac until the egg was neatly removed. It had been a strange, wordless, intimate contact. Now that Keziah was gone, Freya had no idea who she could ask to remove her jiggers.

Freya did the housework for a week. Jimmy, the garden boy, had watched as she struggled to put the heavy washing on the line and then said, 'Madam, I help do the work for you.' She had laughed at first, thinking that he was far too young. But he said he was fifteen and at secondary school. She wasn't sure if he was telling the truth but she was relieved to have some offer of help. She said she would pay his school fees and, in return, he would clean the house twice a week and do the washing every morning before going to school. Freya did the ironing and the cooking.

Roger was always away, travelling up-country. The other project men hardly ever went further than Kampala or Entebbe. Freya wondered if Roger's going away was his way of getting over the prison incident, an act of defiance, to show that no one could get the better of him. When she tried to ask him about this, he said, 'The machinery still needs fixing. That doesn't stop because of those bastards.'

TWENTY-FOUR

Freya drove carefully along the road to Kampala. Mavis had called round that morning to say that one of the project wives had told her that Jimmy had been caught stealing eggs from their hen house and she should get rid of him. Freya had told her, as politely as she could, that Jimmy always did his work well and that she had no intention of sacking him. Mavis sighed and left.

Freya knew that she had to get away, to escape from the stifling project compound. But where could she go? Perhaps she could pass the time at the charity office. Hardly anything was happening there now. Prudence had left, saying that she was too scared to be alone in the office. People still came and waited patiently in long queues outside, but Satish said that he didn't have time to do very much as he was too busy seeing to his own affairs. Amin was starting to seize the Asians' property and money, and people were queuing all day outside the banks. Others were sleeping all night on the pavement outside the British High Commission, waiting for it to open so that they could sort their passports and visas.

She put her foot down hard on the accelerator and drove faster. She switched on the car radio and heard Amin's voice. She slammed on the brakes as a goat ran in front of the car. He was saying that he would now ask Britain to take responsibility for all the Asians of British nationality in Uganda. He had had a dream and God had told him to do it. They would have three months to leave. She felt her hand trembling on the steering wheel.

She still felt shaken when she got to the office. The door was wide open. Satish must be there, she thought, but there was no sign of him. Through the open door, she saw upturned tables and chairs. Broken glass from smashed windows was scattered all over the floor. Papers, pens and ink had been swept from the desk. There was a strong smell of pee from a puddle on the floor. She retched at the sight of a small heap of shit by the door.

The old woman called Sarah who came in and cleaned the office from time to time was sitting on the floor, crying.

'Soldiers did it,' the woman sobbed. Freya tried to comfort her and then together they began to clear up the mess. They jumped at the sound of a car drawing up outside. Satish walked into the office, where he stood silently staring at everything.

'Bastards,' he said. She had never heard him swear before.

Freya struggled to know what to say to him. It was as if she was trying to offer condolences to someone after a death.

'I heard Amin's announcement on the radio,' she said. 'It's awful.'

He didn't answer but started to pick up papers from the floor. Then he moved an overturned office chair and sat down on it.

'You see, it's all hopeless now. Edward Heath is sending some minister out here to try and get Amin to change his mind, but I doubt that will help. The British just don't want us there.'

Freya felt ashamed and helpless and didn't know what to say. She wanted to shout, *It's not my fault, it's the government, the people at home.* But that seemed a feeble excuse.

'It's all over now,' Satish said. 'We'll have to shut this place down. All the work we've done, and it comes to this.' He wiped away a tear with a grubby handkerchief.

Sarah began to sob. 'No job,' she said.

Freya wanted to hold Satish in her arms and cry with him. She was strangely excited by the thought. Was it bad to think about sex in the middle of such horror and misery? He met her eyes for a moment.

'Thank you,' he said. 'I know you have tried your best.'

She wanted him to touch her but she knew he wouldn't. He wasn't the kind of man who was always putting his arm around a woman's shoulders or waist.

'You'd better go home. There is nothing that you can do here now.'

She was afraid that she might not see him again.

'Will you … stay in touch?' she said. It was a stupid thing to say to someone who would shortly be a refugee in a strange country.

'I don't know. Who knows what will happen to any of us or where we will be in a few months' time. But be careful and don't let those project people push you around. Do what you think is right.'

*

When she got home, she was exhausted. She lay on her bed for the afternoon nap which she took every day, as a way of avoiding the boredom of the long afternoons. She thought about the stinking, litter-strewn charity office and the despair on Satish's handsome face as she drifted off to sleep.

She was woken by the sound of Mavis shouting her name. She jumped quickly off the bed and hastily combed her hair.

Mavis was standing in the doorway. Her own hair had become longer and stragglier and speckled with strands of grey since her friend, who was a hairdresser, had left for the UK.

'I did warn you,' she said, 'but I've just seen that boy of yours driving your car on the project road.'

The stupid woman must have imagined it. But when Freya looked towards the baobab tree where the car was usually parked, she saw that it had disappeared.

'You'll be sacking him?' Mavis said.

Freya could still hear Satish saying that she should do what she believed was right. But she hesitated, thinking that perhaps Mavis was right: theft was theft. But was this theft?

'He'll come back. He's just a boy trying his luck,' Freya said.

'Roger should be told,' Mavis said.

If Roger found out, she would tell him that there had been a misunderstanding and that she had said Jimmy could drive the car to the gate.

'The car is pretty old, it's nearly given up,' Freya said.

She could see that Mavis was exasperated. She was trying to hold onto things that were slipping away all around her.

'Well, I suppose it's difficult for you, with Roger being away so much.'

Freya just nodded.

'Anyway, he's being well looked after. Don's old friend David Fox, up at Masindi, said he stayed with them last week.'

Freya tried to hide her surprise. Roger hadn't said anything to her about staying with his friend. Masindi was a place you went to on the way to the Murchison Game Park and the Falls. So why would he be there?

'Oh yes, he told me,' she said. She was getting better at lying all the time. Mavis looked as if she had run out of things to say. She turned and walked away down the drive.

Freya went back into the house, wondering what she would say when Jimmy got back. After half an hour, she heard the sound of a car stopping suddenly outside. Then she heard the pounding noise of the hoe.

She went into the garden. Jimmy looked at her and she saw fear in his eyes. She drew a deep breath, about to tell him that he had done something wrong, and that if he did it again she would sack him.

But she knew why Jimmy had done it. She couldn't really blame him. Amin had told him that everything would soon be his to take. Unless he got a place at senior secondary school, he might have to spend his life working for someone like her. Amin was a bad person, but she could see why people followed him. He gave them all a bit of hope that they could have all the money, the cars and other things that the *msungus* and the Asians had.

So she waved to him and said in Swahili, 'Don't forget to water the tomatoes.' He turned away from her. He was probably laughing at her. Had she been a coward, afraid to confront him? Did it matter?

*

When Roger came home later that day, she told him what Mavis had said about Masindi.

'I didn't think you would be interested. I stayed there on my way back from the North. I didn't want to drive for hours in the dark,' he said.

Hadn't Keziah once said that she was going to Masindi to visit her aunt? She couldn't remember. The old pangs of jealousy came back.

There was no point in telling Roger about Jimmy. He would just want to sack him.

'I went to the charity office today. The soldiers had been in and completely ransacked the place,' she said.

'I'm not surprised,' he said. He seemed distracted by a letter he was reading. He crumpled it and threw it into the wastepaper basket.

'Come on,' he said, 'let's lie down.' The sex was rough and quick and she felt invisible.

TWENTY-FIVE

Freya stared into the scared eyes of strangers as the packed lift swayed and creaked its way up to the nightclub on the tenth floor of the Bata building in Kampala. She hoped it would make it to the top without coming to a sudden halt.

Don had invited them to join him for his birthday party. He had been slow to recover from the trauma of the prison incident. He had lost weight and his skin was yellow. The curfew had been lifted but the project people were increasingly scared of going out on the road at night. In the end, Mavis had persuaded them that the birthday party was the tonic that Don needed, something to get him out of himself. To make sure they were safe, they had all driven in a convoy.

It was dark and smoky inside the nightclub. Tables with small lamps were arranged around the circular dance floor. Freya's eyes watered, as they had always done ever since she was a child when her mother and father had taken her to the Post Office Club, and then told her to sit outside if she complained too much.

It was nine o'clock and already people were laughing and shouting drunkenly and the floor was wet with spilled beer. Army men in uniforms called to the bar girls to come and join them, sometimes pulling them onto their laps. Some tables had people of different races all sitting together and Freya guessed by their casual trousers and brightly coloured shirts and African dresses that they were from Makerere. The people from the project were more formally dressed, the men in white shirts and ties and the women in cocktail dresses. Mavis wore a shiny black satin sheath dress and pearls, and Freya was in a green halterneck dress.

The band was playing and singing Congolese music and a few people were swaying and dancing. Freya recognised one of the songs. It was called 'Malaika', and she had heard it played repeatedly on the radio. Freya had noticed that Keziah laughed when she heard the title. Satish had told her that it was a love song about a young man who couldn't marry his girlfriend because he didn't have any money. The word *malaika* meant infertile, barren, harlot.

It was strange that you could be called a prostitute if you couldn't have a child. As if a woman's body was just there to be used for sex or for having a baby.

Freya had always hated noisy bars and the smell of alcohol. But she knew that she was trapped for the next few hours. Roger was at the bar getting the drinks.

She felt someone brush past and a white woman sat down beside her. She stared closely into Freya's face. There was a strong smell of drink and eau de cologne. Freya tried to move away but the woman put her hand on Freya's arm and moved closer, pulling on the sleeve of her dress. Freya could hardly hear what the woman was saying above the noise of the music and the drunken laughter.

'They all hate me,' the woman sobbed, grabbing her arm. 'I sent them away. Now they hate me.'

Freya didn't know what she was talking about. She just wanted her to go away.

'You don't know what it's like standing there, watching the plane take off. It's like your stomach is torn out.'

The woman tightened her grip on Freya's arm.

'Have you got children?' she asked.

Freya shook her head.

'Then don't. It's too hard.'

An embarrassed-looking man came towards them. 'I do apologise,' he said. The woman sobbed loudly as he led her away.

Freya was disturbed by what the woman had said. If they carried on living this kind of expatriate life, their child would grow up and eventually he or she would have to be sent away. Was there any point in having a child if it was wrenched from you and sent away to sleep in a cold dormitory? Another child would slip away from her. Her heart began to beat faster and she could see the flashing lights that signalled the start of a migraine. It would be an excuse to leave. Roger would be annoyed but it was better than staying and vomiting all over the dance floor.

She looked around for Roger. Then she spotted him standing at the bar talking to a tall man wearing a light blue shirt. She would have to wait now until he came back to the table.

Her heart sank when she saw Roger and the man walking towards her and recognised with a start that it was

Wensley. She had tried to forget what had happened the night that he had stayed. But sometimes, when they made love, she saw his face instead of Roger's.

Mavis sat down by her side.

'Isn't that the West Indian chap who was staying at your house?' she asked.

Freya thought of escaping to the toilet but she knew it would be overflowing and the stink would make her want to vomit. But it was too late.

Wensley offered his hand to Freya as if to shake it. As she took it and felt the roughness of his palm, he said, 'I've just been thanking Roger for letting me stay at the house.'

Roger was smiling. He must have forgotten any suspicions that he had about Wensley. They had been drinking and probably talking about some cricket match. She was always surprised that such a slow, boring game made men like Roger and her father so excited.

Wensley looked at Freya and smiled. Her migraine had gone.

'You don't mind me giving your wife a twirl on the dance floor?' he said to Roger.

Freya wanted to say no. She had never learned to dance properly. People said she had two left feet. If it was the twist or some kind of bobbing around by herself, that was fine. But dancing with a man, trying to keep in step, was always embarrassing. But Roger said, 'Go ahead,' and turned to talk to Don.

Wensley held her formally at first, as if afraid to get too close to her. She could smell a mixture of aftershave and gin. Then he slowly pulled her more closely towards him until she was almost stepping on his feet. It gave her no choice but to move with him. 'Relax,' he whispered and pulled her even closer so that she could feel the buckle of his belt pressing against her ribcage. She gradually stopped feeling tense and let him do the work as they swayed and moved to the Congolese music. She saw through the crowds that Roger was talking and laughing with Don.

Freya's heart was beating fast. She wanted the dance to go on for ever, but at the same time she felt scared and prayed for it to finish soon. As the music slowed, he pulled her towards him even more tightly and she felt his erection.

'Have you missed me?' he whispered. She stayed silent but pressed her hand slightly more firmly into his. She saw, or imagined, that people were looking at them. It was not unusual to see black men dancing with white women in the nightclub, but it still excited and frightened some people.

'Kill us a dog, Kotonu,' he laughed. 'Have you worked out what that means yet?' He was teasing her.

'Only that people sometimes want to do things but they have to make sacrifices for the sake of everyone,' Freya said.

'And sometimes people have to do things because they know they'll always regret it if they don't,' he said.

The music stopped suddenly. The lights went out. A voice shouted in Swahili and then in English, 'Get out now! Police!' She let go of his hand but he pulled her towards him and kissed her. His hands held her firmly behind her back. It was as if she had forgotten where she was and didn't care if the lights came on suddenly. Someone shouted, 'Go now!'

'When should I pass by?' he said. It felt to her as if there was no going back or way of refusal now.

'Most Wednesdays. In the early afternoon,' she said.

It was the time when the project staff had their weekly meeting and Roger was always late back from work.

She searched for Roger in the darkness. When she found him they ran for the door, made their way down the stairs and eventually found Don and Mavis waiting by the car.

On the way home, Freya tried to make normal conversation while her head was wild with excitement and anxiety about what she had done.

'I don't understand what that was all about,' Don said. 'It's this ongoing thing between the police and the army. They're always fighting each other, tribal stuff as usual. That's the last time we'll be going to that place.'

Roger and Freya were sitting in the back seat of the car and Roger took her hand.

Mavis said, 'I saw you dancing with that chappie. Suppose it would have been rude to say no.'

Roger looked at Freya, took her hand, and squeezed it. She wanted to pull it away but she squeezed it back.

*

In the days after the dance in the nightclub, Freya felt variously guilty, scared and excited. She couldn't concentrate and she lost her appetite. What would Wensley expect from her if he 'passed by', as he had said? Anything more than a kiss was unthinkable. The *askaris*, the house servants, and the project people might see him.

She would have to think of an excuse as to why he was visiting. To give her Swahili lessons? To help organise a surprise for Roger's birthday that had something to do with cricket? Everything she thought of seemed more and more ridiculous.

Was this the beginning of an affair? It was a strange, flat word for the feelings that she was going through. Her mother, the girls at work disapproved of affairs, especially for women. They were more forgiving if it was men who had needs that wives couldn't always satisfy.

She knew that the *msungus* often had affairs. Perhaps it was because they were far away from home and could do what they liked without family or friends knowing. If a man strayed and was found out, the woman had to put up with it. She couldn't run home to her mother at every little tiff. If a woman strayed and was found out, she might be sent home or just called the 'local bike' behind her back. White men strayed with black women as if it were their right, the other men covering for them like members of a gang of criminals. If white women strayed with black men, there was something wrong with them, like a strange incurable disease.

She began to pray that it had all been a joke. But she still woke every day with uncontrollable butterflies in her stomach as Wednesday approached.

TWENTY-SIX

When Wednesday came with no word from Wensley, Freya woke feeling relieved that it had all been a ridiculous dream. She would try to concentrate on ways to keep herself occupied now that the charity was closed. Perhaps she would offer to help at the British High Commission. She had managed to persuade one of the project wives who was working there to see if she could track down Satish's papers and help sort out the paperwork for Adam.

Around ten o'clock she heard the sound of a vehicle outside. Oketch knocked on the front door, handed an envelope to Freya and then quickly drove off. There was no name on the envelope. She opened it nervously and took out a piece of folded lined paper. It looked as if it had been torn from an old exercise book. Her hands trembled as she read it.

Come to the Speke Hotel this afternoon at 2pm.

She knew who it was from. She would tear it up and pretend that she had never received it. There was no reason for her ever to see him again.

It would be easy to avoid him as he only came occasionally to the project for coaching, and always took a path along the back road that went directly to the project offices.

The kiss had been a drunken mistake. They were lucky that no one had seen them. She had to forget it all and pretend that nothing had happened, that she had imagined it all or dreamed it. But when she looked at the paper again, heat flushed through her body and she felt strange twitches of excitement. She had no choice any more.

*

The Speke Hotel was an old two-storey building, fronted with elegant archways. The project people went there for beautifully cooked five-course lunches or dinners that usually started with onion soup and ended with crème brûlée. Freya preferred it to the fourteen-storey Kampala International Hotel, which was always noisy with the sounds of music and teeming with shinily dressed bar girls who accosted men, even when they were sitting with their wives.

Freya parked her car some distance away from the hotel. She hoped that her large straw hat and sunglasses would stop people recognising her. She waited nervously outside the hotel for ten minutes. Maybe he was waiting inside? The heat became too much and she went into the

237

hotel entrance area, not knowing what she would say if anyone approached her. She could ask to use the toilet.

In the dining room, waiters were clearing away lunch from the starched white tablecloths. The room was deserted except for an old white couple who sat at a table in the corner, shouting and arguing loudly. She guessed that they could be in their seventies. They were probably from Kenya. Until independence, Uganda had been a British protectorate, a place still ruled by local kings and rulers, a place where foreigners couldn't easily buy or own land. So there were very few old white people living in Uganda.

A waiter came towards her. She felt embarrassed. This had all been a mistake. She turned to walk away as if to leave but he followed her and said quietly, 'Madam, take this key. Room 25. Up the stairs, turn right.'

She walked up the stairs, her stomach churning, and found number 25. It wasn't too late to leave. She had never experienced this madness before. The psychiatrist at the mission hospital had been right. There had been something in her childhood that made her act impulsively and irrationally. She had to leave before it was too late. But the door opened and Wensley was standing there.

'You came,' he said. 'I wasn't sure. Are you okay?'

Inside the room, the furniture was dark, the curtains were drawn and a fan whirred. The air was damp and musty.

'I'm scared,' she said.

'No need. I'm always careful.'

She wasn't sure what he meant. She couldn't talk about taking the pill to someone she hardly knew. Men expected you to deal with that. It was a woman's problem.

'It's okay. No one will find out about this. The guy who gave you the key is a friend. I'm helping him with his son. He's a promising bowler.'

He had planned exactly what would happen. Of course, he must do this kind of thing quite often. Freya hadn't thought about that before. She hadn't asked him if he had a girlfriend or a wife. Now, that didn't seem to have anything to do with anything. Nothing else really mattered.

He came close to her and she could smell soap and aftershave. She remembered the night when he had stayed at the house and how he had taken her arms gently from around his neck. She wanted to touch him but didn't want to make the first move. But he pulled her close to him and kissed her.

Then he said, 'Shall we try?' She nodded and he moved away from her and began to take off his clothes. He folded them carefully and laid them over the back of a carved wooden bedroom chair. She took her clothes off slowly without embarrassment, but she was too excited to do anything other than let them drop to the floor.

When they lay down it felt comforting and natural. His body was firm and smooth. He made love carefully, all the time asking if it was what she wanted, if it pleased her. So different from Roger and his silent thrusting. There was nothing else she wanted other than to be there in that moment. Afterwards, he fell asleep still inside her.

The alarm on the phone rang suddenly and he gently pulled away from her, then sprang out of bed and went to the bathroom for a shower. He dressed carefully.

'Stay here for another hour and then leave. Give the key to the waiter called Vincent. I have to go now.'

Afterwards, she lay on a towel on the bed, feeling the trickle of semen down her legs. He had said little apart from the things he had murmured when they were making love. It was strange how a person needed words to remember, to think about, to make sure that what had happened had been real, not a dream or a fantasy. Was saying very little his way of making him feel no guilt for what he had done?

Her mother's generation was always guilty about sex. Things were changing. You weren't supposed to feel guilty. The pill, women's lib; sex could be like a game of tennis. Nothing to feel guilty about. Wasn't she just trying something out? It wouldn't hurt anyone. No one would know. No harm had been done.

And Roger? What if he found out? It would be the end of everything. She had been stupid.

She saw that an hour had passed. She showered and dressed quickly and walked down the stairs. She looked around, afraid to ask for Vincent. Then the waiter came towards her and said, 'The key, madam? I hope your stay was good.'

The old white couple were still sitting in the dining room. The whisky bottle was empty and they were talking loudly and angrily. How many lovers had they taken out of boredom in all their years in Africa? Maybe they were Mike and Sam's godparents, the tea planters? Could they ever survive anywhere else in the world? Old white people in Africa. That sounded sad.

TWENTY-SEVEN

Freya was resting on her bed in the afternoon after ironing and preparing the dinner for later in the day. She thought about Satish and felt guilty that she had become so self-obsessed that she had forgotten about what was going on outside the bubble of her life. Britain had agreed to accept fifty thousand Asians with British passports. But then Amin had quickly announced that he would expel all the twenty-three thousand Asians who had Ugandan nationality. What would happen to them if they had no right to go to the UK? It was all becoming too difficult to think about.

She heard the noise of a car crunching to a sudden halt on the drive outside. She jumped off the bed, hastily pulled on her dress and combed her hair. Then she heard Wensley's voice. Why had he come to the house? She had tried to forget what had happened at the hotel, to pretend that it had never happened. That way she could hide her guilt.

Wensley stood in the doorway. He was wearing light-coloured slacks, a green Aertex shirt and a black baseball cap, pulled over his eyes as if to disguise himself. Without being asked, he walked into the living room and the old feeling of excitement rushed through her. Not caring if anyone saw them, she went up to him and put her arms round his neck.

'No,' he said as he gently took her arms away. 'The taxi is waiting outside. I have something to deal with first. I wanted to check that you were alone.' His expression was anxious and he was dripping with sweat.

She watched nervously as he opened the back door of the taxi. He bent over and carefully picked something up from the back seat. It was a moving bundle and he held it awkwardly in his arms. She thought it must be a live chicken with its legs tied together. He would have picked it up at the market on his way to the house. People often brought gifts of chickens.

'Would you mind paying the taxi driver?' he said. She fetched some money and went outside to give it to him. As she came back into the house, she heard what sounded like a baby's cry. Was she imagining things? Was this some kind of dream?

Wensley pushed the bundle towards her. She had no choice but to take it in her arms. Her heart beat faster as she pulled back the cloth and saw that it was a baby, wearing only a thin vest and a cloth nappy.

'Please. What is going on? I don't understand. Who? What is it?' she asked.

'It's a she,' he said. 'Someone left her outside my door. I didn't know what to do.'

'But who left her?'

'I don't know,' he said, avoiding meeting her eyes and looking through the window into the garden.

Everything outside looked the same. The sun was shining brightly with its usual mid-afternoon glare. The bougainvillaea, with its bright orange and pink flowers, hung over the veranda. But everything had changed. He met her eyes, but it wasn't a look of desire. It was more like desperation. His eyes were bloodshot, his skin was marked with small sun blisters and she smelled baby poo on his clothes.

'I don't understand. I don't know what you want from me,' Freya said.

'I need you to help me. You *msungus* can do things we can't. You can organise for her to be taken care of.'

So that was how he saw her, just another stupid *msungu*. She was just someone to be ... fucked. She'd never said the word out loud. But now she knew what it meant. He mopped his brow with his handkerchief and pulled his fingers until they clicked.

'This is dangerous. You should take her to the hospital or the police station,' she said.

'I can't do that. You know what they're like. If you report anything to them, they immediately arrest you as the suspect. Everyone knows that.'

She had heard that story before. Maybe it was true. The heat in the room was stifling. The child woke, stretched her arms, clenched her tiny fists and began crying. Freya felt the wetness of her pee-soaked nappy seeping through to her dress.

Freya looked at her properly for the first time. She

had tight curly black hair but her skin was pale. People said that all babies began life with pale skin. Her heart was pounding in her chest. She moved closer to Wensley, still clutching the child.

'I think you're not telling the truth,' she said carefully. 'Why did you bring her here?'

'I couldn't think of anything else to do.'

He had changed from the man she had fucked – the word seemed easy now – and daydreamed about, into a stranger.

'Tell me the truth.' Her voice was strained.

Wensley looked at his watch and got up as if to leave.

'Look, I need to go.'

'No!' Freya shouted and moved to block the doorway.

'Please. If she can just stay with you for a couple of hours until I can sort something out, then I'll take her,' he said.

'Then tell me the truth. Why did you bring her here?'

Wensley stared at her. He took off his baseball cap and sat down on one of the dining room chairs. He seemed to shrink in size.

'All right,' he said. 'I thought her mother might be here.'

'Her mother?'

'Your girl, Keziah. She left the baby.'

Freya began to doubt her own sanity. Was the illness coming back?

'Keziah? But she left here weeks ago. I don't understand. Why would she leave the baby with you?'

'I don't know. Maybe because I helped her a little, a while back.'

'How?' Freya asked, afraid of what he might say.

'Can't say.'

An image she didn't want to see flashed through her mind: the way that he had looked at Keziah the night he had stayed at the house. She blurted out the words she didn't want to say.

'Are you ... the father?'

Wensley shook his head.

The room began to swim around. She felt sick.

'Did you know her before you met her here?' Freya asked.

'Not exactly,' he said.

She wanted to raise her hand, to slap him across the face. Instead, she clenched her fists and took a deep breath.

'She works in a bar sometimes,' Wensley said. 'Paradise, the one on the Kololo Road.'

'She's a ... prostitute?' Freya looked at the dust that had settled on the coffee table.

'No, not exactly,' Wensley said.

What did he mean by that? An article in one of the old *Transition* magazines said that African prostitutes weren't like prostitutes in Europe. Sometimes they just took a liking to their customers and wouldn't ask for money. Sometimes they just wanted someone to go dancing with. Freya thought about the street girls at home, standing about under the station bridge shivering in the cold and fog of winter. They wore short, tight skirts stretched over their bulging stomachs, and their feet were crammed into teetering high-heeled shoes.

Fierce-looking women argued on TV that all women were prostitutes if they married men and relied on them to keep them. Her mother had said, *What rubbish!* and changed the channel.

Some men wanted sex so badly that they would pay for it. The women who did it just needed the money to survive. Or maybe there were some women who enjoyed sex with a lot of different men? Freya thought about how she sometimes used sex to distract Roger or to get him to change his mind about something. And when he brought her material or flowers from Kampala, she knew it usually meant that he wanted sex.

'What happened? With you and Keziah?'

The baby cried out and Freya stood up and walked about patting her back, trying to calm her down. She would need feeding soon. Freya desperately wanted Keziah to be there, to take the child away.

'Tell me what happened and then perhaps I can help you,' she shouted above the baby's screams. The crying stopped and Freya laid her carefully on the sofa.

Wensley's face was sprinkled with beads of sweat. He looked away from her as he spoke.

'I went to the bar some months ago, just to get a drink, after cricket practice. She was there, sittin' at the bar.' He hesitated. 'She reminded me of an old girlfriend.'

His face softened and Freya felt an unexpected pang of jealousy.

'I knew what she wanted.'

Is that what he'd thought about her after they had kissed in the nightclub? The romantic ideas she had been playing out in her head were blowing away like rubbish in the *murram* dust.

'I was a bit lonely. I was a stranger, like you, remember?'

Freya knew he was trying to soften whatever he was about to say.

'We talked a bit. She said it would be free. But I couldn't do it. It didn't seem right. Then I felt bad and so I just gave her some money.'

Freya wasn't sure if she could believe this. Had he been lying all along about everything?

'After that, I forgot about her. But then she stopped me one day when I was walking down the project road on my way to coaching. I had no idea that she worked here. Tell you the truth, I didn't recognise her at first, especially in that uniform. When I asked her what she wanted, she said she was havin' a baby. Asked me for money. She said she didn't know what she was going to do as she'd be out of a job. But I was a bit wary of it all so I just refused.'

'So that night you stayed, when you spoke to her in the kitchen, what happened?'

'She asked me for money again. I said no. But then when I was leaving after staying the night, I thought things weren't gonna get any better for anyone, so I just gave her some as I was leaving. I didn't see her after that.'

So that was the explanation, if she believed him, of the envelope she had seen him give Keziah as he left the house.

He fumbled in his pocket and took out a crumpled piece of pink notepaper and gave it to her. Was it the same pink stationery that she kept in her bedroom drawer? The writing was childlike.

Mister pleese look after her. Cant keep her. I get beaten. The daddy not to know. You give me money. You kind I can tell. Give her to someone who look after her. Give her to the msungu woman. She knows. Keziah

'I did think of just leaving her outside the hospital. But I didn't really understand what she meant by *she knows*. So I thought I'd bring her here and ask you.'

'Well she can't stay.' The words came out of her mouth but she hardly believed them herself. She stroked the baby's head. She was beautiful. Wasn't she the reason that the child was lying there, gurgling and clenching her fists? She clutched her more tightly.

There was the sound of a car outside. For a moment, Freya thought she could try to hide the baby in the spare bedroom until whoever it was had gone away.

The door opened. Roger stood in the doorway. Jock ran into the room, lay down and growled at Wensley.

'Could you call your dog off me?' Wensley said. Roger ignored him.

'What is going on?' he said. 'Whose is that … baby?'

'Thought you might know,' Wensley said.

Roger's freckled face turned red. He stared at Wensley. There was a tiny bald patch on the back of Roger's head. She hadn't noticed it before.

'What do you mean, I might know?'

'He thinks it's Keziah's. He came here looking for her,' Freya said, desperately hoping that Roger would calm down.

The two men faced each other like boxers in a ring. She hugged the baby closely to her, afraid that one of them might snatch her.

'Why has he brought it here?'

'She left her on his doorstep,' Freya said. As she said it, she knew it sounded like a ridiculous story.

'You can't believe that rubbish,' Roger said. 'Can't you

see? He's trying to get money out of us. I suppose you're the father?'

Wensley clenched his fists and moved towards him until his face was almost pressed against Roger's.

'Please stop,' she said, standing between them. The baby was crying loudly again. Freya looked at Wensley. 'I really think you had better go now. You can see how upsetting this is.'

Wensley took the baby from her arms and she felt the smoothness of his skin brushing against her. Then he walked out. Freya wanted to run after him but she was transfixed on the spot as if in a nightmare. She pinched her arm to see if this was all a bad dream and felt her nails dig into her flesh.

Roger was trembling and he took out a cigarette and lit it.

'I told you not to get involved with these people. You should never have let him stay the night.'

She wanted to cry, to run away, to get away from the stifling heat of the bungalow.

'That's not fair,' she said. 'He was the one who helped you all get out of that terrible prison.'

'That's his story. The High Commission says they got us out.'

She wanted to scream '*Liar*' at him.

'What did he mean?'

'About what?' Roger said. His face was still blotched with red marks.

'He said that you knew something about the baby.'

'I don't know. Can't you see? These people lie through their teeth if they think they can get something out of us. They're all the same, doesn't matter where they come from. It's in the genes.'

It would be like that for the rest of her life, hearing him say awful things without knowing what to say in reply.

'And if he comes near this place again, I'll tell the *askaris* not to let him onto the compound. They'll set the dogs on him if necessary.'

He collapsed into a chair. He had the same haunted look that he had when he came back from the prison. Jock lay down beside the chair and Roger patted and stroked him.

'I'm sorry,' he said, beckoning to her to come and sit with him. 'I know it's not your fault that you got caught up in this. He seemed fine, the cricket and everything.'

She took his hand. It was limp and sweaty.

'I've got a lot on my mind at the moment. I'm worried...' he said.

'What about?'

'Nothing. I can't talk about it, not now. Let's lie down for a while,' he said. She knew that if she agreed it would make him feel better and show him that she could forgive and forget what might have happened. She decided she would no longer let him use sex to make her change her mind about something.

'No,' she said. 'I don't want to, not now.'

'Suit yourself,' he said as he let go of her hand. 'What's the matter? Don't let all this baby stuff upset you. Keziah's gone now. He's gone.'

Roger pulled himself wearily from the chair. 'I'm going for a rest,' he said.

Freya started to tidy up. The room smelled of the baby. She saw something on the floor. It was Wensley's baseball cap. She picked it up and held it.

She'd had sex with two men. She was taking the pill, but if something had gone wrong she would never know who the father was. She didn't really want sex with either of them ever again. Both of them had just used her. She had thought that Wensley understood what she was feeling about the difficulties of living in this strange, troubled place. But had she ever really meant anything to him? And she would never know if Roger had really wanted to marry her.

She put the baseball cap in the desk drawer, locked it and hid the key underneath a brightly coloured paperweight.

TWENTY-EIGHT

Freya dreamed that she was pregnant, but the pregnancy lasted for years and the baby refused to come out. When it did, it was a shrivelled little animal that turned on her and taunted her like the monkeys that threw things at visitors in the Entebbe botanical gardens.

When she woke, she knew what she had to do. After breakfast, and as soon as Roger had left for work, she took the baseball cap out of the desk drawer. Then she got into the Hillman Imp and drove down the road to Kampala. She was waved through three army roadblocks. She guessed that they were not interested in her or her battered old car because it was unlikely that there would be anything much to take from it. Asians were better pickings.

She drove along the Kololo Road looking for the row of flats where Wensley had said he lived. She stopped the car. She had no idea which block it might be. It had been a stupid idea. As usual, she had done something without thinking it through. A houseboy and a house girl were smoking and chatting outside the entrance to one of the blocks. She sat in the car trying to pluck up courage to speak to them. She got out of the car and said, 'Excuse me, I'm looking for the cricket man. Do you know where he lives?'

They looked at her and shook their heads. They probably thought that she was crazy.

'*Bwana* Wensley?' she said.

It sounded stupid but the woman laughed and then said, 'Maybe school.'

School? What did she mean? Then Freya remembered that he had said that he sometimes coached children at the secondary school. She tried to remember the name of the school. It was no use. She would give up and go home and just pretend she had been shopping. But then a name floated up from her memory. The Aga Khan school. Satish had been a pupil there. Maybe she could just try the school and see if he was there.

When she arrived at the school playing field, she saw him straight away. He was standing with his arms crossed, watching the game attentively. There were two school teams, both made up of African and Asian boys. Groups of parents stood around watching and occasionally shouting, 'Well played' or 'Out'.

The Asian parents stood in small huddles. They would be talking about the expulsion and what was going to happen to them all, and about having to find new schools for their children in strange new places. The African parents stood in strangely silent and subdued groups. It was easy, she thought, for people who had got along well together before to quickly become enemies.

Satish had told her that the school had performed

Romeo and Juliet, with the Asian and African students playing the two conflicted families. He said his brother still remembered how shocked they had been to see an African student kissing an Asian girl on the stage. It had been at a time in the sixties after independence when everyone was still hopeful that things would change and that all races would be able to live happily, side by side. *Didn't last long. Bit of a pipe dream*, Satish had said.

Freya sat in her car and watched Wensley as he winced and then shouted out as the ball slipped through the fingers of a fielder. A smartly dressed Asian woman went up to him and whispered in his ear. He laughed and lightly rested his arm on her shoulder. Freya felt a lurch of jealousy. This was a stupid idea. She would leave now before he saw her.

But it was too late. He turned suddenly and stared at her. He said something to the woman and then walked towards Freya's car.

'Why are you here? What do you want?' he asked.

She opened her bag and took out the baseball cap. 'You left this,' she said.

He lifted an eyebrow as he took it from her. 'You came all this way, just for that. Thanks. But I'm a bit too busy right now to chat.'

She knew then that there were certain things you could say or not say, or do or not do, but they would change your life for ever. Like not saying that she didn't want to marry Roger.

'The baby,' she said carefully. 'I came because I've decided that I can take her and look after her.'

'And what do you think he will say about all this?'

'I've decided that I'm going to leave him. It'll be just the baby and me.'

'So you think that will solve your problems?'

'My problems?'

'So you want to take a child to your country, where they don't want the Asians to come to, where they don't like blacks?'

'People do it all the time, adopt black children. It's quite common.'

'She's not yours to take,' Wensley said. She wanted to say, *Yes, she is mine*, but the story was too complicated to tell him.

'It's too late, and I can see now that I shouldn't have come to the house or bothered you. It has just made things bad between you and the husband.'

'Where is she?' Freya said. Surely he hadn't given the baby away to someone else?

'I left her with my houseboy's wife.'

Freya began to panic. 'How could you do that? Can you trust her?'

'I've found a way out of all this. I called my sister last night, back home in Dominica. She can't have children. She has wanted a baby for ages. She says she'll take her. She'll be well looked after, loved.'

'But you can't just take a baby out of the country. It's … not legal,' she said.

'The minister I coach says he can sort things. I just have to add her name to mine on the passport.'

That was it, then. There was nothing more that she could do. She would have to go home to Roger and make some excuse as to what she had been doing in Kampala.

She looked into Wensley's eyes, half hoping that she would see what she had seen at the nightclub and when they had made love. She saw only fear and sadness. She turned to leave. But she still needed to ask him something.

'The other day at the house, you said something about Roger knowing something. What did you mean?'

'Oh, I don't know. Just something said in anger, I guess. He's got no manners.'

She could tell he was lying by the way he had answered so quickly.

'Forget it all,' he said. 'You should just start thinking about leaving this place before things get worse. It's the Asians now, but you'll all be next.'

'Please, I need to know.'

He shouted 'Howzat!' as a wicket fell and applauded the batsman off the field. He turned and looked at her.

'Why is it so important to know? Some things are best left alone.'

She felt she had to change her tactics, as he might have done at the wicket in the face of a fierce, fast bowler.

'Did you have any feelings for me?' she said.

He looked irritated at being distracted from the game.

'Yes, of course. I like you. Another time it might have been different.'

'Then please tell me what you meant. About Roger knowing something about her.'

Everyone at the cricket ground was looking at them. A voice in the distance shouted, 'Hey, Wensley, come over here, man.'

'It's nothing. I was just angry with how he treats me. I wanted to annoy him,' Wensley said.

'That's all?'

Wensley sighed and then faced her directly.

'All right. Perhaps you should know. When I met him at the party at the High Commission, I thought I'd seen him somewhere before. It was in the Paradise Bar. I think I may have seen him talking to her, your house girl. They looked … close.'

Her heart beat faster. What did he mean? She was too afraid to ask him.

'I may have made a mistake. A lot of white men look like him. It doesn't matter,' he said. 'Things are difficult right now. People sometimes do crazy things.'

He met her eyes and she felt his hand brush gently against hers.

'Forget it all and go home. Make it up with him and be glad you've got a man.'

She felt the anger welling up inside her. It was the same anger that she had felt in the market, and when she had broken the porcelain figurine. She raised her hand as if to strike him but he took her wrist firmly and pulled her arm down. A woman was staring at them. Freya wanted to cry, ashamed that everything was getting out of control.

'If Roger is the father, then she's my stepdaughter.' She knew she sounded ridiculous but she was grasping for some way out of all this.

'You're young, you've got everything ahead of you. One day when you're old, you'll look back on this and it will be a tiny speck, a little bit of the learning curve of your life. You came here thinking things would work out but you just couldn't find where to fit in. I feel the same. We're a bit alike. Don't use that baby because you want to change the world. Let her be cared for by people who want a baby they can love and bring up decently.'

She thought she might cry.

'The best thing you can do, all of you, is go back to your country.'

'That feels like running away.'

'You asked me that night whether I thought you people were doing any good.'

'Your eyes were closed. I thought you were asleep. You didn't answer.'

'Well I'm tellin' you now. You people have fenced yourselves in. Hundreds of years of being the big white *bwana*, and you still can't see what's in front of you or how people resent you.'

'Me as well?'

'Yes. You think you're helping but when things get tough, you get back in the Land Rover, close the windows and drive like hell back down the road. You stay here with all this stuff going on and you'll cause more trouble. Hundreds, thousands of Africans getting beaten, killed, tortured, no one does anything. But one of you goes missin' and it's in all the newspapers.'

She remembered the letter in *Transition*. It said that the West always sent rescue missions whenever whites were being attacked.

She could hear what her mother would say. *I didn't think it would work out. Those places are full of savages. I've seen them on TV. You're better off here.*

Someone shouted 'Howzat!' and the stumps fell. Wensley began clapping and walked across the pitch to congratulate the players. She knew the conversation was over. She went back to the car, hoping that no one could see that she was crying.

She didn't want to go home but she had nowhere else to go. She still had the key to the charity office. She would go there and think about things before she went home.

*

She slowly unlocked the door of the charity office, afraid of what might be inside. The room was bare and smelled of disinfectant. She sat on the floor in the stuffy room and stared at the air conditioner that was hanging off the wall.

She was about to leave when Satish arrived.

'What are you doing here?' he said. 'Everything is finished now. We've closed down. I just stopped by to check if everything's okay. We're still paying rent.'

She started to cry and then told him about Wensley and the baby. She wanted to tell him about sleeping with Wensley and her suspicion that Roger was the father of Keziah's baby. But she was afraid of what he would think about her.

'Look, you've just got caught up with something. The world seems crazy at the moment. But he's right about you not taking the baby to the UK. I heard Enoch Powell on the radio today. He said that there was no legal responsibility for Britain to take us in with our "so-called" passports. I hope Heath will stand up to him.'

Her mother had smiled and nodded when they had heard Enoch Powell's speech about the rivers of blood on the radio. What would her mother say if she arrived home with a brown baby?

'Go home now before the traffic builds up,' Satish said.

For a moment, she thought she saw the same look that she had seen in Wensley's eyes. It would be easy to be in love with Satish. But he was married and she couldn't think of him in that way.

'Will I see you again before you leave?' she said.

'Probably not,' he said as he locked the door.

She drove home with tears streaming down her face. She had lost everything that was important to her.

TWENTY-NINE

When Freya's car drew up, Roger rushed towards it, almost falling over Jock as he opened the car door.

'Where have you been? Jimmy said that he hadn't seen you all day,' he said, cursing as he tried to jam the door shut. 'You could have left a note.' His hair was thinning at the front, leaving reddened patches across his lined forehead. Had she ever really found him attractive? There really was nothing left. She wanted an excuse to be alone, to think about what had happened.

'I had to go and meet Satish in Kampala. He wanted to talk about the charity. It took longer than I thought it would. I'm really tired.'

'I thought you had finished with all that,' Roger said. He struggled with the lighter as he lit a cigarette.

'The smell of your cigarettes makes me feel sick.'

She had never dared say it before.

His face turned pink and she almost felt sorry for him.

'I'm helping keep an eye on the place, until Satish gets back.'

'I wish you'd stop. It's dangerous. He won't be coming back, not while Amin is around. You still aren't well enough.'

'Well, I'm going to do it and there is nothing you can do to stop me.' She was trembling.

Roger picked up a piece of paper from the table and gave it to her.

'Anyway, it doesn't matter any more what you want to do. This note has just come from Don.'

The attacks on the Asians are getting worse. And there have been some incidents with msungus. The watu can't always tell the difference between us and the Asians. There was a report last night that a white man was shot in the arm at a roadblock. The High Commissioner has asked me to put us all on alert. You need to get plenty of supplies in, just in case we can't get to Kampala. We need to prepare in case we have to leave in a convoy. You should get the PWD chair cushions ready to line the windows of the car. From now on, only go out if you have to. Some of the women and children might have to leave quickly if things get any worse.

Were things really that bad? Don liked to exaggerate, to make himself sound important. He had told the story more than once about the time in 1966 when the Kabaka of Buganda had been thrown out of his Palace at the Lubiri by Obote's men. Don and the other project men had patrolled around the compound at night with guns, while all the women and children gathered together and camped on old mattresses in Don and Mavis' house. But the gang of villagers who were said to be marching towards the compound to attack it with *pangas* had never appeared.

'Is it really true?' Freya said.

'Don knows what he's talking about.'

He took the paper from her and turned it over.

'Read this,' he said.

Whether we like it or not, we Brits are caught up in it. He's going to punish us for what the British Government is doing. He is saying ridiculous things, like the British should have employed Africans to build the railways instead of bringing in Indians all those years ago. If any of the women and children from the project want to leave now, the High Commission has said they will do all they can to help them get flights.

'The British Government should do more to help the Asians,' Freya said.

Roger had the same alarmed look on his face that he had when she had confronted Bobby about the bilharzia.

'I think you should stay out of the politics,' he said. 'It's not easy for the government. Mavis says that the High Commission has been told to try and keep down the numbers of people leaving. But don't tell your friend Satish. It's a very tricky situation.'

'Do you know what will happen to people when they get to the UK if they haven't got friends and relatives to stay with?'

'They are thinking of setting up reception centres, sort of camps, for them to go to.'

Camps? The word scared her. As a child, she had seen flickering black and white images on the small screen of their newly bought TV. They were pictures of terrified, skeletal people in concentration camps. She had cried uncontrollably. Her mother had said, *That's the war, it's over, we've got to forget it and get on with things.*

She imagined Satish and Adam, cold and shell-shocked, sharing a bunk bed in an old army barracks in the middle of the English countryside.

'So you've got a chance to get away from all this nonsense. I assume that you'll want to leave with the others.'

Freya tried to fight back tears as Roger put his arm around her.

'I'm sure you'll feel better when you get home to the UK. You can forget all this stuff. I'll have to work out my contract. But the time will fly by.'

He drew on his cigarette and puffed out the smoke.

'Look, I know it has been difficult for you to settle in and that you just want to help. That's what we are all supposed to be here for. But you have to accept that there isn't much you can do. These people aren't like us. They never will be. They are way behind us on the scale of evolution.'

Freya's stomach lurched with anger.

'That's just a stupid idea that you and the others all keep telling each other so often that in the end you think it's true. You would just hate to think that the ... *watu* might be cleverer than you are. If you did think that, it would take away your reason for being here.'

He had the look on his face she had seen the day he kicked the dog when it growled at Keziah. He was trying to control his temper. She usually just walked away when he was like this, to let him cool down. But instead she looked him directly in the eye and said, 'Actually, I lied. I saw Satish but that's not why I went to town.'

He sat down, and then slowly crumpled into the chair.

'I really am tired of all this. Oh, all right, it was a lie. You had your reason, I suppose. I don't think I want to know any more. Let's just forget it all and have some supper.'

She knew that supper would be eaten in silence, a punishment for what she had done. She would have preferred to have a fight with him like those she used to have with her brother when she was a child. They were fierce and painful, but over quickly.

'Actually, I went to see Wensley,' she said.

'What on earth for? What is going on?' He became red in the face and sat upright.

'I went to ask him if he would give me the baby.'

'What? And what were you going to do with it?'

'I wanted to take her and bring her up as my own.'

'You really are crazy.'

'But he says that his sister will take her and bring her up in Dominica.'

Roger stubbed out his cigarette and stood up.

'I'm sorry, so sorry. I can see now that you really are ill, like you were before. We'll get you to a doctor tomorrow.'

'I wanted that baby.' Her voice was a strained scream.

He tried to put his arm around her but she pushed him away.

'I know it might be my fault that you can't get

pregnant. Maybe there is something wrong with me. I'll get it checked out. Being in this place doesn't help. When we're back in the UK, we can try again. It'll be easier at home, to relax, to get things right,' Roger said.

There was a rumble of thunder. The wind began to blow. The washing waved and tugged at the line until pants and shirts blew around. Freya saw a shirt fly off the line. She ran outside and chased and picked up the clothes as they scattered around the garden. Jimmy laughed as he watched her. Had he been listening to their argument?

'Come inside, leave them,' Roger said. 'He'll get the rest.'

'No, he won't. He's hopeless. I'll have to sack him. He keeps hiding things. On purpose.'

'Stop it!' Roger shouted. 'What is the matter with you?'

She began to cry. 'I can't go on like this any more.'

'What do you mean?'

'I think I want a divorce.' She didn't know where the words had come from.

Her mother had said that she should be grateful to get a husband. To leave him would be seen as failure. And who would want a divorced woman? But she had said it, and now nothing would be the same.

'Don't be ridiculous,' Roger said. 'It's this place. It does things to people. Changes them. Plays with your mind. This is not our country. Not our home. When you get away from here, you'll see things differently. You'll go back to normal. It's my fault. I've neglected you. You don't understand. There are things that have gone on with me.'

'What things?' she said.

'I can't really talk about it. I just want you to know

that's why I haven't been able to give you much attention. Everything is such a mess here.'

'Wensley says that we're all partly to blame for this … stuff, with Amin and the Asians.'

'Wensley? What?' Roger hesitated, as if afraid to go on. 'When have you been having these conversations with him?' He sighed. 'Of course, I remember now.'

There was an awkward silence.

'What happened when he stayed the night?'

She blushed and turned away from him.

'I saw the way you danced with him at the nightclub.'

Why hadn't he said anything before? Telling him the truth now would just make things worse. She wished Keziah was still there to burst through the door and interrupt them. When she was working quietly around the house, she had always been there as an excuse to stop talking, a reason to make them control their feelings.

Freya thought about the chessboard. She was the king trapped by a rook and a knight. She had to make some kind of move to escape, to distract him.

'And what about you and Keziah?' she asked.

'I don't know what you mean.'

'Mavis and the others tried to warn me about her.'

'They're just gossips,' he said. 'They think all the *msungu* men are just waiting for their chance to sleep with African women. Not surprising, the way some of them look.'

'That night, after the dinner party,' Freya said slowly, 'you gave her a lift, with those VSOs. And you didn't come back till the morning.'

'I told you there are things I can't tell you about.'

'Tell me the truth,' Freya said.

'Nothing happened. Nothing important.' He looked away, avoiding her eyes. There was a long silence.

'But I did kiss her, once.'

Freya picked up the small Victorian paperweight that sat on the desktop. Her grandmother had given it to her when she was a child. She held it between her hands and gently moved it in her palms. It was brightly coloured, with the swirling colours of a peacock. If she threw it at him it might knock him out, with the blood streaming down his face. She let it slip from her hands and it bounced on the stone floor and then landed unbroken. Roger picked it up and put it carefully back on the desk.

'When?' Freya said.

'It was when she first started working for me. One evening I tried to talk to her about her home, her family, her boyfriend, the usual things. She just misunderstood and kissed me, thought I wanted sex. I was lonely. It was nothing.'

'She's a prostitute.'

'No, she isn't.' He looked angry.

'She works in that bar.'

'Who told you that?'

'Mavis and the others. Everyone knows. Wensley told me he had seen you with her in that place.'

'Oh, him again. Well now you can tell me the truth about him. I just hope you haven't slept with him. I've heard that he's always in that bar. You could have caught something.'

Her stomach lurched. Now she just wanted to punish Roger, to tell him that, for the first time in her life, she had really wanted someone, so much so that in that moment she hadn't cared what happened. But Roger had spoiled everything, dirtying the thought of Wensley in her mind.

'I don't believe you didn't sleep with her. Get out. Go and find another whore.' She could hardly believe that she had used the word.

Roger stubbed out his cigarette.

'If that's what you want?' he said.

She didn't really want him to leave. But it had all gone too far. She could stop him from leaving, say she was sorry and ask him to forget everything and ask him if they could just start again. But it was too late. He got up and walked out. She heard the car engine revving up and roaring as he left the house.

She sank into the chair, too exhausted to cry. Everything was spoiled. It was true what people said about Africa; it was full of darkness, horrors and pain. It could rot your soul. That's what she'd read somewhere. Marriage wasn't supposed to be like this.

She would have to leave and go home along with the other wives. That was the only answer.

Had she really said that she wanted a divorce? The baby, Wensley; it was already beginning to feel like a bad dream. The cold winters, the power cuts, the strikes; that was what was real. Everything would be different when they were at home together, settled in their new house, maybe pushing a pram together to the shops. They could forget the horrible things they had said to each other. When he got back, she would confess to him that she had kissed Wensley. There was no need for him to know that she had slept with him.

She needed a drink. She took a tonic water from the

fridge and searched at the back of the cupboard for the *waragi* bottle. It was half-empty. Who had been drinking it? Surely not the pregnant Keziah? It was probably Jimmy. Roger would have marked the bottle to try to catch him out. She knew she could never do that.

THIRTY

The gin and tonic made Freya drowsy and she fell asleep in the chair. She woke with a start, confused for a moment as to where she was. The wall clock showed that it was ten past midnight. There was no point in waiting up for Roger. If he had gone to find a prostitute, it would be her fault. She would have to live with it and say nothing. She had been angry, accusing him of doing something that she had done herself. Her own guilt had made her angrier than she should have been. Roger wasn't a bad person. You had to work at marriage. You couldn't just run away.

She heard footsteps on the veranda. She jumped up quickly and tried to smooth her crumpled, tangled hair.

'Where have you been? I was getting worried,' she said. There was silence and then a knock on the door. She was scared. Who could it be so late at night? Perhaps it was the *askari*?

'Hello Freya, can I come in?' a voice said.

Don stood in the doorway, mopping his brow. What on earth did he want so late at night?

271

'Don, come in,' she said. 'Roger isn't here. He went to town. I don't know when he will be back.' Don looked unwell, old and drained of life. His clothes were covered in mud and sweat stains.

'Don, what is it? It's late. Sit down, please.' Don put his head in his hands. His hands were trembling.

'Are you ill, what is it?' Freya asked.

'Freya, I have some terrible news. Mavis and I …'

'Oh God, is it Mavis? What's happened?'

Don spoke slowly. There were tears on his cheeks. Freya's heart raced, afraid of what he was going to say.

'We were on our way back from the cinema. We stopped. A crowd was standing around something in the road.'

Freya remembered the dead dog in the road. Why would Don be so upset about a dog, a goat, or even a body in the road?

'I don't understand,' she said.

'My dear, I'm so sorry. There's been an accident.'

'Who?' One of the project workers? People were always driving when they were drunk. Don must feel responsible.

'My dear, I don't know how to tell you. It's Roger. He's had an accident.'

'Oh my God. Where is he?' Freya said.

'At the hospital.'

'What's happened? I have to get there. Can you take me? I'll get my things.'

'No dear, I'm sorry. I don't know how to say this. But he's dead.'

'Dead?' Freya repeated it as if she didn't understand what it meant.

'No. It's a mistake. Where is he? It'll be okay when he sees me.' She dug her fingers into the skin on her wrist. I'm dreaming, I'll wake up in a minute.

'They couldn't do anything to save him. It was a huge lorry; it smashed into his car head on.'

Don put his arm around her shoulder.

'I'll take you to the hospital now,' he said.

'No, it's a lie. You people all hate me,' she screamed. But she knew that she was the one who had caused him to die. She had started the argument by telling him the truth about Wensley and the baby. She had always known that the dead dog in the road had been Roger. In her head a voice said, 'Kill us a dog, Kotonu; kill us a dog, Kotonu.' The gods wanted a sacrifice. It was all her fault. She screamed and then fainted.

*

She was in the back seat of a car. Please God, let it be a dream. Let it be a mistake so that someone else would be lying there. She wanted her mother. She would have known what to say to comfort her.

'There, there, it's not your fault, we'll manage,' Mavis said. Her arm was around Freya's shoulders.

*

The big, modern hospital was usually a comforting sight, a place to treat the symptoms of malaria, dengue fever, gut-wrenching stomach bugs or any of the other strange and mysterious tropical diseases. Now it was a place of terror.

Freya's body was rigid and glued to the car seat. She couldn't move to get out. The night was warm as usual but she was shivering.

'Come on, dear,' Mavis said, gently helped her stand, and then linked her arm with Freya's.

They took the lift to the sixth floor, to the private wing where the expatriates were treated. Everything was eerily quiet except for the beeping of machines and the occasional shout or sob from a patient. A heavily pregnant nurse was slowly mopping the floor in the hospital corridor. The stench of urine was mixed with the smell of disinfectant. Water was flowing from under a toilet door. The murky water seeped into her sandals. Freya stopped and retched and tears filled her eyes. She slipped and Mavis reached out and caught her.

They stopped outside a side ward. She was scared of how she would feel when she saw him. He had been alive just a few hours before. It must be a mistake. The nightmare would end soon and she would wake up.

The blood-covered bodies that she had sometimes seen lying by the sides of the road had never seemed like real people. When her father had died, she and her mother had decided not to visit the undertaker to see him the night before the funeral.

Better to remember him how he was. He wouldn't have wanted it, her mother had said. But was her mother just scared that the dead body would make her confront thoughts of her own death? When they had watched the coffin slowly disappearing as the curtains closed, Freya had felt guilty that they had left him all alone.

They were taken by a nurse to the side ward where Roger was lying on the hard hospital bed. He was never ill and he hated hospitals. A large cut on his head was covered in dried, congealed blood. Apart from that, he looked the same. She thought she saw a twitch in his cheek.

Her heart beat wildly, and she fainted again.

THIRTY-ONE

It was a long walk up to the church at the top of the hill. Don walked quickly with his head bowed. Freya and Mavis, wearing high-heeled shoes instead of their usual sandals, struggled to keep up with him. Freya kept stumbling and wanted to turn back. Mavis took her hand. Freya wanted to pull away from her but Mavis gripped it tightly. She could smell her flowery perfume and it made her feel sick.

The graveyard was well looked after. A man dressed in ragged shorts and a torn shirt slashed the grass with a *panga*. There were European names on most of the headstones; graves of men, women and children of all ages, killed by tropical diseases or by terrible accidents.

All these dead people were so far from home. The village people in Uganda buried their relatives in their compounds, keeping them forever with them. Soon there would be no one to visit his grave. Freya thought about Roger's mother. He had been her only child. She hadn't known what to do to stop her sobbing on the phone. Freya remembered that she had said she would take a photo of the service but in the end she was too embarrassed to take out her Polaroid camera.

The church was full of shadowy figures. There was a smell of sweat from the rarely worn suits and dresses. She looked straight ahead as she walked behind the coffin flanked by Don and Mavis. The South African priest she had met in the village officiated at the service. After Roger's death was reported in the *Uganda Argus*, he had contacted her and offered to do it.

Freya started sobbing as they lowered the coffin into the grave. Don held her arm. Mavis looked anxious and drained. People from the project who had come to pay their respects looked uncomfortable in their dark suits and heavy day dresses. Satish stood apart from everyone. She wanted to talk to him but he waved and walked away down the hill.

The priest said how sorry he was. 'Africa is like a beautiful unfaithful woman,' he said. 'She can seduce you and then destroy you.' It sounded like something he said to everyone. Roger's death had nothing to do with Africa. It was her fault. She suddenly wanted him to be there. To catch his eye and signal to him that it was time to leave and go home. Instead, she had to stand alone, waiting for Don to finish his conversation.

She was a widow now. It sounded strange for a young woman of twenty-three to be called that.

THIRTY-TWO

3 SEPTEMBER

Pictures, wooden carvings, books, ornaments, kitchenware and crockery were set out on the wooden floor ready to be packed up. The carefully chosen blue pottery and linen was a sad reminder of the excitement Freya had once felt at the thought of going to another country and trying to start a new life, of trying to forget the miscarriage. Now everything would go back to the council house and her mother would complain that there was nowhere to put anything.

After the funeral, Mavis and one or two of the other wives had come round to see if she was all right, and to ask if they could do anything. But she didn't know what to ask for and they struggled to find something to talk about, and seemed anxious to leave as soon as they could.

As she took the last picture off the wall and laid it on the floor, she heard the sound of a car outside. Her mind still played tricks and for a moment she thought it was Roger. She wanted to hide away from whoever it was.

Jock barked and growled and then she heard Satish

saying, 'No, go away.' She hadn't seen him since the funeral. She had forgotten about what was happening in the world outside the bungalow and she was confused and guilty about whether she wanted to be reminded of it.

Satish's pale blue safari suit hung loosely on him and his forehead was more lined than she remembered.

'I'm sorry to disturb you,' he said. 'I can see you're busy. I can come back some other time.'

The sound of his voice made her want to cry, to sob, to ask him to explain what it all meant, to say she didn't know how she could face the future and going back home alone. But instead, she said, 'No, please come in, it's good to see you.'

He was silent for a few minutes.

'How are you feeling? It's hard to believe that something like this could happen to someone so young,' he said.

She had forgotten what he must have been going through. It was a death for him too; the death of his life in the country he had always known. It was the opposite for her. She would be going back to the place she called home. But was it really home any more? Would her thoughts and dreams about Keziah, Wensley and the baby disappear when she got there? Would they just die along with Roger, buried in a faraway place?

'I'm getting used to it all, slowly. The nightmares and the sleepless nights are still the worst part. But how are things with you and Adam?'

'We are getting ready to leave. No one knows the exact dates yet. Arrangements are being made for us to depart. It can't be too soon. Amin is threatening to put us in army concentration camps if we don't go.'

At least she was alive and no one was threatening her.

'I didn't really want to bother you. I can see you are busy. It's just that I've got some things and I wondered if you could take them to the UK for me and keep them until I can collect them. We can only take a couple of suitcases with us.'

She saw tears in his eyes.

'But I can see you've got enough stuff to pack up,' he said.

'No, no, it's fine. We … I have quite a big freight allowance.'

'If you're sure. Thanks,' he said.

He went outside to the car and came back carrying a large musical instrument inlaid with an ivory pattern. Freya had seen one on the cover of a Beatles album. Then he fetched a carved wooden statue with a large head. There were raised lumps on the chest that could be breasts. It was difficult to tell if it was a man or a woman and it was different from those she had seen in the market and the craft shops.

'We think it came from the Congo,' he said. 'There is a lot more stuff. We'll just have to leave it behind. But my father gave me the sitar and the carving and I just can't bear to give them away to someone I don't know.'

Freya nodded. She was touched that he trusted her to look after and care for things that were so precious to him.

'Thank you so much. I'll always remember our friendship,' he said.

His eyes met hers. She looked away quickly.

'You'll be with your wife again soon.'

'It's not that simple,' he said.

Was there something wrong with his marriage? She

didn't think that she could cope with a confession of some sort from him. She didn't want to get into something deeper. Perhaps they would meet up somewhere one day. But that wasn't really likely. And things would be different in the cold light of home.

'I heard that the British High Commissioner is getting into trouble for what he's been saying and that he is being sent home as well,' Satish said, as if he was trying to change the subject. She had found it difficult to listen to the news since Roger's death. When she got home, people would ask her questions about what had happened and there would be no way of explaining anything to them that they would understand. Or maybe they would have no interest, preferring to ignore things that were happening in a far-off country.

'But what about you? Do you know what you will do … when you get to the UK?' Freya asked.

'Getting Adam and myself out of here seems the only thing that matters at the moment. After that I'm not really sure. My sister has settled in Coventry. She says she has heard that there might be a job in Warwick for someone to work as a clerk at the Council Offices. She's even found a little house for us to rent but the neighbours are already complaining that they don't want too many Indians living in the street.'

'Did you sort out Adam's papers?'

'Yes, thank goodness. I suppose I'm worried about him and how he'll settle down. But I hear the schools are good.'

Freya wanted to reassure him that everything would be all right for them, that people would accept them. But she wasn't sure.

'What will you do?'

She was surprised by the question. She hadn't thought beyond the trauma of packing up and getting a flight back.

'What I was doing before, I suppose. I'll have to find some clerical work. I'll need to stay with my mother at first. But maybe I'll try and find my own place when I have enough money.'

'Well,' Satish said, 'you could think of doing some further studies.'

'I'm too old.'

'There is a thing called the Open University,' he said.

She remembered that one of the women she worked with had done it, and now she was training to be a primary school teacher.

'I'm not clever enough,' she said.

'That's not true. I saw the things you were good at. Sympathising with people. Always trying to work out what made them tick. You can study that kind of thing. Social work, psychology, maybe.'

She realised that he was the only person she had ever known who had said that she could do things.

'Can I have your address? I'd like to write to you.'

'Yes, that would be nice,' she said, smiling at the thought of what her mother might say if she brought an Indian home for Sunday afternoon tea. Maybe coronation chicken sandwiches instead of salmon would be served.

'You are looking better,' he said.

There was silence. He stood up to leave. She fought back the tears.

'You shouldn't blame yourself,' he said.

'It was my fault.'

'No,' he said, 'don't say that.'

'If we hadn't had an argument, he wouldn't have gone out in the car.'

'You mustn't think that, please.' He hesitated, as if he wanted to say something.

'Look, I think that there may be another explanation.'

What did he mean?

'That's partly why I came here. It wasn't just to ask you to take the things for me.' He looked at his watch. 'I need to pick up Adam now. But I have to go to the office tomorrow to sort out some bills. If you meet me there tomorrow at ten, we can talk.'

Freya heard his car revving as it drove away. He always drove too fast. He meant well but she couldn't imagine that he had anything to say that would make her feel better.

THIRTY-THREE

Freya drove up the road through the university campus and remembered how nervous and excited she had felt the first time she had visited the charity office. Now it all looked different. Soldiers were everywhere, standing nervously holding their guns or crouched on the ground, smoking. They glared at her as she drove past them but no one stopped her.

Most of the staff houses looked deserted, with the doors closed and the shutters down. The lawns were turning to brown dust.

She parked outside the office. Satish's car wasn't there. The door of the charity office was locked. Where was Satish? Had something awful happened to him? She was about to leave when the door opened.

'Come in,' Satish said. 'I locked the door to be on the safe side. My car is parked round the corner.'

'I was scared for a moment,' she said.

The room was empty apart from a few cardboard boxes piled up in the corner.

'Is everything finished now?' Freya said.

'Yes. But I've asked someone from the Rotary if they will just keep an eye on things until we have to close. I don't think the army will be interested in ransacking this place again for a few cardboard boxes and an old typewriter. But you never know.'

The bare, yellow-painted walls of the office were littered with lumps of Blu Tack and old drawing pins. The room always smelled damp and stuffy. But she realised that it was a place where she had felt in charge of her life and was not always waiting for someone to criticise her. She was sad that she might never see it again.

'Let me get you some tea,' he said.

The tea usually tasted awful but it seemed rude to refuse the offer.

Satish boiled the water on an old gas ring and then poured it over the tea leaves. He picked up a tin of condensed milk and splashed some into the cup. The smell of gas and the sight of the whitish-yellow milk made Freya feel sick.

'I asked you to come so that we could talk, but I'm not really sure now if I should tell you,' Satish said.

There was only one small window in the room. Through it, she studied a crumbling brick wall. She was afraid of what he might say. She wanted to move on to another life as soon as she could, to forget everything that had happened, to start again.

'Maybe I should leave,' Freya said, wondering if it had been a good idea to come.

'No, please,' he said. 'I think you should know. It may make you feel better. Help you heal.'

She wasn't sure that she wanted to know the truth or whatever he was going to tell her. It couldn't bring Roger back.

'What I'm about to tell you … it is just a suspicion.'

There was a poem she had read at school about an old … an ancient mariner. He wouldn't let someone go until they had listened to his story. She picked up her bag as if to leave.

'No, please, stay.'

She took a deep breath and sipped the sickly-tasting tea.

'It was at one of those parties at the High Commission,' Satish said.

Freya thought about Wensley and was afraid of what he was going to say.

'Well, a friend of mine, Sony Patel, saw me talking to Roger and asked me who he was. He thought he'd seen him somewhere before. Then, after the party, he rang me and said he'd remembered where he'd seen him.'

Freya's heart began to beat faster. She didn't want to hear any more.

'He said he'd seen him a few times in a bar in Masindi.'

Freya saw the Paradise Bar and the men with the cigarettes hanging from their mouths.

'He said that Roger was always with the same person,' Satish said. 'An American guy, a lecturer from here at the university. You might have seen him. He has long blond hair and a beard. He drives around on a motorbike and always wears those wide trousers and bright-coloured shirts. He's usually got a couple of female students riding on the back.'

Freya remembered seeing him one day on the Kampala Road. She had been jealous of the way that he roared along the road, his hair flying behind him as if he didn't care at all what people thought about him. He wasn't the kind of person she thought that Roger would want to mix with.

'It seems that there have been a lot of rumours about this guy.'

Uganda was full of rumours. She didn't want to hear any more.

'People said that he could be a spy, maybe a double agent.'

Freya thought this sounded ridiculous. That only happened in stories.

'A spy? Why would anyone spy?' she asked.

'Since independence, a lot of countries in Africa have turned to Russia, to communism. At first, the British were happy with Amin because he was so pro-British, pro the West. But now he's turned against you, and the Soviets are trying to get control here.'

What did this have to do with Roger? The word 'spy' sounded too glamorous for Roger.

'So, you see, it's just possible that Roger was doing a bit of spying for the High Commission. There is a lot of it going on. Just very small stuff. People being asked to keep an eye out for things, pick up what they can from people in bars.'

A piece of tea leaf stuck in her throat and she coughed and retched. Satish fetched a glass of water.

'I'm sorry, I didn't want to upset you. But what I really wanted you to know was that he may not have died in an accident. He could have been deliberately targeted by someone, maybe thinking he was more important than he was, or even mistaking him for someone else. Those kinds of mysterious car accidents happen all the time.'

It was too difficult to understand, to take in.

'I just wanted to say that you shouldn't blame yourself for his death. It could have been other things,' Satish said.

She felt faint and clutched her head as she sat down.

'Sorry, I hope this hasn't made things worse for you,' he said.

She knew that Satish was a good person. He always wanted to do the best thing for everyone. But it was no use. She knew that she would always blame herself for how Roger might have died. In any case, how could they have known he was going to leave the house that night? But maybe he had gone to the bar and someone had seen him there and followed him? She would never know. Her head was spinning.

'Thank you for telling me,' she said.

Satish's face was taut and worried.

'Perhaps our paths will cross somewhere in the UK,' he said. She knew that was unlikely. She just nodded. She wanted to be alone to think about Roger.

She sat for a few minutes in her car, trying to calm herself. Was it ever possible to know someone else properly? Even her mother probably had dark secrets. She had known someone called Roger, but only that part of him that he wanted her to know. Would relationships always be this difficult?

THIRTY-FOUR

Freya could still smell Roger's aftershave and his cigarettes, and the odours of grease and oil were everywhere. When she finally left the house, she would have nothing left of him. Had she ever really loved him? They had got married hastily to make the best of things. Maybe it would have worked out in the end. Happily ever after, like the fairy stories. He had helped her to enjoy sex. He had made her laugh, sometimes. Maybe that was enough in any marriage.

She had lain awake for hours thinking about what Satish had told her. If it was true, there was a whole part of Roger's life that she didn't know about. If he had lied about all this, what was the truth about Keziah and the baby? She wanted to forget it all. She tried to focus on leaving, on what she needed to pack, on what could be thrown or given away. Images of Keziah kept floating into her mind. Then she remembered the night of the first dinner party. Perhaps someone might be able to help her.

She drove to Mulago Hospital and sat in the car park. She felt dizzy. The last time she had been there was to see

Roger's body in the private wing on the sixth floor. Mavis had complained that the top floor was now overrun with drunken army officers and all their wives.

She looked up at the large, modern, six-storey hospital. Everyone in Uganda was proud of it. People still used traditional medicines, but the hospital was there if everything else failed. The hospital was like a village or a marketplace, with relatives bringing food and sitting around all day in big family groups.

She went in through the main entrance doors and walked through the Accident and Emergency department, past a long queue of coughing, feverish-looking, emaciated and injured people. A woman with a baby on her back called out 'Doctor' to her and pulled on her sleeve. Freya pushed the woman's hand away and walked more quickly. She stepped round the cleaners and their pails of dirty water and torn old cloths.

People were lying on the floor in the corridors. Inside the wards, she glimpsed patients, still wrapped in their own clothes, lying on bare mattresses on rusty bed frames.

'Excuse me, I'm looking for the administrative offices,' she said to a tall, thin, heavily pregnant nurse who was limping slowly down the corridor as if she was weary of all the chaos and commotion of the hospital.

'Wrong place. It's at the old hospital. Go that way,' the nurse said.

The path was steep and narrow. Freya walked carefully. She stepped aside from time to time to let the porters and their trolleys pass. She hoped that the patients wouldn't fall off on the way down.

When she reached the old hospital, one of the porters directed her to an office. It was the wrong one. She began to despair of finding him and then she saw him in the room next door. He was sitting at his desk sorting through papers.

'Mike?' she said.

He looked puzzled. For a moment, she wasn't sure if it was him. His hair was cut short, close to his head. He was dressed in a white shirt, tie and cotton trousers. The John Lennon wire-framed spectacles made him look older than she remembered. His desk was covered in neat piles of papers.

'I'm Freya,' she said. 'Do you remember? The dinner party?'

'Of course. We had only just arrived, hadn't we?' He blushed. 'And, of course, I heard about your husband. It was a terrible thing to happen. I am so sorry. It must be awful for you.'

Freya was afraid that she might start crying. She had made a mistake in coming to find him. It was unfair to try to get him involved with her obsessions.

'Can I help you with anything?' he asked. 'I expect there's a lot of paperwork to do before you leave.'

'Yes, I hadn't realised…'

'I think you'll need to go to the almoner's office on the third floor of the new building. I can take you there.'

'Thank you,' she said and got up to leave, trying to control the tears she could feel coming.

'No, please, sit down for a moment,' Mike said as he stood up and put his hand on her arm. 'I can see you're upset at having to come to this place again.'

'No, it's fine. I am sure I can find it,' she said.

'Please, just take it easy for a few minutes,' he said. 'Everything is so difficult for everyone.'

He put his head in his hands.

'I came here thinking it would be fun, as well as useful, of course. I thought that a hospital would be a safe place to be. But you can see what it's like. All these unpaid bills, for a start. The nurses do their best but you can't blame them if they would rather sit in their offices than look after the patients. And people use this place as somewhere to hide from the army, or from the police and Amin's men. But the thugs still come inside the hospital trying to find people. I expect you noticed the bullet marks on the walls.'

Freya hadn't realised that the dents on the peeling, dirty paintwork were caused by guns and she shuddered.

'What will you do? Will you leave soon?'

'Well, Sam has gone home. It all got too difficult in the village where he was staying. The army trashed it and some women were raped and a couple of children just disappeared from his class.'

Freya wanted to vomit. She knew that he was talking about women and children that she might have met in the village. She touched her neck. The necklace and the earrings that had been stolen from her seemed small and insignificant now.

'But I'll stay for a bit and see how things go. It would be like failure if I went home. I wouldn't be able to stop thinking about it all the time.' He hesitated. 'And I've got a girlfriend. She's a nurse, a *muganda*, from around here and I'm frightened to leave her.'

The phone rang and he answered, speaking in what

sounded like fluent Luganda. Then it rang again but he didn't pick it up.

'Look, it's my morning break. Shall we go outside and get some air?'

He made two cups of instant coffee with condensed milk and they took them outside and sat on two old plastic chairs under a large baobab tree. She didn't know why, but for the first time since she had arrived in Uganda she felt relaxed and at home. It was as if she didn't want to be anywhere else at that moment.

'It's a shame all this is happening,' he said. 'I heard from Sam that he had seen you in the village and that people there thought you were a good person.'

She knew he was just trying to make her feel better about things. The people in the village had hardly noticed her, apart from Miriam, the woman who had given her the herbs.

'I was thinking about the dinner party at your house the other day. So much has happened since then. It seems like years ago.'

He smiled at her and she saw the young boy she had met that evening.

'I could see you were a bit uncomfortable with what that guy Don was saying. I suppose when someone has been here as long as he has, he can't help himself. It's difficult to change, to admit that you might have been wrong.'

The midday sun overhead came in glimpses between the leaves of the tree. It beat down on her bare head.

'I felt a bit sorry for you, stuck in that place.' He looked at his watch. 'Sorry, maybe I shouldn't have said that.'

Freya moved her chair into the shade.

'It has been difficult. There is so much to try and understand. But now I'm scared that when I get home it will all drift away and when I try to explain things to people, they will just see things in the same old way. An invasion of coloured people that they don't want. That it's somehow the Asians' fault.'

'I don't know. I'm not so sure. Not everyone is like that. People are changing quite fast in the way they see things. It's just that not everyone's caught up.'

He was right. She didn't have to listen to those people. She could find new friends who thought like she did. Or get a job where she could use what she had learned.

'Look, you need to go to the almoner's office before they close for lunch.'

'About that dinner party,' Freya said, trembling slightly and still unsure if she should ask him, but the words came spilling out.

'There is something I want to ask you.'

'Oh, sure,' he said, sounding surprised.

'After the party, Roger gave you both a lift,' she said.

Mike looked puzzled for a moment. 'Oh yes, I remember now,' he said.

'He didn't … come back that night.'

Mike frowned and she was embarrassed that she had lured him into something that he didn't want to get involved with, but she couldn't stop herself.

'Would you mind telling me what happened?'

'I'm not sure what you mean. He gave us a lift back into town, that's all.'

He looked at his watch. She had made a mistake. He didn't want to talk about it.

'I'm sorry. I shouldn't have asked. I can see that you are busy. You have to go back to the office,' Freya said.

'Well, I do remember something.' He looked at her as if judging how she might react.

'We stopped at a bar, the one called Paradise. He, Roger, said he needed to just pop in to see someone. Sam and I did think it was a bit strange because it was quite late by then. But we were both feeling a bit tipsy so we went in with him.'

'And Keziah, did she go in as well?'

Mike looked away as if he was avoiding her eyes.

'Keziah? Oh, you mean the house girl. Yes, she did.'

Freya's heart started pounding.

'When we got inside, Roger went straight up to this guy. You might have seen him around, long hair, always on a motorbike. They shook hands as if they had arranged to meet. There was another guy with them. I didn't know who he was. But since then, I've seen him here. He works for the High Commission and they come to the hospital from time to time to monitor the British aid programme. Well, I think it's the same chap. I can't really be sure.'

Freya knew that was probably all she needed to know. It fitted in with what Satish had told her. She knew that she should just leave it there but she couldn't help herself.

'The house girl, Keziah, what did she do?'

He hesitated. Freya's heart sank again.

'There was some music and we danced ...'

Freya interrupted him. 'Roger and her?'

'I can't really remember. Maybe ... but only for one quick dance, and then I ...' He stopped. 'I danced with her after that, for quite a long time. We kept on drinking. So it's all a bit of a blur.'

'And after?' Freya said, her heart beating faster.

'Sorry, I can't really remember. I think he just dropped us off at our friends' flat where we were staying. It was very late by then.'

'And Keziah, where was she?' Freya said.

He hesitated. 'I think she was still in the car after he dropped us off. But I honestly can't remember.'

She would never know if he was telling the truth.

'Look, strange things happen in these places. People do things they wouldn't normally do. I do have to go back to the office now. I hope everything goes well for you when you get back to the UK.'

Was he making some kind of excuse for Roger and whatever he had done? Mike seemed like a nice person. But he was a man, and didn't men always back each other up?

'Thank you,' she said. 'You have helped me.'

THIRTY-FIVE

Freya unlocked the entrance gate to the club. A fence and a tall hedge surrounded the clubhouse and the swimming pool. The gate was always firmly locked to make sure that only the club members could get in. Soon, Freya thought, the lock would be broken and anyone would be free to come in and use the pool.

A thin green layer of slime covered the water in the swimming pool. The pump had stopped working. The men who looked after the pool had left and no one knew where they had gone.

Freya lay on the ground, sunbathing. The project people hardly ever went to the club any more and so she felt safe lying there. No one would disturb her. She was packed up and ready to leave so she was free to escape from sitting, staring at the bare walls of the bungalow.

Her body was smooth and tanned and she knew that she looked good in her black and white striped bikini. She wanted Roger to be there, to look at her as if he wanted to make love.

In a few days' time she would be at home without a husband, living once more in her mother's house. She would have to find another office job, probably in a typing pool, alongside women who had no idea of what life could be like outside a small, rain-drizzled town.

Freya was disturbed by the noise of a gate opening. She opened her eyes and turned to see Mavis walking towards the door of the clubhouse. She pretended to be asleep. But she heard footsteps coming towards her.

'Hello, dear,' Mavis said. 'I'm just collecting some glasses and plates, before everything disappears.'

Freya prayed that she would go away, quickly. There was no longer any need to get into conversation with her. After a year or so, Mavis would be a distant, hazy memory.

'I'm really sorry that things have turned out so badly for you. It's really terrible,' Mavis said.

Freya was glad that her sunglasses covered her eyes. She could pretend to be asleep. Mavis went into the clubhouse and a few minutes later came out carrying two heavy bags, rattling with the sound of glassware.

'Is everything all right?' Mavis asked. She hesitated, as if afraid to go on. 'It's just that the *askari* told me some story about that man, the cricketer, arriving at the house with a baby. He said he heard people shouting at each other.'

Freya felt weary and confused about why she was asking about this. Roger was dead. Couldn't she leave him to rest in peace?

'You see, Don doesn't want to have to deal with anything complicated. Not at this stage,' Mavis said.

Freya remembered the market woman, and felt the old anger she had tried to control since she was a child.

Princesses in fairy tales didn't get angry. It was only old witches who were allowed to scream and shout and have tantrums. Why shouldn't she be angry without feeling ashamed? She stood up and faced Mavis.

'It's none of your business. Please just go away and leave me,' Freya screamed, surprised at the sound of her own voice.

Mavis' expression changed quickly. She looked frightened and in pain and Freya wished that she had tried to control her temper.

'I'm sorry you feel like that. I can see you're grieving. I'll go,' Mavis said tearfully, as she stooped down and slowly picked up her bags. Freya had a sudden image of Mavis back home in England, waiting in a supermarket queue of screaming mothers and children, and then realising that she had to pack her shopping herself into plastic bags and then push a broken-wheeled shopping trolley to her waiting car.

Mavis began walking towards the gate and then stopped and turned round to face Freya. 'I'm sorry,' she said. 'I might not get a chance to say this again. I know I've said things that have hurt you. But I think it was just my way of trying to protect you.'

Protect her? From whom? Did Mavis think she needed protection from being criticised and blamed by the expatriates who desperately wanted to hang on to their comfortable way of life, and couldn't bear it if anyone told them that they might have got it wrong?

'I'm sorry,' Mavis said again. More flecks of grey were beginning to appear in her dark brown hair. She was getting to be an old woman, probably nearly as old as Freya's mother, who would soon be fifty-two. Perhaps she had confused Mavis with her mother and been too hard on her? Things had changed so quickly in the sixties. Women like Mavis and her mother felt left behind, unsure of what they thought any more.

'I didn't need protecting,' Freya said. 'At first it was difficult, but after a while I didn't really care what they said or thought about me.' Freya could hear herself sounding angrier than she had intended.

'No, I didn't really mean that. I just wanted to protect you from the kind of pain I had to go through.'

What was she talking about? Freya wanted to put her hands over her ears, to scream at her to go away. But Mavis fetched a canvas chair from the clubhouse veranda and sat down.

'When I met you, you reminded me of myself when I first came here. It was something about the way you wanted to stand apart from everyone else.'

Mavis took a deep breath.

'I've never told anyone all this before.'

Freya didn't want the burden of her confession, but it was too late.

'Do you remember I told you that I first came to Uganda because I had a job as a Woman Administrative Officer? I said I enjoyed the work, and I really did.'

Mavis pushed her hair from her eyes and Freya thought that she saw tears. There was a thudding sound of someone hoeing outside the club compound.

'But I didn't tell you how lonely I was. When I came home in the evening, the only person I had to talk to was the houseboy. His name was Alex. He taught me Swahili. I helped him sometimes with loans or bits of money to help his family.'

There was a distant rumble of thunder and the sky suddenly darkened. Freya remembered that Mavis was frightened of storms. There was no shelter in the area where they were sitting. Maybe she should suggest that they go inside the clubhouse.

'I often had to drive up-country for work. Alex always came with me. It made me feel safer to have someone in the car with me. We usually stayed at rest houses and he would cook for me and clean the place before we left.'

Did women like Mavis ever stop talking about their house servants? She was probably going to say that he stole something.

'Of course, I don't know if he is still alive. And I don't suppose I would even recognise him if I met him.'

Mavis went on as if in a kind of trance.

'When I first saw him, I thought he was good-looking. But he was the houseboy. I told myself that it was like looking at a picture. Something you could just enjoy from a distance.'

Freya's heart beat faster, wondering what she might say next. She remembered the painting in Mavis' house, of the man with the corn cob on his head, and how handsome but passive he looked. And she remembered how guilty she had felt when she had first seen Mavis' cook and thought him handsome.

'I can still see his arms,' Mavis said. 'They were very muscular with a sort of blue/grey vein running down them. I often felt I wanted to touch his arm but the thought just made me ashamed.'

Mavis could have been one of the girls in the office where Freya had worked. Freya never liked talking about her boyfriends, or what she had done with them. But some of the girls had no shame and wanted everyone to know all the details. She wanted to shut her ears but Mavis went on talking as if she was in a trance.

'Then one night when we were staying at a rest house up-country, I was woken by the noise of something rustling around in the room. I jumped out of bed and saw that it was a large rat. I've always hated them and so I screamed loudly. Alex was staying outside in the boys' quarters and he ran in to see what was happening.

'He chased the rat round the room with a knife, but it took ages before he managed to kill it. Then we both started laughing. Sort of relief, I suppose. He made some tea. There wasn't a teapot so we put the tea leaves in the kettle and boiled it all up. I remember that it tasted horrible. Then we found a half-empty bottle of whisky.'

There was a loud clap of thunder and Mavis cried out in fear. This could be the excuse for them to both leave. But Mavis carried on as if nothing could stop her.

'I don't usually drink whisky, but I had had a fright, and it tasted good. I soon got tipsy, of course. It's not an excuse, I know. We had never really talked about anything personal before. But he told me that he had been to a mission school and had wanted to be a priest. But when his father died, he had to look after the family, so he started working as a houseboy. And after that it was difficult to do anything else.'

Mavis stopped, as if afraid to go on.

'I remember looking at him and just wanting to touch him. I was wearing my nightdress and I took his hand and placed it on my breast. I felt as if I was going crazy. He looked terrified. But I just nodded and pulled him towards me. Even now I wonder if he just did it because he thought it was part of his job and he couldn't refuse.'

Freya was shocked that a man would have sex with a woman he hardly knew just because he felt obliged to do it. But perhaps that was what she had expected deep down from Wensley when she had first put her arms round him, that he would respond because he would be grateful for her attention?

'And that's what I can't forget,' Mavis said. 'For me, it wasn't just sex. I really wanted him to have feelings for me. I have never felt anything like it since then. But there was no way that there could ever be any kind of relationship with him. And they would have sent me home in disgrace, of course.'

Freya could see that it was all painful for her.

'Afterwards,' Mavis went on, 'we just pretended it had never happened. Then, two months later, I realised I was pregnant. So I sacked him. I accused him of stealing some jewellery. He said nothing, showed no feelings and left the next day. Of course, I gave him good references.'

Freya was afraid of what she would say next.

'So I found a European doctor. He helped me get an abortion. After that I just wanted to leave and go back to the UK. But then I met Don. Of course, I have never told him about any of this.'

It began to rain heavily and the two women ran to the doorway of the clubhouse and went inside to shelter.

Mavis took a half-empty bottle of whisky from behind the bar, poured herself a glass and drank it quickly.

Freya felt angry. Did all women have a story like this, somewhere in their lives? A story that was hidden away. About sex with the wrong person, or about anxiously waiting for the signs of period blood, fear of miscarriage, or abortion.

Whatever the story, it was always a woman's fault unless it was rape, and even then it could be your fault for being with the wrong man or wearing the wrong clothes, or staying out too late, or walking in the wrong place. Had this place turned her into a feminist, a bra burner? The girls at the office would laugh.

'So, when I saw that Roger had taken on that woman, you know, all alone in the house with her, before you arrived, I suppose it all came back to me. The guilt, the pain, the pleasure. And I didn't know what to do, except confront you with it. I suppose I knew it would hurt you. So, you see, that is how I was trying to protect you. I'm so sorry. It was inexcusable. Please forgive me.'

Mavis hesitated. 'And then there was the West Indian who stayed the night. I saw the way you danced with him at the nightclub. Maybe I was jealous.'

Perhaps she was dreaming? She would wake from her snooze in the sun and Mavis would come through the gate complaining about everything as usual. But she knew it wasn't a dream, and she felt confused about what she was supposed to do with the information.

'I'd better go now,' Mavis said. 'Don't forget to lock the gate when you leave – you know what the *watu* are like; they'll be in there like a shot the moment we have all gone.'

After she had left, Freya poured herself a glass of

brandy. She smiled to herself. It had been an emotionally draining, painful confession. But Mavis had quickly gone back to being her old self.

THIRTY-SIX

Freya left the car at the church gate and walked up the hill to the graveyard. The headstone said:

ROGER TEMPLEMEAD
1945–1972
DIED AGED 26 ON AUGUST 18, 1972
BELOVED SON OF VIOLET AND ERIC AND
HUSBAND OF FREYA

Freya shivered in the heat as she realised that this was the last goodbye. She was leaving Roger thousands of miles from home. Her mother's brother Richard had been killed in the war in North Africa but they had no idea where the grave was. His photo in his army uniform stared at them from the mantelpiece. *He's always with us*, her mother said. Freya had no idea what kind of a person he had been. Only good things were said about him. Would Roger always be with her? The fear of forgetting someone was almost worse than the death itself. In some of the African stories she had read, the rituals went on for weeks, even years, to keep the person alive in memories.

She was alone except for the man who was slashing the grass. She began to cry. It came from deep down and had no words with it. She sat down on the grass and stared through her tears at the view of Kampala and the lake in the far distance. The man stopped his work, looked at her and said something to her in a language she didn't understand.

She heard the church gate opening. A few moments later, someone tapped her on the shoulder. Freya looked up and saw a smartly dressed woman wearing a long, silky, patterned dress. Her hair was covered with a matching turban. Freya saw the familiar row of scars on the woman's forehead. Keziah looked older, almost middle-aged.

'Thank you for coming. I didn't know if you would,' Freya said.

'Oketch found me. Give me the letter. I want to come. Roger was good to me.'

Freya had never heard Keziah say Roger's name before. It was unexpected and intimate and brought back the old anger and jealousy. She shouldn't have asked Keziah to come. She should be trying to forget everything, not raking up the past. She started to cry.

'No. Sorry. It's a mistake. Please go and leave me,' Freya said.

Keziah sighed and shook her head. She stood in silence in front of the grave for a few minutes, made the sign of the cross, and then she started to walk away down the hill.

Freya knew that she had done the wrong thing. She had asked Keziah to meet her because there were things

307

she wanted to ask her. She might never have a chance again. She couldn't let her go.

She called after her. 'No, please come back.'

Keziah ignored her at first and then slowly turned round and walked back.

'What you want?' she said.

'The baby? Why did you do it?' Freya asked.

Keziah looked directly at her. Did she understand what she was saying? Small pale patches were dotted on her skin, as if she had been using skin-lightening cream. Her eyes were sad and full of pain.

'Why did you leave her?'

'You know about it?'

'Wensley, the man you left her with. He came to the house. He had the baby. He was looking for you.'

Keziah swayed and Freya thought she might faint. She reached out and touched her arm and the two women sat down on the freshly cut grass.

'When she came out, my man saw her and said she was *nusu-nusu* and not his. He beat me. Told me to take her away, get rid of her. Then I could stay with him. Had no choice, got no job. And I think he going to kill me.'

Freya could see the fear in Keziah's face and she knew that she was telling the truth.

'They don't want her in the village. Already too many people to feed. Some people say I'm a witch. They might throw her in the river. I scared.'

Freya tried to take in the horror of what she was saying.

'Then I think, maybe the cricket man will help. He's kind. I went to his house. He wasn't there. I was so scared so I left her. Told him take her to you.'

Freya could see the pain and fear in her face and wanted to help her but didn't know how.

'Where is she now? You know?' Keziah said.

'Wensley, the cricket man. He is going to take her to his country. To give to his sister.'

'She's fine then?' Keziah said. Freya thought she saw tears on her cheeks but it could have been beads of sweat.

Freya nodded. She didn't want to say it but she couldn't stop herself.

'Is he the daddy, the cricket man?'

'You think I sleep with anybody?' Keziah said angrily.

'You work at the bar, the Paradise.'

Keziah shook her head. 'I help my friend when she want time off, when her kids are sick.'

'Oh', Freya said, 'I didn't …'

Before she could finish, Keziah said, 'You people think we're all bad. You know everythin' but nothin'. Things are goin' to be better now you all goin'. You should have got that cricket man to give you a baby. That's what you wanted. I see you that night. You like a prostitute, eh?'

Freya felt as if she had been punched in the stomach. She had forgotten that they were standing by Roger's grave. Perhaps this was the moment to confront her and to ask her if it was Roger's child. But she couldn't. She wasn't even sure if she wanted to know. She knew she should leave things as they were. Everything was over. The child would be well looked after. She just wanted to leave, to go home and rest.

But Keziah stood facing her and said, 'Don't understand why you gave me money to keep the baby?'

At that moment, Freya saw another woman who had lost a child. Keziah's life was harder than hers by far. At least

Keziah's child was still alive, even though she had given her away and she would never see her again. Everywhere, the loss of a child was always a death from which a woman would never recover.

The two women stood facing each other.

'Before I came here to Uganda, my baby died in my belly. Four months old. It was my fault. They took her away. Buried her somewhere … I don't know where. No grave. I thought everything would be all right. I would forget when I came here. But it gave me a pain I can't get rid of. Made me sad, so I can never feel happy again.'

She began to cry and Keziah reached out to touch her and gently stroked her arm.

'So when you said you wanted to get rid of your baby, it all came back to me. If you got rid of your baby, it would have been my fault.'

She wasn't sure if Keziah understood, but as she sobbed, Keziah put her arms around her and hugged her like a child.

Then Keziah said, 'If you give me money for a chicken, I can do a sacrifice for the baby. I get a chicken. We kill it. Make sure she is with the ancestors.'

Freya searched in her bag and gave her a few notes. Keziah put the money inside her bra. Then she said, 'Goodbye, Madam,' and walked down the hill. As Freya watched her go, she felt a strange sadness and wondered if she would ever feel happy again.

THIRTY-SEVEN

Freya stood on the driveway of the bungalow with her case by her side, waiting for Oketch to take her to the airport.

Jock sprawled limply on the veranda. Since Roger's death, he had lost interest in barking at the *watu* who occasionally wandered into the garden. Freya had never felt much affection for him but she didn't want him to be deserted and neglected after she had left. Pets belonging to the departing Asians and expatriates were being put down. It was too expensive to take them to the UK and the quarantine period was long. It seemed unfair to expect them to get used to cold weather and cramped living conditions.

Don drove up to the house and Mavis got out of the car. She was dressed as if she was ready to face the autumn chill of Gatwick Airport, in a heavy brown polyester skirt and a grey and yellow patterned blouse. Simon, the cook, walked slowly up the drive and then stood patiently watching them.

Mavis had two battered suitcases made of leather. She kept bending over to touch them as if she was afraid that they might disappear. One of the locks on the suitcase had come undone and she struggled to close it, looking around for help. Simon took the case from her and fixed the lock.

Don kissed Mavis on the cheek.

'Take good care of Milton, and make sure he gets the right meat,' Mavis said.

She looked at Simon as if she was about to say something. But he turned away. He touched the corner of his eye. Maybe he was crying? Or just feeling the effects of peeling onions?

Jock wagged his tail and jumped into the back seat of Don's car.

'Don't worry, Freya dear, I'll look after him until we can find him a good home,' Don said.

Freya wondered how Don would cope without Mavis. But Simon and the houseboy would look after him. He had been used to being alone for long periods of time during his life in Africa. As long as he had his whisky, the record player and the BBC World Service, he would be quite content. Maybe a local woman would move in temporarily. No one would say anything. And when he eventually got back to the UK, they would pick up their life where they had left it, without any questions asked.

Freya felt too embarrassed to look directly at Mavis but when she caught her eye it was as if Mavis was saying, *I said what I said, but we will never talk about it again.* She looked anxious and tearful. Soon, she would find herself in a place where she didn't want to be. She had that in common, at least, with the Asians.

What would Mavis do in the UK? Settle into a cottage in a quiet village and take on a local woman to clean every week? Tell stories about Africa that no one wanted to listen to and complain about the immigrants that were taking over the cities. After a year or two, maybe she and Don would emigrate to South Africa, a place where they could feel comfortable again, a place where the old order was undisturbed, where the *watu* knew their place.

Or maybe she would become a feminist, leave Don and join a commune of other unkempt grey-haired women, taking drugs and having free sex. Freya found it difficult to hide a smile at the thought.

Freya locked the front door. Jimmy ran up to her. He was wearing a shirt that was too big for him. Freya realised with a shock that it was Roger's green and white patterned shirt that she had packed up with the rest of his clothes and given to Simon.

'You pay me,' he said.

'I thought I gave it you.'

'I want more,' he said.

She opened her bag and gave him a few shillings. He ran off laughing. She thought she heard him say, 'Good riddance to white devils.'

The Land Rover turned into the drive. A white woman and two small blond-haired children were crammed into the back seats. They looked tired and tearful.

Freya and Mavis climbed into the front seat. Freya was pressed close to Oketch. His bulky body was wet with sweat. This would be the last time she would have to squeeze herself in next to him. She struggled to say something to him, to thank him or to show that he was

313

someone she would remember or miss. She saw the scarred markings on his temples, similar to those on Keziah's face.

'Will you be okay?' she said to Oketch. She felt Mavis become tense beside her as she looked away from them through the window.

Oketch stared straight ahead.

'Could take long time today. With this long convoy.'

'I mean for work,' Freya said. 'Now the *msungus* are all leaving.'

'Always want drivers. Specially the big men. And there's more of them around these days. All gonna get big Mercedes, they say.' He laughed.

'Are you …' She hesitated. 'From his area?'

'From the North. Not his tribe.'

'Is that a bad thing?'

'Could be. Just got to stay smart. Could end up in that stinking prison or thrown in the Nile to the crocodiles.'

'That's awful.'

'Lot of people getting away from the town, going back to the land. Safer there. I like to go but got three kids in Primary in Kampala. Can't leave them. One of the wives, she's gone back already.'

A child in the back of the car started crying. Mavis had fallen asleep.

'That girl of yours. You meet her?' Oketch said.

'Yes. Thank you.'

He didn't usually ask questions.

'She liked the minis, the bars and the *msungu* men.' He sniffed as he said, 'Bad women. They make men bad.'

Why was he saying this? What did he know?

314

They reached the main road to Entebbe. The traffic slowed down. People lined the roads as if waiting for a funeral to pass. But they were waving and jeering. She remembered the dense curtains of banana trees and the fear she had felt on the day she had arrived. Now she saw dense curtains of angry people.

They were in a convoy of vehicles of all sorts taking the Asians and a handful of Europeans to the airport. Police on motorbikes and in cars escorted them. Soldiers manned the roadblocks. Freya lost count of the number of times they were stopped along the twenty-mile drive to the airport. Undeterred by the police escort, the drunk, wild-eyed soldiers stopped the vehicles, ordered people to open the cases at gunpoint, pulled out cases, opened them and scattered the contents on the floor. The soldiers picked over and sorted through the contents until they found things worth taking. Anything left unwanted by the soldiers had to be repacked by the scared, weary Asians.

After six hours, they arrived at the airport. Long queues of vehicles hooted their horns as they dropped off their passengers. Hot, sweaty, bedraggled families pushed and struggled to get inside the densely crowded terminal. The queue for Customs and Immigration was an endless snake. Cases were emptied and repacked again. Exhausted-looking Asian families stood or sat where they could, or just lay down on the floor. Cases and other belongings were piled or scattered around.

Some people carried heavy-looking coats in preparation for the weather that would greet them. What would it be like for those who got off the plane wearing only saris or light shirts? Freya just hoped people in the UK would be kind.

No one seemed to know what time the plane would leave. Mavis' face was pale and blotched with exhaustion and her dress was stained with dirt and sweat marks. Freya went to find some water and biscuits for her. But the small airport shops and stands had run out of everything. People began making beds out of clothes and bags.

After a wait of five hours, a voice shouted, 'Board now.' People quickly gathered up their things and ran or limped wearily towards the door to the ramp. It was strangely quiet.

Freya joined the queue. The man from the BOAC airline waved in her direction. From behind her, she heard Mavis say, 'Look, he's calling to us to go first. Thank goodness.' Mavis pulled on her sleeve.

'No, he can't do that. I'll just wait here with everyone else.'

'As you like', Mavis said. She rushed to the front, pushing past the men, women and their crying, half-asleep children. Getting all these people on board would probably take hours. Freya turned to look at the long queue behind her and at the sea of Asian faces. A few Africans and white people were dotted amongst them.

Someone was calling out names and people were pushing forward. Then something clicked in Freya's head. One of the men at the back of the queue looked familiar. She squinted in the glaring light and saw that it was Wensley.

She wanted to speak to him, to touch him, to say goodbye. People were pushing her forward. She waved at him but he kept disappearing into the crowds around him. She knew it would be foolish to try to struggle back through the queue and speak to him. Her life in Uganda was over. She would never see him again. Getting on the plane was the most important thing to think about.

Then she remembered something. Where was the baby? She looked for him again and spotted him chatting to an Asian man, but there was no sign of the baby. Perhaps he had given her to someone else to hold for a moment.

Mavis was now at the front of the queue. She waved at Freya as if to say, *Come on, don't wait there, come to the front.*

Did it really matter where the child was? Wensley's sister would make sure she was well looked after. But there had already been so many things in her life that were unfinished: the pregnancy, the marriage, the job at the charity.

She knew then that she couldn't leave this unfinished. She had to find out where the child was, to speak to Wensley before he left. She turned round and struggled and pushed her way back through the queue. Confused and angry faces stared into hers and she was jostled and bruised when she finally reached him.

He looked startled.

'What are you doing? This is foolish. You'll get hurt,' he said. He looked worried and tender and it reminded her of the day they had made love.

'You're leaving too?' he said. She had to shout above the noise of the queue. They were both pressed forward.

'They said that the wives and children could leave with the convoy. Where is the baby?'

'You had better go back or you'll lose your place. You don't want to get left behind,' he said.

'So where is she now?'

'I should have told you, but I didn't think it would be a good idea to come to your place to try to find you. Your girl, she came to take her back. My sister is disappointed, of course. But she just accepted it was God's way. Better for her to be with her real mother.'

Freya couldn't speak, her heart was racing so fast.

'Oh, I heard about him, the husband. I am so sorry for your loss. But you're young.'

'Where did Keziah go? Do you know?'

He looked away from her and shook his head. 'I don't know.'

Was he telling the truth?

'Look, I think she might have said she would go back to your house for a while.' Wensley put his hand on Freya's arm. 'You can't do anything about it. Go now and get on the plane with everyone else.'

'Why are you leaving?' Freya asked.

'Same as you, scared of what might happen. They'll be a bit wary about touching you people. But I'm not so sure about people like me. So I'm going back home for a while, to relax.' He looked away and then met her eyes again.

'But I'll be coming to the UK next summer for some county cricket. You never know, our paths may cross. What's your address?'

Everything around faded away. She wanted to kiss him, to forget what had happened.

'I don't think so, I can't,' she said.

He smiled at her and said, 'I understand.' He took her hand and scribbled a number on the back of it with a biro.

'This is my friend's number. I'll be staying with him. Just in case you change your mind,' he said.

She turned round to see what had happened to Mavis and when she turned back, he had disappeared.

He had said he thought Keziah had gone back to the house. She knew then what she had to do.

She pushed and shoved her way back through the throngs of people until she was finally out of the airport. Then she hailed a taxi, jumped in the back, and sank into the torn leather seats.

'Take me to Bugelere on Masindi Road,' she said.

'Be long time,' the taxi driver said.

She didn't care any more. She wasn't in a hurry.

THIRTY-EIGHT

17 SEPTEMBER

The taxi drove out of the airport onto the dark road. They faced an endless convoy of vehicles still crawling in the opposite direction. Even though night had fallen, people were still dancing and cheering along the sides of the road. The taxi slowed down to a halt and two men ran towards it and banged their hands on the roof of the car. The taxi driver screamed at them to go away. Freya pulled a wrap over her head and tried to disappear into the back seat of the car. She was drenched with sweat and dust when they finally reached the turn to the project.

As usual, the *askaris* stood to attention and saluted as they opened the project gate. Nothing in their expressions suggested that they might be surprised to see her returning in a taxi, so soon after she had left.

The dawn sky was already turning pink. The day she had arrived, the house and garden had looked neatly kept, like a safe, calm oasis, protected from the dust and bustle of the world outside the project gate. Now the lawn was brown and patchy. The shrubs and flowers were dying and the white paint on the walls of the house was beginning to peel and fade.

Freya took her case out of the taxi and unlocked the door. The lounge was empty except for the PWD furniture. Someone had been in the kitchen. There was a tin plate in the sink with traces of *posho* on it.

She felt exhausted, drained of feelings, her mind as confused as it had been the day when she thought that she had lost her memory. For a moment, she struggled to remember why she had come back. She went into the bedroom, now stripped of everything, and lay down on the bare mattress. She fell into a deep sleep and dreamed again of the cat scratching at her heels. It was skinny and dying but still something stopped her from feeding it.

The noise of rattling tins outside woke her and she forgot where she was. The heat told her that it was already well into the day. Her watch showed eleven o'clock. She jumped up from the bed and heard laughter.

Through the living room window, she saw Comfort, sorting through the rubbish and putting things into neat piles. There were pens, pencils, small wooden ornaments, assorted items of clothing, plastic cups, knives, forks and spoons, old shuttlecocks and used tennis balls. The books had been set aside carefully in a separate heap. Close by, a bonfire smouldered. Charred bits of blue airmail paper floated and drifted around. Freya remembered that she must have left her mother's letters at the back of the drawer. Now they were gone. It didn't matter. They had never said anything very important.

On the ground outside the servants' quarters, there were cooking pots, rolled mats, Tilley lamps, bags of rice and *posho*, tins of food and a few wilting tomatoes and green peppers. It looked as if someone was getting ready to move out.

A woman came out of one of the houses and called to Comfort, who ran to her and took a slice of bread and a mug of tea. Freya heard a baby cry and saw with a beating heart that the woman was Keziah.

Freya opened the kitchen door. Keziah turned and saw her and ran back into the hut. Freya went out into the garden and knocked hard on the door. The baby was screaming loudly now.

The door opened. Freya remembered how Keziah had looked when she had first seen her, and the jealousy that she had tried to squash deep inside herself. Keziah no longer looked like a young girl. Her belly was still plump and rounded. The faded, patterned cloth that she wrapped around her waist was grubby with stains of food, grease and charcoal. She looked afraid.

'I thought you people all gone. Why are you back?' Keziah asked. She clutched the baby tightly to her chest, rocking her as she spoke. 'I leaving soon. Government will want this place back for Africans, now you whites have gone.'

'It's all right,' Freya said, 'you can stay.'

Keziah gave the baby to Comfort, who put her on her hip. Freya looked closely at the baby. Did she have Roger's broad shoulders? Were her eyes like Wensley's?

What was she doing? Had some strange instinct taken hold of her, like the birds that migrated not knowing why or where they were going? Or was it just her illness coming back? The doctors at the mission hospital had said that some women took time to get over miscarriages. Would she ever get over it? She would always know deep down that it was all her fault. Was this baby her punishment? Or her reward?

She panicked at the thought that project people might see her and that she would have to explain why she had come back to the house. The wives and children had left but Don and the other project men were still there. She would have to think of an excuse for why she had come back. After the illness, she knew that they had all thought she was strange, even a bit loony, as her mother would have said. They would just think that Roger's death had finally tipped her over the edge.

What she was doing was crazy. There was no logic or point in it. She had to pull herself together, go back to the airport and wait for the next plane. By now, the first plane would have taken off. Everyone, no matter how squashed they were in the overcrowded plane, would have been relieved to be finally leaving, enjoying the cool of the air-conditioned plane and putting off thinking about what might be waiting for them in the cold, misty dawn of Gatwick Airport.

Her brother and mother would be waiting at the airport. When she wasn't on the plane, they would be worried, terrified that something awful had happened to her.

Freya went back into the house to start collecting her things together. Keziah followed her and began sweeping the floor.

'You don't need to do that any more,' Freya said.

Keziah ignored her and carried on, even though the floor was clean and spotless.

323

'Where will you go?'

'Stay with my auntie in Kawempe till I get work again.'

'At the bar?'

'No, that finished. I still got the money you gave me. Going to start my own shop now the *mahindi* gone. Hairdressing, beauty? The brother, the one you see in the garden cutting hair, he help me.'

'What about your man?'

'Still might kill me if he comes back from the North.'

Comfort came in through the kitchen door. The baby cried again, moved her small hand in a kind of wave, and smiled.

'You could stay,' Freya hesitated. 'Here in the house.'

No one was likely to come and take the house back for a while, so why shouldn't they stay?

'You crazy. What do you want? Is this a trick?' Keziah said.

Freya could hear Wensley saying that *msungus* like her just got in the way; thought they were doing good but just made things more difficult for everyone else.

'She has a name?'

'Yes. She called Cheryl.'

Freya thought Keziah must have found the name in a book, or heard it on the radio.

'The cricket man call her that. It come from his country. I just keep it,' Keziah said.

Freya needed to know something. She hoped Keziah would understand what she was asking. For the first time, she looked directly into Keziah's eyes. She had always found it difficult to make eye contact with people. Only really confident people could do this without fear of what they might see or of what might happen. Looking people in the eye had something to do with falling in love, with letting go and not knowing what might happen next. Looking a house servant in the eye was the first step towards losing power and control, seeing things you didn't want to see. She thought she might have read that in one of the orange-covered African novels.

Keziah's eyes were pained and frightened.

'Why did you fetch the baby back?' Freya said.

Keziah shrugged her shoulders.

'Please tell me,' Freya said.

'After the grave, when I see you, I know I want her back. Don't know anything about the cricket man and his sister. Just want to make sure her life better than mine. Proper school, job. No need for a man who'll beat her up. But I can try.'

Freya felt ashamed. When she had thought about having a child, it had all been about herself, about pleasing Roger, about making her mother happy or having something to do to pass the time. She hadn't really thought about what kind of life the child would have. She thought about the woman in the nightclub and the pain she had seen in her eyes when she had talked drunkenly about the children she had been forced to send to boarding school.

Keziah said something to Comfort in their language and walked away to go back to her house. Freya couldn't believe that this was the end. She wanted to hold the child one more time and she put her arms out to take her. Comfort hesitated and shook her head. Then she nodded and handed the baby to Freya before she ran away as if she was scared at what she had done.

Freya laid the baby carefully onto the settee, so that she could watch her as she put her night things back into her suitcase. The baby began to cry, a whimper at first and then more loudly. Freya picked her up and rocked her but her screams became louder. She panicked and called for Comfort but no one came. Freya took her out into the garden and walked up and down until the baby stopped crying, gripped her finger and smiled.

Freya's feet were bare. Only local varieties of grass flourished in the tropical climate and the blades were sharp and spiky under her feet. She tried to avoid the small holes and mounds made by the black safari ants that people said could march like an army over a body sleeping at night.

A new family, friends of Amin or a soldier would soon move into the house. Plantains, bananas, cassava, okra, pumpkins and corn would replace the grass and flowers. Goats, chickens and ducks would roam freely in the garden.

The small Asian shops, the supermarkets and the restaurants in Kampala would change hands or close down. Nothing would be the same. She wondered what her life would be like without them. Could she survive without these things if she had to?

She thought about the sanitary towels. She hadn't really needed to stuff her case with them. You could buy them in the supermarket. The women in the villages used rags that they washed afterwards. She could do the same.

Her dress felt wet. She went back into the house and carefully took off the matted, yellowed nappy. She had seen second-hand nappies like these on the market stalls, alongside the piles of brightly coloured clothes.

Her stomach sank as she thought about it. Would that be the child's life from now on? Second-hand clothes, maybe not enough to eat, rice and beans, *matooke* and scrawny chicken if she was lucky. How could she leave the child like this? She was responsible for her being alive.

There was a knock on the kitchen door. Freya felt afraid to open it. She heard two raised voices arguing. The door was pushed open and Keziah and Comfort stood there. Comfort was crying.

'Stupid girl. I told her not to leave the baby. It time for her feed. Give her to me.'

'No,' Freya said as she clutched the baby closer to her and moved towards the bedroom door.

'What happening?' Keziah looked straight into her eyes. 'You a bit crazy like when you went to the hospital?'

'I can help look after her.'

Keziah laughed. 'You people stupid.'

Freya heard Wensley's voice again, saying, *People like you always think they can solve everything. Your way of life has always got to be the best. You can't understand any other way of doing things. Everyone has to fit into your ways. I pity those Asians. You won't be happy until they are all like you.*

She had been hurt that he thought that she was just like all the other *msungus*. She had wanted to say, *But when you put on your cricket whites in Surrey, weren't you joining those people, pretending to be like them?* He had said he kept away from politics. But wasn't that politics, to just stay there on the pitch, accepting the names they called him as just part of the game?

The old familiar feeling flushed through her body as she thought about Wensley. The number that he had scrawled on her hand in biro was still there. She needed to wash it off. But she would leave it for a little while longer.

She needed to stop using other people to sort out her problems. Hadn't she just used her relationship with Roger as a way of escaping from her mother? Perhaps she had known deep down that getting pregnant would be her only way out of a dull, drab life. Did women always need men if they were to escape? And did it really matter any more what her mother might think?

'Give her to me,' Keziah said. Freya held the baby tightly but Keziah gently prized her from Freya's arms and then wrapped her in a cloth before swinging her onto her back.

'You want food?' Keziah said.

Freya felt as if she was being treated like a child. She wanted to refuse, to show that she understood that Keziah was no longer a servant. But she was hungry.

'Got chicken stew and rice, if you want?'

Freya nodded and Keziah went into the kitchen and she heard the sound of rattling pots and pans. Freya's heart beat faster and she saw the flashing lights at the corners of her eyes. Her mouth felt dry.

'Please,' Freya called to her, 'will you come in here?'

Keziah appeared in the doorway, holding a wooden spoon.

'You want?' she said.

'Yes, please sit down.'

'No I stand,' she said as she jiggled around to stop the baby whimpering.

'I said you could stay,' Freya said, 'but I meant that you

could stay in the house. You have the key. No one need know. It will take a long time for people to sort things out.'

'Don't want your help. It's a trick,' Keziah said.

A voice from outside called, '*Hodi*. Anyone there?' Before they could answer, Don came in through the veranda door. He looked tired and his usually smart shorts and safari jacket were crumpled and stained.

'Freya,' he said as if he had seen a ghost. 'What on earth is going on? Why aren't you at the airport? What happened?'

She searched for an excuse.

'I'd forgotten the death certificate. I had to come back.'

'Oh, I am sorry,' he said, 'that's so upsetting for you.' He tried to put his arm around her but she moved away.

'But there are planes going all the time. I'm sure we can sort something out. I can take you to the airport myself.'

He looked at Keziah as if surprised to see her. He spoke to her in Swahili and she nodded.

'I've told her she's got to go right away. I only came round here to make sure everything had been cleared out so that I could lock up and hand over the keys to the PWD.'

Keziah stood up to leave.

'Sit down,' Freya said.

'What is going on? Why is she sitting in here with you, anyway? Is that a good idea?'

He had become wizened and frail. He looked half-alive, as if something was missing without Mavis by his side. Freya thought about what Mavis had told her. She could destroy him by telling him the story. He would never believe her but it made her feel stronger, more in charge and no longer afraid of him.

'Actually, I've decided that I'm not leaving,' she said.

'Oh.' Don sounded puzzled. 'Well, there's probably another plane tomorrow we can get you on. This stuff is all so awful. I'm not surprised you're a bit confused about things. But she'll have to go.'

'No,' Freya said. 'I mean I'm staying here in the house for a while and she's going to stay here in the house with me.'

Don frowned and scratched his head.

'Why would you want to do that? It's dangerous. I just don't understand. Are you ill, my dear?'

The baby screamed.

'She want feeding,' Keziah said.

Don stared at the child. He hesitated and then shook his head.

'Oh, I see. It's something to do with that child.'

Freya knew then that Don and the others must have suspected that Roger was the father of Keziah's child. They had tried to warn her or hoped Keziah would just disappear.

'I don't know what's going on but you aren't going to put things right by staying here,' Don said. 'This is something for her to deal with. It's not your problem.'

'Yes,' Freya said, 'but I want to stay and help.'

Don clenched his fists and wiped the sweat from his brow. His hair was greasy and flecked with dandruff.

'This nonsense has to end now. You have no right to be in this house any more, now that Roger has gone. The government has to take it back.'

'Well, they'll have to come and remove me. Keziah has friends in the army.'

'This is ridiculous. You are deliberately putting

330

yourself in danger. But I wash my hands of it. You're not my responsibility any more. But I will have to let the High Commission know.'

Freya knew that the High Commission would be too busy with other things. The High Commissioner himself had stood up to Amin and been expelled alongside the Asians.

Don's face reddened even more.

'You've been nothing but trouble since you came here,' he said as he slammed the mosquito door shut.

'We staying?' Keziah said.

'Yes, Comfort can stay in the house too ... and that brother who cuts hair.'

She felt as if she had drunk too much.

'You crazy,' Keziah said.

Freya thought that was probably true. People had been telling her that ever since she had arrived in Uganda. But it felt like the right kind of craziness. But there was something she still wanted to know.

'Will you tell me something?' she said to Keziah.

Keziah frowned. 'What you say?'

'Who is the father?'

Keziah laughed and shook her head. 'Don't know.'

'You must have some idea?'

'It wasn't him, Roger. I know that's what you think.'

Freya would never be able to tell if she was lying. But it didn't really matter. The baby was alive because of her. She had some kind of right to some part of her life. She wasn't sure what it would be.

Then Keziah said, 'Could be ... Bobby?'

Freya was astonished. But then it suddenly made

sense. Bobby made visits to the project every few months. She had thought it strange when she had seen him taking Keziah home after the project party.

'But he's old,' Freya said. 'Must be fifty at least.'

'Make no difference to me. He was always nice to me. Brought me nice clothes from England. But it wasn't easy for him. And he got a small one.'

Freya began laughing. She had often thought about what she might say to Bobby if she met him again, even thought about some kind of revenge. But this wasn't the kind of revenge she had expected. Keziah started laughing as well.

'This baby mine now. You won't take her,' Keziah said.

'No,' Freya said. 'But I can help with her.'

She had no idea what was going to happen or how long she could stay. Maybe she could get a job and rent a house now that so many people were leaving. She would go to the charity office and open it up. Lots of people would need it. The Europeans would say she was putting everyone else in danger by staying. Her mother would think she'd lost her mind. The local people would tell her to go home. It was time for *msungus* to leave so that they could have the things they had, do things their way.

Keziah said, 'At the grave, you tell me about your baby. It make me sad. Baby with no name.'

Freya tried to hide her tears.

'I did the sacrifice for Roger. And I did one for your baby that died. She with the ancestors now.'

Freya started sobbing.

'Don't cry,' Keziah said. 'She need a name.'

Freya was silent for a moment.

'Beatrice,' she said. That was the name she had planned

if the baby had been a girl. It had been too painful to think about it at the time. But now she felt relieved just saying it. 'Beatrice, yes, that is her name.'

Keziah said, 'I'm goin' to the market. Comfort gone to school. Can you take her?'

'Yes, give her to me.'

Keziah took the baby from her back and handed her to Freya. *Maybe I could learn to carry her that way*, she thought.

Wensley's number was still on her hand. Perhaps she would write it down somewhere, before she washed it away.

A dog barked and growled outside. It was Jock. She smiled. Even he had had enough of Don. Freya pushed him away as he tried to lick the baby's face. He lay at their feet. We're like a little family, Freya thought. Dogs weren't really so bad.

An old woman was walking up the drive of the house using a gnarled piece of wood as a walking stick. Freya realised she had seen her somewhere before. As she got closer, she saw that it was Miriam, the old woman from the village.

This book is printed on paper from sustainable sources managed under the Forest Stewardship Council (FSC) scheme.

It has been printed in the UK to reduce transportation miles and their impact upon the environment.

For every new title that Matador publishes, we plant a tree to offset CO_2, partnering with the More Trees scheme.

For more about how Matador offsets its environmental impact, see www.troubador.co.uk/about/